A SAVAGE

GRACE

A NOVEL

A SAVAGE
GRACE

A NOVEL

VELDA
BROTHERTON

SOLASTA
PRESS

an Imprint of
OGHMA CREATIVE MEDIA

OGHMA

C R E A T I V E   M E D I A

Solasta Press
An imprint of Oghma Creative Media, Inc.
2401 Beth Lane, Bentonville, Arkansas 72712

Library of Congress Cataloging-in-Publication Data

Names: Brotherton, Velda, author.
Title: A Savage Grace/Velda Brotherton.
Description: Second Edition. | Bentonville: Solasta, 2019.
Identifiers: LCCN: 2018944145 | ISBN: 978-1-63373-434-0 (hardcover) |
ISBN: 978-1-63373-433-3 (trade paperback) | ISBN: 978-1-63373-065-6 (eBook)
Subjects: | BISAC: FICTION/Horror | FICTION/Occult & Supernatural |
FICTION/Gothic
LC record available at: https://lccn.loc.gov/2018944145

Solasta Press trade paperback edition June, 2019

Cover & Interior Design by Casey W. Cowan
Editing by Greg Camp, Gil Miller & Cyndy Prasse Miller

This book is a work of fiction. Apart from the well-known actual people, events, and locales that figure in the narrative, all names, characters, places, and incidents are the product of the author's imagination or are used fictitiously. Any resemblance to current events or locales, or to living persons, is entirely coincidental.

Acknowledgements

THIS IS MY first horror novel. It's something I worked on between other writing projects for several years. I have no idea where the idea, the demon, or the story came from. I have seen signal trees, rock drawings, red chert arrowheads in a land where no red flint exists. And I have walked the paths where early Americans trod for eons.

One day in a grocery store, I was staring at the headlines in one of those ridiculous papers found at the checkout line and began to wonder what would happen if one of those featured in a story influenced my actions. And the idea took off. All my experiences came together in this novel. It was just there every time I opened up the file and began to write. All of the Biblical mentions are true. Many of the places mentioned are real. They exist in the Ozark Mountains, but all of the things that happened here are fiction.

There really is an Indian Trail off Highway 71 near Artist Point where the Ozark Highland Trail passes. If there ever was an iron cross buried in the ground, I do not know about it. However, it is entirely possible. The setting for this story exists, but the town of Summit Falls is fictional. I enjoy setting my books around and about where I was born and have returned to live.

I'd like to thank the staff of Oghma Creative Media for giving me the opportunity to take this nearly-forgotten manuscript from its box under the bed and see it published. Special thanks go to my publisher, Casey Cowan—who also happens to design my kick-ass covers and layouts—and my editor, Gil Miller. I also want to remember the rest of the Oghma gang, Venessa, Gordon, Amy, Mike, Dennis George, Cyndy, Vivian, and Andrew. They say a small group of dedicated people can change the world. After having the privilege of being a part of this group for the last few years and seeing them work, I believe it.

For M. G. Miller, who urged me forward with this one long after I'd put it away. And he didn't even think there was too much sex in it.

Thanks, Mike.

1

LENORE KICKED BACK the covers and moved to the window, stood in a shaft of early morning sunlight and gazed toward the surrounding woods, the leafless trees hunched like bony sentinels. Shadows of night retreated beneath their feet. A serenading cardinal's song muted the despair that too often followed her from sleep.

In the kitchen, cupboards banged and pans clattered. Herb fixing breakfast. Throwing on a robe, she tiptoed past the closed door of the room where her mother had died, not wishing to rouse the imprisoned spirit that often appeared like a shimmer of mud-spattered rainbows.

Herb always cooked after a pleasurable sexual romp, as if she bought his help by satisfying his passions. That was okay with her, none of his appetites were demanding, and that too was okay. Most of the time.

The aroma of bacon and eggs and coffee filled the cabin. She watched him a moment before entering the kitchen, an alcove cut from a corner of the living room. Tall and broad shouldered, he managed not to look out of place there. His competent hands worked an egg beater as expertly as they operated the tools of his trade. He heard her and turned, a smile lighting his boyish features.

She went to him and kissed his cheek. It was warm and smooth, smelled of the Stetson aftershave she'd given him for Christmas.

"Mmm, bacon and eggs."

His hazel eyes regarded her a moment, the doubt there familiar. He got that from his mother, the need to make sure he was not being criticized. The entire family had no sense of humor at all, always presumed they were being ridiculed.

She filled the teakettle and set it on the electric coils.

"Sorry," he murmured. "Tea. I always forget, don't I?"

"Nothing to be sorry for. This is wonderful." She reached past him for her own mixture of chamomile and green tea, spooned leaves into a small metal tea ball and dropped it into a blue pottery cup.

"You were wonderful last night, my dear—as always." He kissed her on an earlobe.

His warm lips tickled an unsatisfied need that lingered from the night before. She shook it off. Herb was a good man, and she would marry him someday. Her idea or his, she could no longer remember.

The teakettle hissed while he took up the eggs and bacon, fingered toast to their plates, and poured himself a cup of coffee. They sat at the minuscule table near sliding glass doors and enjoyed the blissful silence of an Ozark morning.

Perfection. Or at least it *should* be. Why did she always pick away till she found something wrong? With her life… with herself… with Herb?

"I won't be home till around seven. You'll be here." He glanced over his coffee cup.

It wasn't a question, and resentment gathered, but she shook it off. Herb's way. "Of course. It's such a beautiful day. Maybe we'll grill some steaks and veggies."

"Well, okay. Best if you don't start till I'm home. Maybe you ought to fix something you could warm up. We've had some delays on the house, and I'd like to have it framed in by tonight." He watched her, waiting for an agreement.

Why not? What did it matter what they ate? "Okay. I'll just put something in the slow cooker before I leave."

A nod, and he finished, sipping at his coffee while rising. "See you tonight, then. You going to the shop?"

"After I run some errands."

An arched brow asked the next question. He always wanted to know where she was and what she was doing. She often felt as if she were tied to him with a gossamer thread, invisible but unbreakable.

Feeling a bit put-upon, she replied to the silent question. "Post office, hardware store, groceries, deliver to the shop, then home to work."

She glanced toward the area that was once the dining room. Herb's moving in had caused a few changes. Her workroom had become his office, thus the dining room mess where she worked.

They'd had a fight over that. He couldn't understand why she didn't move her "junk" into her mother's old room. When she'd told him that was out of bounds, even forbid him to put anything in there himself, he told her she was in denial and needed to face facts. Dead people were dead, and that was that.

Thinking back on the argument, she wondered again why she'd ever let him move in. She'd been happier here alone with the wandering spirit of her mother.

The door slammed at Herb's back, and she grabbed up an empty packing carton, dropped it on the floor in the cluttered space.

Along one wall, a table held tins filled with herbal tea mixes, each affixed with a hand-designed tag of curlicues and Victorian lettering. No computerized designs for her products. How satisfying the smooth flow of colored inks from the fine nib of her drawing pens, while the fra-grances of the dried leaves and roots embodied her in nature's perfume. Her chosen work. What Herb called her little hobby.

How wonderful if she never had to leave this remote, peaceful place and deal with life in a world in which she felt ill-equipped to function. Out there, something dark and foreboding frightened her in ways she didn't understand. She hated that she saw the auras of everyone she came in contact with. Despite that, every Friday she ventured out to shop in Summit Falls and deliver her wares to Delilah, her business partner at The Craft Basket, located just off the exit of the new Inter-state that slashed through the once serene mountains.

Teas and herbs packed in the cardboard carton, a roast in the cooker, she dressed in a denim skirt and white blouse and slipped on a sweater and sneakers. She carried the box out to the shiny new Jeep Grand Cherokee Herb had bought to replace her derelict Volkswagen Bug. She'd liked that old bug, missed it. Everything he did bound her to him all the more, left her gasping for air, for freedom, for the peace of being alone. They weren't compatible, and she'd known it the first time she studied his chakra and realized he was a prophetic. A deadly combination. Prophetics tended to destroy feelers like her.

Herb chastised her for such nonsense, said that people didn't have auras, and what was this chakra nonsense anyway? Her argument that auras were a scientific fact meant little to him. When Herb believed a thing, well, then, that's pretty much how it was.

Despite such disagreements, they were in love. Weren't they? The answer to that question eluded her.

The canopied lane wound for a mile or so to the blacktopped county road that meandered through the hills to the small mountain hamlet of Summit Falls. She parked, dropped by the post office and the hardware store, then strolled along the sidewalk to the grocery. Inside, she wrestled a cart from those lined at the entrance, headed for the fresh vegetables and fruits, and plucked up an assortment of both.

Several people spoke to her. She nodded in return, once in a while passed a few words. Different people's auras shimmered around them, some like wings of angels. Seeing muddy colors told her that person was having a rough time and unnerved her. But she was not a counselor and didn't care to admit to her intuitive abilities. To let people know she sometimes caught glimpses of their future would have been devastating to her already wobbly reputation. Imagine what they'd think... what they'd say. That talent was best kept secret. They gossiped about her enough, she was sure. The daughter of that crazy poet who had killed herself. If it wasn't for her love of the wilderness, she would live in a large city where no one knew anyone else's business. You could be invisible, no one would care.

Topping off her purchases with a loaf of whole wheat bread, she headed for the check-out line where two people waited. Old Mrs. Compton, widow of the past mayor, behind the Baptist minister's wife, Jean Mallory. On her left, just beside the tempting display of candy bars and chewing gum, stood a rack of tabloids with their disgusting photographs and headlines. She glanced across a splash of words proclaiming the perversity of a well-known actor, then turned away. Pure trash.

From a place deep inside her head a harsh voice demanded, *"Look at me, bitch."*

The command hit her hard, shocked her into an abnormal posture that made her jaws hurt and sent a flash of pain through her shoulders. Like a robot, she twisted to scan her surroundings. No one in line behind her. Plump Mrs. Ramey strolled up a nearby aisle, stopped to pluck down a box of Cheerios and study the label. Jean Mallory closed her pocketbook and followed the bag boy out. Mrs. Compton chatted with the checker who ran her purchases over the scanner.

The savage voice spoke again, *"I said look at me. Over here. Come here."*

A snake coiled around her spine. A yelp escaped her lips, and she whirled to look behind her. No one there. The words came from nowhere and everywhere.

"Shut up," she muttered, then covered her mouth. Talking to herself in public was not a good idea.

Calm down. Surely someone playing a trick. A child who'd learned ventriloquism, or someone she knew who thought such a bizarre joke was funny. She leaned to one side and peered behind the display at the second cash register.

No one there.

In front of her, Mrs. Compton wrote out a check, glanced nervously at her, and smiled.

Had she truly heard the voice? Was she losing her mind? Just like her. Every time something strange happened, that was her first thought.

"Well?" she said aloud.

The clerk—wasn't her name Diana?— paused with Mrs. Compton's check in hand, shot her a worried look. Lenore smiled, and Diana frowned, but went back to her job. A pale yellow aura ringed her head and shoulders.

In search of the source of the voice, Lenore shot a frantic glance toward the tabloids. She'd pretend to be reading the awful stuff, maybe that would convince everyone she was sane. Scanned the headlines of *The Comet*, read a few sentences.

DEMONS WALK THE EARTH TO DWELL IN KILLERS

by Christine Carle

Memphis, Tn., March 14, Eric Adair sits in the West Memphis Institute For The Criminally Insane, where he could spend the remainder of his life. He claims he is not alone. A demon possesses his soul and is responsible for the thirteen barbarous murders he has committed.

A photograph buried in the text snagged her attention, stopped her cold. Like a black and white film overlaid in a color movie, a hideous scene distorted racks of bread, potato chips, and packages of cookies that wavered as if trapped under water, then cleared. Repugnant flashes of butchery, as if vomited from the bowels of hell, made her stomach heave. She wiped perspiration from her face and neck, fought dizziness and leaned on the counter.

"Lenore? Miss Maine?"

Another voice. *"Leave me alone. Stop doing that."*

"What?"

"Your stuff. I can check it now."

Lenore glanced at her basket, grabbed the items and tossed them on the moving counter. The bread bounced and fell on the floor at Diane's feet. She glared, picked it up, and slashed it over the little window.

Once more Lenore checked out her surroundings. No one else had heard the insistent, evil voice. That was evident. The shoppers all went about their business. Immersed in her task, the clerk continued to slide her grocery items over the scanner.

The voice spoke to her again, louder, more insistent. *"Bitch, I said look at me. Now."*

Sheer terror threatened to explode her heart, her brain shuddered as if a demon indeed poked it with a clawed finger. The rack of tabloids blurred, grew fuzzy. The clerk—Diana, she was sure of it now—moved her mouth, widened her eyes and stopped checking groceries. Saying something Lenore couldn't hear. All she could do was stare at the news photo of a haggard but handsome young man with madness in his eyes. Eyes that drilled into her thoughts.

Her vision cleared… disjointed words assaulted her. **DEMONS WALK EARTH**, followed by a stupid, childish picture that looked as if it had come from a cheap horror movie.

The penetrating gaze of the killer snagged her like a sharpened hook. She scanned the article. Disgust rose like bile. Only a beast—an unholy monster—would do the things this man had done.

"Nail him to a tree by his balls, leave him there to die. Pour acid in his eyes and mouth, drive needles under his fingernails."

Lenore clamped a hand over her mouth, breath hot and wet in her palm. What ugly thoughts. She had never experienced such hostility, such ugly hatred for another human being. The pungent smell of apples and celery turned sour in her nostrils.

"Are you okay, Lenore?" Diana shouted. "Should I call someone? An ambulance? The police?"

She shook her head, gazed vacantly at the groceries, some sacked, the rest waiting.

What would Diana do if she told her everything was fine, she was simply going stark-raving mad and conversing with a demon-possessed madman? A disjointed giggle choked at her throat, threatened to bubble out and put fact to the statement.

The voice came at her again, spouting words so filthy she wasn't sure of their meaning. She stumbled backward into old Mr. Stiles, who had joined the line, frail arms folded around a package of bologna and a quart of milk. He dropped the plastic carton, and it split open, gushing white fluid over his tattered shoes. Staring at the mess, he let go the pack of bologna. It hit the floor with a loud smack and splashed milk up the legs of his threadbare overalls.

She stared at him, speechless, ashamed, frightened.

At last she found enough of a voice to blurt, "I'm sorry, oh, I'm sorry."

The wrinkled farmer gestured at the pool around his feet and swamped her in tobacco breath. Fire would spout from his mouth at any moment. A terrible black hole swirled in his muddy aura, and she wanted to grab his arm, shout at him to beware what was to come, but she didn't.

"*Pick up the paper, bitch,*" the voice commanded, and she forgot all about Mr. Stiles's black hole.

"Shut up," she screamed.

The poor old man blanched and tottered away, leaving white tracks on the floor.

She whirled, put her nose against the photograph on the tabloid's front page and hissed, "Who are you? What do you want?"

Someone grabbed her arm, and she yelped, jerked away, peered through a slimy red haze at the owner of the store, Bill Crowley.

"Let me get someone to take you home. I'll bring your groceries."

Her distraught mind wouldn't admit Crowley's offer, though she knew him well. A kind, hardworking man filled with good deeds for his community.

Just like him to take care of the dead poet's crazy daughter.

Shaking her head, crying out, "No, no, no." She pivoted, grabbed a gallon jug of orange juice and swung it, hitting Crowley in the stomach so hard he gasped and bent double. The jug fell to the floor and split open, juice curdling into the milk.

"*Take me with you,*" the voice commanded, and she could not think of doing otherwise.

In stilted acquiescence, she grabbed a copy of *The Comet* and shoved her way through the astounded bystanders and out the door into a metallic sunlight. She barely heard Diana call out in a plaintive voice, "Wait a minute, Lenore. Don't you want your stuff? What am I gonna do with all this stuff?"

Outside, a fresh breeze dried the coating of perspiration that slicked her face. She ran, the handbag strapped over her shoulder slapping at one hip, her sneakers scraping over gravel-strewn asphalt. Her breath came in great gasps that tore at her lungs. She had to escape, yet even as she flung open the door of the Jeep, threw herself inside and pounded at the automatic lock button, a horrid reality told her she carried the enemy with her.

Hateful words verified the fear. *"Well, my sweet Lenore, alone at last."*

The paper, crumpled in her fist, grew hot, twisted against her palm like a live, wild thing. Why had she brought it with her? Why?

"Because I told you to."

With a screech, she flung it to the floor where it curled out flat so his face stared up at her. A sly grin twisted the countenance frozen in black and white. Had he been smiling before? God, she couldn't remember. Both hands over her eyes, she hunkered into the corner of the seat, the armrest digging into her ribs. All she could do was wait for him to take her, drag her into the madness that had been waiting there all along.

Chapter 2

A **CAR HORN** blared, and Lenore jerked back to her senses, groggy and disoriented. Through slitted eyes she peered at the clock. After one? Impossible. She couldn't have been in town four hours. Only minutes ago she'd made a complete spectacle of herself inside the grocery store. That would make good telling around town. Should last everyone several months, the story of that nutty poet's daughter going berserk while shopping.

Runs in the family, you know.

And when it got back to Herb, what would he think? His snooty mother never let up on him about wanting to marry her, for surely she must be as insane as her mother. Sometimes she thought he actually believed some of what the nagging old woman told her only child, conceived and born in the autumn of her life. At odd times Lenore caught him watching her when he thought she wasn't looking.

"Hateful Herb. Snooty bitch of a mother." An evil, insistent whisper. In her head, but surely not her own thoughts.

Lenore raised her chin from her chest and peeked at the clock, as if doing so might change what it said. Momentarily bewildered, she rubbed her eyes. One thirty? She must have fallen asleep. What was she doing sitting here in the car outside the grocery store?

Sighing, she adjusted the rearview mirror and with trembling fingers poked the key in the ignition. Her glance flew back to the reflection of the few purchases she'd made at the hardware store and the carton of packaged teas she hadn't delivered to Delilah at the shop. Where were her groceries? Sure that the mirror lied, she turned to take a closer look. She filled a cart in the store, so where were the groceries? She swung the door open to see if the cart was outside. A stupid thing to do. Why would she have left a full cart sitting in the parking lot, crawled in the car, and fallen asleep?

Dear God, what was happening to her?

A crippling panic rose in her throat.

Frantic, she twisted the key in the ignition. The engine roared to life, but she held the starter until its shattering protest made her let go the key as if it had burned her.

Infuriated by her own stupidity, shaking uncontrollably, her gaze darted to the paper lying on the floor on the passenger side. It was his fault, the filthy, dirty, rotten, fucking son of a bitch.

"Oh, my god," she cried and clamped a sweaty palm over her mouth. Had she actually imagined such vulgar words? Never… never in all her life had she used such obscene language, never even let it enter her mind. Once when Herb said the "F-word" in front of her, she didn't speak to him for a week.

"You're such a prude, Lenore. Such a fucking prude." The voice, the god awful, terrifying voice, spoke from her own inner self.

Of course, why not? She was crazy, wasn't she?

"Ah, but don't worry so, my little dove. It's all right. Let me make it all better for you."

Something warm and moist trailed over her face. A worm covered in slime squirmed between her lips, moved about inside the moist recesses of her mouth. She gasped and scrubbed at her tongue with fingers that felt like clubs, gagged until bile surged into her throat and spewed out onto the pavement.

Wild with fear, she slammed the door and jerked the shifter into reverse. She yanked the transmission into drive, tires screaming from the lot onto the highway. The Jeep rocked from side to side. Horns blared, splitting apart the peaceful spring morning. Hands throbbing, she grasped the wheel and leaned forward in the seat. Lips moved in silence, her chin almost touched the steering wheel, as she barreled out of town and down the county road.

The frantic flight didn't end until she tumbled from the bucket seat, raced across the yard and into her cheery yellow kitchen. Breath coming in great sobs, she regained her senses standing in the middle of the room, legs spread, one hand clutching her purse, a sweat-dampened fist around wads of the tabloid page.

No, she'd thrown it away. She had, hadn't she? It clung to her palm.

Each breath seared deep into her lungs. Her mouth, dry and hot as a dragon's breath. With one last burst of energy she staggered to the sink and filled a glass with icy water, gulped it down past the fire in her throat. Retching, she leaned over but nothing came up. After a miserable few moments she touched her forehead with the back of one hand. Burning up. She was coming down with some kind of bug, that was all. A bug, a virus, the flu. Yes, please let it be a gut wrenching, feverish, head pounding case of the flu. A much more curable ailment than madness.

Feeling vague and disconnected, she gazed at the wadded paper, still clutched in her hand like something of value. Comet? The name skittered through her consciousness. She never bought this trash, so what was she doing standing in her kitchen holding the piece of filth? And where were her groceries? She remembered filling a cart, waiting in line…. Her grip loosened, and the paper floated to the counter, landing so that the eyes of the man in the photo stared at her. Whatever bug she'd been exposed to took fresh hold of her guts when she looked into that face again. She wanted to curse him, spit on him, set him on fire, bury her fingers in his flesh and rip out his heart, burn out those eyes with a hot poker.

The telephone rang.

A sharp yelp erupted from deep in her chest like a massive hiccup.

Jesus!

She had to get hold of herself. Taking a long, calming breath, she picked up the receiver, but couldn't speak.

"Lee, is that you, honey?" Delilah's syrupy tones created a semblance of reality, yet she had trouble replying.

Finally she croaked out a weak, "Yes."

"What's wrong? You sound sick. When you didn't come in, I got worried. Why didn't you call or something?"

"Del." Her voice bubbled out like a frog being squashed.

"Lee, my God, what is it?"

She cleared her throat, tried again. "Nothing. I mean, it's something, but I guess I'm sick."

"Quite mad is more like it."

She squeezed her eyes shut against the sarcastic comment from inside her head, strained to hear Del.

"Sick? How can that be? You're never sick. I've never even seen you with a cold. What is it?"

"Lord, I don't know. I'm hot, and I want to throw up and…." After a short pause she related in disconnected sentences what had happened— or as much of it as she could remember. There was more, but it had flown from her mind, and that was probably a good thing. She already felt enough of a fool.

When she finally wound down, Delilah said, *"Well my goodness, darlin'. This sounds serious. Have you called a doctor or Herb?"*

"No, I just got home." Dizzy again, she grabbed at the counter to keep from falling, closed her eyes to shut out the whirling kitchen. Numbed fingers let go of the phone. It bounced off the counter top and onto the floor. Appalled, she gazed down. Del's voice shouted her name over and over in a tinny echo. She reeled up the receiver by the cord, thunked herself soundly on the cheek with it and cried into the mouthpiece, "Del, it's okay. I'm fine. I dropped the phone."

"I'm coming over there this very instant."

"No, no, don't do that. The shop. You can't close down in the middle of the day."

"Richard's here. You know he's always here on Friday to do the books."

"Richard?" Lenore whispered the name.

A hot tingly sensation clutched her between the legs. She moaned. Richard's handsome features, his fingers moving low over her stomach. The husband of her best friend. Grinning at his wife not twenty feet away while he felt up Lenore behind the kitchen counter. Cocky, so cocky. And Lenore had allowed it, harlot that she was.

"Cheap slut."

"Shut up."

His touch again. Her nipples hardened, and desire gathered low in her belly, exploded in a shower of exquisite delight.

"If you want him, a touch of hemlock in her tea, bitch, or if not, then perhaps in his. Every problem has a solution."

"No, stop it! God, just stop it!" She lashed out with the handset, batting at the invisible enemy.

"That does it, I'm on my way," Del shouted, and the line went dead.

"Brew her up some special tea, dear, before she arrives. Do it now, and get it over with. Sooner or later, you will."

She threw the instrument against the cabinet, grabbed up the crumpled paper, screamed into his vile face, "What do you want with me?"

His eyes stared back at her, and he remained silent. Bastard.

So this was what it was like to go mad. This was how her mother had felt when she.... Lenore couldn't finish the thought, had never been able to put that last day of her mother's life into coherent images. Besides, this was her madness. All hers.

With trembling fingers, she spread the article out on the counter, smoothing the wrinkles with slow deliberation.

"So, let's take a good look at you, filth." She failed to recognize her own grating voice. With one palm she covered the disturbing photo with its overlying image, someone's grotesque version of a demon, and read the accompanying article. She had to know more about this man whose photo had exposed her lurking insanity.

She scanned the boring account of Eric Adair's mundane life. Why and how had he found her? Didn't care that he'd attended church and been a kind, pleasant family man, for God's sake. People said that about every killer. There it was. He'd gone mad.

Adair's killing spree began late one evening when he returned home from the high school where he taught, locked himself in with his wife and two children, and spent the night methodically butchering their bodies.

Evidence shows that he then took a shower, dressed, packed and left the house, climbed in his Oldsmobile Cutlass, and drove away. He would not surface again for nearly five years, when police in Atlanta arrested him in a motel with the body of what they soon learned was his thirteenth victim.

Her stomach churned. What did he want with her?

Tracing the lines with one finger, she stared at the blurring words and read on.

What turned this peaceful man into a perverted monster?

He says the devil made him do it, claims the demon that possesses him came into his body the night the notorious mercy nurse, Josie Lange, died in her cell in a Pennsylvania institution for the criminally insane. It seems Lange claimed previous possession by the traveling demon.

Detective Burt Manson, who arrested Adair in 2005, after a five-year manhunt following a trail of butchered bodies, had this to say:

"When I interrogated Adair, I became convinced that evil is out there and has a presence in this man. It's real, and it's been with us since the beginning of time. I'm not sure about his claims of demonic possession, but I do know that evil dwells in Eric Adair, and if the authorities are smart, they'll put him to death."

Adair claimed he'd pled guilty to the crimes because he wanted to be locked away where he could never hurt anyone again.

Well, he got his wish. They put him in the institute for the criminally insane in West Memphis where he would spend the remainder of his life.

The mercy nurse, Josie Lange, whose demon spirit he claimed possessed him, had carried on quite a murderous binge of her own some forty years earlier in Pennsylvania before passing on her demon to Adair.

It was in 1952 that Josie Lange began her spree and did away with twenty patients under her care before being arrested some three years later. She claimed they were mercy killings. After the police searched her home and found a collection of body organs preserved in formaldehyde, she was charged with twenty counts of murder. She then changed her story, claiming to have been possessed by an evil that has walked the earth for two thousand years.

In an interview published in The Comet *fifteen years after her
incarceration, Lange said that the demon moves into an innocent person's mind and body and causes them to commit unspeakable deeds.*

Lenore shivered. Was that what Adair was doing? Preparing her for
his demon's obsession? Had it happened to him in this same way? Lange
had died around the time Eric Adair claimed he'd been possessed. Maybe Adair had died and the demon was searching for its next victim. Her.

Good God! How could she buy into such a story? Everyone knew these
rags never printed the truth. Still, she couldn't keep from reading on.

Speculation by a well-known psychic that there might be such evil—a
demon who could pass from one person to another and force them to
commit unspeakable crimes—awoke new terror in Lenore.

She came to herself staring out the window into the golden, silent
afternoon, unsure how much time had passed.

Be sensible. Think. What had she been doing in July of 2006 when
the authorities put Eric Adair away? She would have been nineteen years
old that summer and out of high school a year. Not yet set in the direction of college, but floating from one job to another all over the state.

Four years later her mother crawled into a tub of warm water, slashed
her wrists, and left the mess for Lenore to find. By then she'd had her
fill of the life of a wanderer and become immersed in a fine arts course
at the university. But after her mother's death, she never went back to
school, never got her degree. Instead shut herself away in the small remote cabin where her mother had killed herself.

Her life had nothing to do with this man Adair. She wadded the of-
fensive paper into a ball and tossed it in the trash can. What complete
nonsense. She had allowed a bout with a flu bug to ruin her planned day,
that was all. Since she was never ill, she hadn't known what to expect. A
simple explanation. No telling what she had done in town, what Herb

would hear. But it didn't pay to worry about it now. She felt faint, her heart pounded so hard she could hear it in the quiet room, and a burning fever imprisoned her.

Grumbling about her own weakness, she crept to the bathroom, swallowed a couple of Tylenol, slugged down a dose of Herb's Mylanta, and stumbled into the bedroom. She had scarcely crawled onto the unmade bed before she fell asleep.

Sometime later, she came to her senses, kneeling on the cool tile of the bathroom floor, hugging the commode while her stomach roiled. Sweat saturated her burning body and soaked her clothes. She fought her way out of the suffocating sweater, tore off the skirt and blouse. What was wrong with her? As if without bones, she slumped onto the floor and into a world she had never imagined existed. A world that threatened her sanity.

She was in some sort of damp, dark cage. Hurting. No way out. No one to love—pure self-hatred, as thick and cloying and nauseating as the dreadful stench. Over her flushed cheek a touch, a caress, a vile kiss.

Chapter 3

ERIC JERKED UPRIGHT on the hard bunk, gasped for air. A woman! He had touched a woman's soft breast, smelled her musk, tasted her honey sweetness. Walls of the gloomy cell shrunk around him, wrapped him in a pain so excruciating he could no longer allow his consciousness to remain out. He closed his eyes, retreated into the deepest, darkest recesses of the demon's brain where he curled into a ball and slept. Perhaps she'd return, this ethereal wraith.

Otherwise occupied, the demon blinked, sniffed at the fetid, open mouth of a limp, still warm body draped over one arm. No breath there, only the vague odor of sweet death. He could escape to relive the pleasures only in his dreams. With reluctance he shed remnants of the enjoyable illusion like an old skin.

Tendrils of feminine desire trickled through his mind, wispy as light perfume. What had the man been up to? What fantasy had he fetched for his own amusement? A bare breast, flat stomach, soft flesh under a searching palm. Smooth muscles that twitched as she moaned.

He roared and flung away the lingering ghost of death. Had Adair been messing with his woman? The puny little cretin. It was time to rip free of the man's hollowed shell, for he had used him up until nothing of interest remained. Women's bodies were so much more interesting, erotic, meant to carry new life. His new life. He preferred them over men any day and was ready to cast off this feeble host. He would fit so cozily within the security of a womb, a cradle to assuage his hungers. An erotic desire filled him. He wanted her, the woman he'd tested so briefly. She would ease this hateful lust. Lips on hers, hands roaming over her tasty parts. Flames licked at his heart, burnt his flesh. Adair could not have her, this he would not allow, except as it would further his own needs.

In the afternoon the demon slept, and Eric stumbled to his knees on the hard floor of the cell, crawled into a tiny splash of sunlight that fell through the high slit of a window. So good, its fleeting warmth. His own desires had spewed forth a foul venom that sated the demon's perverted needs. He had to stay away from the woman, the one called Lenore, whose dreadful fears gripped him. Though he yearned to save her from the horrible fate the demon planned, Eric sensed no part of himself remained that could do so. He waited only for the day he could pass into whatever the afterlife had to offer. What frightened him most was that the demon was only one of many who dwelled in Hell, and because of what he had done, Heaven wasn't an option. So all he could do was join their legions.

Without warning his eyes snapped open. He had slept. The sunlight had gone, starlight twinkled. The demon nudged him, took over. Time to awaken and be out and about. His gaze focused on the cement wall, a spreading stain. Concentrated. Bored into the hard rock. Through it and away to freedom. To that foul place where it roamed, and Eric, too weak to stop it.

The dreaded voice, the pull of its wicked mind.

"I am here. Come with me. Without the depths of Hell there is no reason for Heaven. Open to me, and I will take you away from this place. Together we will play."

Moaning like a helpless, wounded child, Eric followed, with no true sense of a choice. A growling reverberated through his senses, filled with promises of exquisite torture to which, God help him, he had become addicted.

"She is not yours, but you may watch if you like."

A woman, after all this time. Lips in a rictus, Eric struggled to communicate, watched hands like reptile claws reach out to touch her. His own, yet not his at all.

"Say don't hurt me. Say it, say it, say it, or I will." A claw poised at her throat.

"Don't hurt me. Please don't hurt me." Her pitiful, frightened voice.

The demon smiled. *"It'll only hurt for a moment before a release of pure, passionate joy. A baptism. A savage grace."*

He locked his mind on hers and yanked viciously.

She screamed, fought back.

Scaled digits brushed over her soft, pliant breast. He nudged her mind again, tasted her essence flowing into him. The sweetness of her sensual being slithered into the hollows of his soul. Warm and sweet and pure. Eric writhed with the knowing.

With a ferocious bellow the body he shared with the beast from Hell stiffened into a rigid crucifix on the clammy, concrete floor. Arms thrown wide, legs clenched. His mind held her essence as long as it could, then released her to an exquisite pain. A birthing, a climax, an orgasm that emptied his body and soul.

Tears trickled from the corners of his eyes. Eric's brittle, ice blue eyes that the demon could change at will until they glowed like midnight lamps.

4

DON'T HURT ME, please don't hurt me." Lenore lay on the bathroom floor, exhausted. Daylight flashed at her senses with the pain of a migraine, pushed away the darkness, so bright it drove a torment of spikes into her eyes.

"Don't hurt me," she shouted. Her teeth clattered over each word, increasing the jolts of agony. Though she had been on fire, she was suddenly cast into a frigid, unimaginable cold. She couldn't move, the tile beneath her naked body brittle as ice. She ached inside as if violated.

"Lenore, what on God's earth is wrong with you?"

"Herb? Herb, where are you?" In a blind panic she groped the air around her.

Another voice, feminine and wispy. "I couldn't get here sooner. Oh, my Lord, what's happened to her?"

Delilah.

"The cunt knows, she knows about you and Richard, bitch."

Lenore waved both hands in an effort to slap away the excruciating light and filthy words. She shaded her eyes with the crook of an elbow, felt herself being lifted, cradled in familiar arms.

"Leave me alone, you bastard." She gritted the expletive through clenched teeth. Who was she and what was she doing?

"Sweetheart, it's Herb. Dear God, what do you suppose happened?"

"I don't know. Honey, it's Del, please, what is it? Tell us."

Lenore's head lolled back over Herb's arm so that she focused on her friend's upside-down features, oh so concerned and caring. The mass of red curls, beseeching green eyes, pale pretty face. Delicate, long-nailed hands fluttered from crimson lips to pat Lenore's sweat-soaked mop of hair. *Lying, two-bit whore.* Had that come from her mouth?

Herb carried Lenore to the bed and laid her down, perching on the edge of the mattress to press her hand to his lips. Del peered over his shoulder, face a mask of distress.

The voice grew quiet at last, and Lenore coiled up against Herb, sighed and floated off into the darkness.

5

A NAKED FIGURE, MORE *animal than man, lurched upright, lifted a twisted iron casting, and bellowed to the rising blood-red moon. Forlorn as a wolf's call, the baying moan rode astraddle a gust of wind. A black wind that touched the gleam of trembling lips and sucked a curse from them.*

"Sic pereant omnes inimici tui, Domine."

The apparition raised its head to glare straight at Lenore with ancient yellow eyes like midnight lamps that glittered in the remote darkness to life. Silent screams clogged her throat, and a body paralyzed with fear refused to respond to its terrorized, thundering heart's desire to flee. With a cry born of awesome despair, the creature dropped to all fours and pawed a cavity in the dank earth. There he cradled the coil of iron and raked musty soil over it like a dog covering a treasured bone.

From the surrounding umber forests surged a mass of red, hairless beasts, babbling incoherently, firing arrows in a rain of fury. Chert points thunked into muscle, flesh, and bone, and the naked beast crumpled across the burial ground.

The crimson moon cleared the skeletal trees and splattered the field of carnage with a fiendish glow...

… that pursued Lenore, sent her leaping from a tangle of covers into the darkness, poised to do battle with the hellish nightmare. She stumbled across the floor and fell forward onto the window seat before coming fully awake. Outside, a rising wind lashed naked tree branches against the glass and a skiff of clouds blotted a peaceful, silver quarter moon. Raw fear burnt her nostrils. Its stench hovered in the room to smother the sun-sweet fragrance of line-dried linens and a vague, clinging aroma of sex.

On his side of the bed, Herb stirred, snorted softly, and threw one arm into a crook on the pillow above his head. Here in the vast dark countryside, far from the vague glow of city lights, moonbeams glowed brightly.

Drenched in perspiration, she shivered and massaged chill bumps that erupted over her flesh. God, what had that hideous dream been about? And the language of the vision, expressions that might have been plucked from an old book. Mary Shelley, perhaps, or Bram Stoker. Probably payback for reading classic horror novels as an adolescent. No nightmares in years, not since… since the months immediately following her mother's death. What had caused this one?

She searched her memory, tried to analyze the inexplicable night terrors and put some sensible meaning to the horrid scene that had played out in the dank pit of her dreams. It reminded her of nothing she had ever read or seen.

Oh, dear God. The frightening incidents of the previous day. Her bout with the flu that had left her totally defenseless. The nightmare had no doubt come from the same place as the earlier hideous delusions.

Yet how could she harbor such evil images in her subconscious when her days were spent walking alone in the tranquil woods, evenings passed with the only man in her life? Herb often accused her of living in another world, but not like that of the dream. She might be a bit zoned at times, but she wasn't the kind of person who would devise such dreadful nonsense.

She had been named after one of Poe's heroines by a mother who spent much of her time writing essays and poetry so obscure and morbid not even the most stalwart lover of the macabre could comprehend her efforts. Yet with the exception of the two or three years as a child when Lenore herself had become engrossed in dark nineteenth century literature, she had led a life sheltered from the realities of malevolence. Perhaps this was the first sign that she was going as mad as her mother had finally become.

In the bed, Herb stirred.

Goosebumps played across her shoulders and down both arms, and she hugged herself. How long had she crouched at the open window? The damp March night had turned her flesh frigid. Whatever the dream had meant, she wasn't going to figure it out by freezing to death. She crawled into the warm covers and snuggled there until the electric blanket chased the chill from her bones. But she didn't sleep.

Morning dawned brightly golden, the day tinged with a definite hint of spring. Sunlight splashed across the creamy kitchen countertops and floor. By the time she started coffee for Herb, the hideous nightmare and the happenings of the day before had faded to the deeper recesses of her mind. Yet she felt weak. Odd sensations assailed her imagination, shadow haunts skittered beyond the periphery of her vision, trailing on dread feet along her spine, wavering in the coffee-scented air like a vague suggestion of smoke.

"Feeling better?" Herb asked through the steam from his cup. His aura glowed in brilliant hues of blue, green and red.

Did she dare tell him what had happened before he had found her lying in the bathroom out of her head? Sooner or later she'd have to, but she couldn't bring herself to do it yet. She swallowed thickly, glanced from his gaze down at the table. Scrambled eggs lay scattered over his toast, and a huge blob of strawberry jam hugged an empty spot on the blue ironstone plate. Blood smeared against a summer sky. Engrossed in the combination of colors and the fascinating mix of textures, she didn't answer right away, and finally he asked again.

"If you're still sick, I could stay home."

"No, of course not. I'm fine."

She almost told him about the terrifying nightmare, but then shrugged and smiled. Any suggestion of madness was to be avoided. In the light of day she felt a bit doubtful about the episode until she glanced through the window. Beyond the glass, furtive creatures darted through the trees, only to disappear on closer inspection. Nothing out there but daffodils nodding cheerfully from nests of new green grass and the stark, silent, leafless forest. Awaiting birth. A rebirth after the death of a long winter. She hugged herself again, smiled weakly at him.

Already looking forward to his day, he failed to meet her glance. "Ummm, maybe you ought to go back to bed, rest. I must be off. Have to make hay while the sun shines."

She smiled at the tired cliché. Delilah often said Herb was a total bore. How could she even think seriously for one second about marrying him? Was it true that she now pursued him, like the evil voice said? No, of course not. That was a trick. Del was good. Herb was good.

Like everything else in Lenore's carefully crafted life, he represented security, a protection from instability. With his large, strong hands he built houses and during slack times did remodel jobs. He worked very hard, but never complained, and he made a lot of money. In his spare time, he had begun to build them a home. She hadn't the heart to stop him. He wanted to leave this place that had such painful memories for her. Still, she hesitated. Why? What was wrong with her, other than the madness in her blood?

He wanted a baby as soon as they married, but she was too frightened of the gene her mother might have passed on to her. Terrified that she might in turn pass it on to their child. She hadn't told him how she felt. Considering yesterday, perhaps she was already a bit crazy.

Refusal to accept that inevitable conclusion grew in her. She could fight it… she would, if somewhere she could find the strength.

Or maybe she'd just stay here alone in her cabin with her teas and go quietly insane.

6

AFTER HERB LEFT, Lenore gathered his plate, smeared with yellow egg yolk and sticky preserves, turned and stepped into the scaly arms of a monster who raked claws that dripped blood over her breasts and down her belly to dig about between her legs.

An excruciating pain enfolded her into a dark cavern where dwelt all the demons ever to walk the earth. They passed her around until blood ran from every orifice. She could not move without experiencing ice picks driven into her flesh, striking bone and organs. When she could no longer breathe or scream or move, they were gone.

She awoke in her bed surrounded by the thunder of silence. God, what a nightmare. A slight movement revived tremors in her arms and legs, as if she had jogged five miles along the side of a hill. Vague pain memories trailed over her. For a while she lay still, listened to the peaceful morning, gazed at a patch of sunlight on the gleaming hardwood floor, breathed in the aroma of coffee. Wondered what day it was, what she had done the day before. She had been ill, but hadn't that too been a dream?

Though her brain sent the message she should move, terror held her captive. A beast tread within her psyche, disturbing secret sexual desires held in bay most of her life. She feared awakening those beasts, allowing them into the reality around her.

Dishes rattled in the kitchen. She should get up, fix breakfast. Herb would be annoyed at having to cook. With a groan she swung both legs over the side of the mattress and perched on its edge. Her insides lurched, threatened to spill out. The bed teetered, sent her grabbing at pillows and linen to keep from slithering to the floor. What in the world was wrong with her?

Arms propped at either side to steady herself, she waited for the rotating room to calm down. God, her mouth tasted as if she'd been gnawing on dirty socks, her lips and breasts throbbed. Inside she felt as if she'd been hollowed out by some sort of digging tool. Raped. Nothing left inside but the slime of his leavings. His? Whose?

She must not think of him. *Would* not.

On the bedside table sat a glass half-filled with water and a prescription bottle. Fingers trembling, she picked up the medicine and strained to read the label.

Lenore Maine Valium Take one three times daily with food. Doctor C. M. Beecher.

Doc Beecher must be happy now. He'd always complained that she was so healthy his services were seldom needed except for the occasional check-up he insisted upon since he'd cared for her mother. But Valium? Why would he give her that?

The label's date, March 14, distracted her, might have helped get a fix on the day's date if she had a clue about how long she'd lain here. Felt like a month the way her muscles ached.

Okay, get serious. Friday. That'd been the tenth. She'd gone to town for supplies and to drop her herbal teas off at Delilah's shop and then... and then she'd come down with a raging case of the flu. Horrid visions tapped at her memory. Only fever dreams, surely. What had been Friday's date? Not the tenth. The eleventh. But the next day she'd been much better. Arose, fixed Herb's breakfast. So what was she doing in bed, weak as a kitten? Surely she hadn't been so out of her head she couldn't even recall what had happened since.

A shadow loomed in the doorway, sent frantic bugs scrabbling under her skin. She cried out, then saw it was only Herb.

"Sorry, didn't know you were awake."

"You startled me."

"How do you feel?" He carried a tray to her. "I only brought hot tea, but I can go down and get you something more if you feel up to it. How about some toast?"

Her stomach heaved. "No, this will do fine. What time is it?"

With a wry grin he glanced at the clock on the bedside table. "Two-thirty. Now ask what day it is."

"All right, what day is it?"

"You have been out of it, haven't you? Beecher said those pills would keep you way under, but I had no idea—"

"What day is it, Herb?" She could scarcely speak intelligibly past clots of something vile in her throat, and grabbed at the half-glass of water, gulped it down. Struggled to keep from upchucking.

"Thursday."

She stared at him. "But it can't be. I remember… I mean, I distinctly remember Friday, and you're telling me it's not here yet. I went shopping like I always do and took my..." Horrified, she stared at him. " ...and that's the last I remember. The rest was a dream, tell me it was a dream."

Instead of a reply, Herb sighed. He was good at that. Gave him time to think up a lie.

"That was last Friday, Lenore. Saturday morning I went off to work because you told me you were fine. When I came home, I found you puking and screaming and... well, bleeding. You've been here in this room since, out of your head. Now, I don't want you to worry, but Beecher thinks you should see someone."

"Out of my head? See someone? That's ridiculous, I'm fine. See?" She swayed on her feet, hands on hips, glaring at him.

"Well, I don't think you're fine."

Despite her resolve, weak knees dumped her on the edge of the bed. "What do you think?"

He glanced down at the floor, took a step away from her.

"Herb?"

"I'd rather you speak to Beecher. You know how I am with those fancy medical terms. People used to act like you've been acting, they called it a nervous breakdown. Hell, they called it worse than that. But no, the doc couldn't keep it simple. Now, please don't get upset. I know how you feel about things like this, considering your mother and everything."

Lips numb, she whispered, "Considering my mother? He thinks I'm going crazy like she did? That's nonsense. I feel fine. I feel just fine. How could you let that quack give me these?" She threw the bottle of pills across the room. It bounced and rolled back to her, coming to rest against her bare toes. She stared down a moment, shouted, "You know I don't like to take drugs."

Struck speechless, lost in a whirling darkness, she fingered her eyes shut. For a moment she couldn't move or breathe or speak. Frightened that she was losing touch with reality, she uncovered her face and squinted in his direction. He was still there, in the center of the room, disconnected as if he floated in a stagnant pool of hazy water. All at once she tumbled away, fell into a deep hole while he watched from above. But he didn't reach out and try to stop her fall.

Stomach queasy, she fisted up wads of bed linen, bringing him into sharper focus.

Anger reddened his mild features. "I know you'd rather dig around in the woods for some dirty root you think might make you better, Lee, but dammit you were out of your head, screaming at things that weren't there, shouting out names, fighting invisible demons. My God, you were naked and trying to seduce me."

"Demons? Seduce you? Naked?" She could barely squeak the questions past the raw fear that choked her.

Herb remained out of reach, as if afraid he'd be attacked. "That's what you called them or him or it. Demons. And you kept begging me not to hurt you. And your language. I haven't heard words so vile from a man. So Doc gave you a sedative. What did you expect us to do, let you continue to suffer in that fashion?"

In an attempt to calm herself, she closed her eyes, summoned serene thoughts, spoke over the lump in her throat. "Of course not. I'm sorry."

She had to get past this, return to some semblance of normalcy. She was not going crazy. Absolutely not. Doc Beecher had told her over and over that people didn't go crazy. They might develop symptoms of a mental illness, but they didn't go crazy. Her mother killed herself because she had severe depression. She refused to get proper care, that was all. How many times since her death had he said that, like maybe she thought it was his fault and it really wasn't? Lenore struggled to believe it, like she had always done in the past.

Okay, fine. He wanted her to see someone, she would see someone. "All right, I'll talk to Doc Beecher. But now I want to get out of bed and dress. Take the tea back to the kitchen. I'll have some in a little while."

His glance told her he didn't approve, but he carried the tray away nevertheless, leaving her alone.

For a long while after the door closed, she sat with her face in both hands. Somehow she had to gather enough strength to prove she wasn't a raving maniac. Food would take care of the physical, but how would she handle the other? Holding on to the bed and then the wall, she worked her way to the bathroom door and there caught sight of herself in the mirror above the dressing table. Pale as a sheet, black hair in nests all over her head, blue eyes bloodshot in cave-like holes. She reached out, tottered toward the security of the sturdy vanity, but could not take her gaze from the image in the glass. Stains marred the front of her white sleep shirt, as if she were a child who had eaten without a bib.

Oh, sweet Jesus.

Leaning over the high rim of the claw-footed tub, she turned on the shower and crawled under the spray. Before it could get hot. Before she drew the curtain on its circular rod. Before she could manage to remove the dirty shirt. Arms wrapped around both knees she sat in the cold tub and rocked beneath the pounding water as it went from cool to tepid to hot.

"Stay away from me, don't you come back. You just stay away." Over and over the litany dribbled from slack lips. Trying to make a deal with the devil.

Illusory arms enclosed her, hands cupped her breasts. Breath hotter than the water spilled over her neck, across her shoulders, ran down her torso.

"Oh, can't do that, sweet Lenore. Welcome back. We have missed you."

The scream began in her mid-section, traveling upward, convulsed her throat.

No, she mustn't scream. He'd come. Get her. And Mama would know. Don't scream. No, no, no. Hot tears mixed with the shower spray. "Help me, someone please help me."

"Lenore, hush now, I will try to protect you, not let him hurt you." Another voice, soothing, but forlorn and lost.

Dear God, how could she be sure she'd heard anything at all? Herb and Doc Beecher were probably right—she needed to be put away and right now. They had names for people who heard voices, used to burn them at the stake, for God's sake. But no more, no more. Now there were drugs. Mind-numbing drugs that turned you into a drooling—

"No, you're not crazy. Hush now."

Him again. The kind one.

The hands, the arms, the hot breath gone away, and in their place a lingering touch, a whisper of solace. Then nothing. No one. No one but herself and the water that grew cold as the old tank drained.

A sharp rapping on the door. She jerked. "What? Who is it?"

"Are you all right?" Delilah's comforting voice.

"Oh, yes. I'm fine." Go away, just go away, and leave me be, bitch.

The door squeaked open, Delilah's face and shoulders appeared through the dissipating cloud of steam.

"Oh, darlin'. Fine indeed. What're you doing? Let me help you."

The rest of her materialized, graceful hands shut off the tap and stripped the soggy shirt off over Lenore's head.

"Just look at you." She cupped Lenore's chin and lifted her head, stared at her with green eyes that swam in unshed tears. Pushing bedraggled hair out of Lenore's eyes, she chuckled dryly. "Honey, it was a good idea to take a bath and wash that limp old hair, but I don't think you're going about it quite right. Let's get you dried off and back in bed. I brought up breakfast. We'll let that little old tank warm back up while you eat, then give you a proper bathing. You'll feel worlds better."

As she spoke Delilah toweled Lenore's hair dry and helped her to her feet. "Come on, out on the rug."

Lenore obeyed and was soon dried, gowned, and propped up by pillows with a tray across her lap.

Del tucked a white linen napkin under her chin. "I wasn't sure what you'd want, being your first day back among the living. Hope you don't mind, I sent Herb on a long errand. I swear, every time I turned around in that itty bitty kitchen I ran smack over him, and he's as useless as tits on a boar hog."

Lenore gazed at the food—two coddled eggs in a blue soup bowl, yolks peering through hot milk like gigantic yellow eyes, buttered toast, and three strips of crisp bacon on a matching plate. To one side steamed a large mug of tea, to the other a glass of orange juice. Nausea boiled into her throat.

"Now, honey, you eat all you can manage. It's time we got your strength built up. No wonder you haven't been eating, Herb sure isn't much of a cook, is he?"

Lenore swallowed harshly, gazed at the chattering woman. She had never seen this side of the normally aloof person who ran The Craft Basket. Though several questions dotted the one-way conversation, Del didn't allow her time to answer them. With a shaking hand she picked up the mug. Del guided it to her lips.

"It's a little hot. Blow first," she said and puffed out her cheeks to help.

"Oh, Del." She wouldn't cry, she mustn't, but tears pooled, anyway, in spite of her efforts.

"Hush, not a word yet. First eat, drink, then talk."

And so she ate, polishing off half of the egg mixture, a slice of bacon, and a triangle of toast, sipping the tea between bites. Del lifted the glass of juice, but she waved it away. Something about it disturbed her.

Del shrugged. "Well, maybe later. There, now, I'll bet you feel a whole lot better." She set the tray on the bedside table. "I'll just check on that water, see if it's hot yet. Be right back."

Water ran for a long while in the bathroom, then Del returned. "Your hot bath awaits, madam."

While Lenore soaked in the tub, Del chattered from the other room where she changed the linens on the bed. Then she came into the bath, rummaged around for shampoo and cream rinse, and knelt beside the tub where she shampooed Lenore's hair. After rinsing it with the portable spray, Del wrapped her head in a big towel and helped her out of the tub. Buffed dry, she submitted to being led to the freshly made bed.

"Now, I don't expect to have to keep up this pampering too long, darlin'. You'll be up and around in no time. But for today, you just lay here and read a while, then get yourself a good night's sleep, and we'll see you on your feet come tomorrow."

"Del, thank you. I appreciate all of this. I don't know what I'd have done. You showed up at just the right time." The words came out in a halting stammer.

"We're friends, aren't we?"

Lenore nodded, squinted, but could see no aura around the woman. Odd, Herb hadn't had one, either. Perhaps she was too sick. Oh, God, yes, pray she'd been sick with a high fever. That would explain so much.

She guessed Del was her friend, though they did have plenty of disagreements. They were partners in The Craft Basket in an odd, sort of one-sided way. Lenore had invested a large sum in the enterprise and often ran across items for stock, but Del and Richard handled running the business. The differences in their taste for quality crafts had made a success of the shop. They did not pal around together—the two couples never mingled socially or visited with one another. Yet she did think of Del as her friend, possibly her only one, except for Herb. And as for Richard, she couldn't stay far enough away from him. He was a womanizer with the vocabulary of an uneducated redneck. Just because he was the best looking man in Summit Falls was no reason to like him. He was arrogant, self-centered, and crude. Besides that, he treated Del a little too rough for Lenore's taste, and the fact that she put up with it said something about her own mental stability.

And that one time when he'd fondled her, well, perhaps she had liked how it made her feel, but there'd been nothing to it. Absolutely nothing.

If she had been in need of a best friend, she would not have picked Del. However, she couldn't ignore the good deeds. After a long while she replied to Del's question about them being friends.

"Well, of course we are. Thank you so much for everything. Now, I think I'll get some sleep." Though grateful, she wished Del would leave.

"You surely can, honey. I'll come by in the morning and check on you if you'd like."

Lenore studied this so-called friend, standing in the doorway in what appeared to be a deliberate, somewhat unnatural pose. Like a pup expecting a pat after having performed a clever trick.

Immediately ashamed, she blew Del a kiss. "I'll have the coffee pot perking, just for you," she told her.

Del laughed. "Better not, darlin'. You make a lousy cup of coffee. People who don't drink it can't brew it, but I do appreciate the thought. See you tomorrow."

Okay, so she had acquired herself a friend, whether she wanted one or not. Herb would be pleased. He often chided her for being such a loner and preferring a walk in the woods to spending an evening drinking and dancing. She picked up M. G. Miller's *Seven Devils* from the night table, but only read a few pages before dropping off.

Chapter 7

ERIC STIRRED CAREFULLY to keep from awakening the beast that dwelled within his body and soul. Terrorizing the woman had exhausted the entity he had christened Alf. A harmless enough sounding name, but according to Norse mythology, it meant someone who was dead and living in the underworld. His own name meant eternal ruler, and over the years since he'd come awake in this hellhole, the comparison kept a tiny spark of his identity alive. A spark fanned awake by the beast's experiments with the woman, Lenore.

Alf prodded him. *"Actually, I quite like the name you've bestowed upon me. Otherwise I would punish you as you know I can. But be wary of any desires for sweet Lenore, or I shall trade yours for my own delightful evening of fun and games."*

Eric shuddered. He carried an abiding sorrow for what Alf had forced him to do, but the shame of the slaughter belonged entirely to the demon who had no conscience. Still the threat of being forced to relive the deaths, especially those of his dear wife Annie and their beloved sons

Seth and Andrew, drove him deep into a black pool of remorse where he sometimes wished he might simply let go and drown. That he could never do so distressed him to the point of insanity.

To ease the dreadful thoughts, he tread gently on memories of the woman Lenore.

"Leave her be. She's mine," Alf said immediately.

"Yes, I know."

"What's that I hear? Relief? What do you suppose will happen to you when I join her?"

"I'll be free."

"Fool, you'll simply be dead with no entertainment."

"My God, that's disgusting." A wrenching pain ripped through Eric.

"I have warned you not to call upon your God. He cannot and will not help you. With or without me, this place is your hell, and it will continue. I promise you that."

"And the woman?"

"Lenore. Fitting name. Where have I heard it before? Ah, yes, I do believe that madman Poe who wrote such drivel spoke of a Lenore before his pitiful soul was rescued. Ah, well, that was quite another time, wasn't it? What do you care about this woman?"

Unspoken questions probed at Eric's mind, digging at layers of salient thoughts. Edgar Allen Poe. A brilliant man who'd been quite mad. Had Alf been responsible for that madness? No, surely that wasn't possible. Aloud, he replied, "Care? I don't care. There's nothing left of me to care."

"Liar. You gentled her."

The roar belched fire and brimstone into the tiny cell, choked Eric with its stench, vibrated the stagnant air. He wished he could cover his ears, but his existence forbade it. He floated in a kind of viscous fluid, helpless to command his own arms or legs save when the demon slept. Blind except through the visions of Alf, he dwelled in a comatose world, aware of everything, but helpless to control so much as a twitch. He could think, though, and he sent a puny bequest to Alf.

"You have nothing to fear from my weakness. Haven't you said so over and over?"

Alf snorted. *"And you must keep that in mind. My curse is that I venture nowhere without you. A* ménage à trois *of the most heinous kind. Now, if you were a woman, ah, but I digress. It's time. She's sleeping, and I do so crave a tender touch. Time to convince the pretty little thing that there are many who need killing. What a desirable and powerful reign that will be."* He rubbed his hands together in devilish glee. *"I tire of being within your puny man's body. I wonder how long we can remain free to plunder, she and I? Her lover boy will soon have his way. He has his eye on that lovely redhead. They will make fine first kills, don't you think?"*

Even as Alf dragged Eric out of the body that sprawled on the hard cot at the Institute for the Criminally Insane, Lenore's terror drifted into his thoughts. Her innocence and fragile spirit reached out to him. With her possession by Alf would come his release. Dare he hope that he could survive such a bitter victory?

The dark bedroom smelled vaguely of apricots, apples, wild flowers, a fragrance that stirred poignant memories. The window across from her bed stood open about three inches, letting in chilly night air that promised spring. The woman lay curled, knees to chin, the quilt kicked off to reveal her lovely body clad in a sheer gown. Cold or afraid? Maybe both.

Eric wanted to close the window, cover her, but could do nothing so physical. In this state, nor could Alf, who wouldn't have had the thought anyway. He wanted her to be uncomfortable and needy.

It was her soul and spirit he would control and eventually take over. Manipulating her mind, Alf trailed an imaginary finger between the cleft of her breasts, groaned as only a demon can. Under his touch her skin felt smooth and cool, heart thumping beneath the silken draped flesh.

Obscene and explicit, the demon's lust rippled through Eric's own salient desires. Dear God, to love a woman, to love Annie, a memory so painful he flung it away, tucked himself into an obscure dark cavern of Alf's being. It wouldn't help, for there was nowhere to hide from the wicked lusting desires.

Lenore whimpered in her sleep. Alf moved over her, spoke in her ear, fondled with deliberate roughness each erogenous zone. She rolled to her back, opened her legs, tossed her head back and forth on the pillow. Demonic laughter, sexual arousal hammered at Eric until he could stand it no longer.

Tweaked by her sexual response, he joined Alf, watched, mesmerized, as Lenore raised her hips to the invisible lover, lowered then raised them once more—convulsing, sweating, gasping, at the same time grappling to pull the quilt over her aroused body.

Such piteous cries. "Oh, please love me. Yes, there."

Fists clutched the covers beneath her chin and for an instant she looked right at him, cobalt eyes dark with horrified passion.

The gaze tore at a remnant of pity, made Eric's head ache. Well, at least that's what it felt like.

The pain rumbled when Alf harshly spoke. *"I will love you, sweet Lenore. Herb is with lovely Delilah, the redheaded bitch. I warned you, told you to feed her the tea. You must stop being such a weak, sniveling little whore. Get your back up and fight for what's yours. While her husband chases you, she carries on a hunt of her own. Don't let her get away with it. Don't let him treat you this way. He's a bastard and a fool, Lenore. You deserve better."* He delved deep within her until she writhed, overcome with a sexual need that threatened to smother Eric.

He trembled at the demon's words, the taunting so familiar because he had heard it all himself. Eons ago. For it seemed he'd been imprisoned with this monster for centuries.

With Alf in the throes of his lust, Eric dared speak to her. *"Fight him. Don't listen. He lies."* Had she heard him? Her eyes flicked around the room, searching. How terrible this must be for her. He wanted so desperately to help her, foolish though that might be. She was already lost, and he might as well give up to it.

Besides, when the demon passed to her, he would be free, and she would be trapped in this hellhole. Let it be, just let it be. He could not help her.

Alf twisted and plunged through the woman in the spasms of her mad ecstasy, and Eric struggled to ignore her wild responses, but to no avail. The moist heat of her mouth, the sweetness within, swallowed him up, and for a moment he found himself drawn into the passion. God, he could see what drove this monster to possess another human. It was like being thrust into a world awash with love and desire, hate and torment, compassion and fear, a celestial sphere of incredible beauty and monstrous emotions. Adrenaline flowed like lava from a volcano.

The demon yanked from that comforting womb of femininity. Her spread-eagled body rose several feet off the bed, caught for a final instant in Alf's brutal embrace, then tumbled into the rumpled linens as they fled the bedroom, exploding away into the night. Encased in a dreadful loss, Eric watched her as long as he could, her pathetic form huddled on the bed, arms wrapped around both knees, sobs pervading the room.

Chapter 8

DRIPPING WITH PERSPIRATION, Lenore jerked awake. Immobile, lips moving soundlessly, she repeated to herself the curse of the apparition of her nightmare.

"Sic pereant omnes inimici tui, Domine."

What did it mean? Where was the dream coming from? She sensed a mélange of terrifying scenes, this the only one she remembered.

Amazing, though, how alive she felt this morning. Like she did after she and Herb made love. Except she was sore, and Herb never became that aroused. Besides, he hadn't slept with her since she'd been ill. Was he, perhaps, sleeping with someone else? Delilah? Her so-called friend? The ugly suspicion infringed upon her good mood, and she shoved it away.

Frustrated, she rolled to the edge of the bed and lowered her feet to the floor. What was it she had to do this morning? Something important. The room remained steady. For two days she'd pretended to take the Valium, but instead spat it out the minute Herb or Delilah left the room, until finally the world around her stopped echoing darkness and confusion.

If Del and Herb thought they could carry on their sordid affair under the same roof with his crazy girlfriend while doping her up with Valium, they were mistaken.

No. Mustn't think such wicked thoughts.

Though a bit weak-kneed, she managed to take a shower, wash her hair and dress without staggering like a drunk. Finally she eased open the bedroom door and peered out. All remained quiet. The refrigerator hummed, the pump in the aquarium blew bubbles, and outside birds sang.

"Yoohoo, anybody home?" Leaving the door ajar, she crept into the living room. A blanket and pillow were folded at the foot of the couch. Did Herb really think she'd believe he'd been sleeping there? He and Delilah had probably been using her mother's room. Making love on the bed that hadn't been slept in for years. How dare they do such a thing? But she wouldn't go there and look. She couldn't.

Stricken with thirst, she moved to the kitchen. On the breakfast bar a coffee mug sat upside down on a folded kitchen towel. The largest black iron skillet rested on a stove burner, the inside white with bacon grease. At the sink she filled a glass to the brim, leaned both elbows on the counter, and drank while staring through the window. Here and there green peeked from buds to form a pale emerald fringe on shrubs and trees. A few redbud trees flared vermillion against the dun brown landscape. Higher on the side of the mountain, service trees blossomed like mounds of snow.

And in Lenore's heart grew an ugly hostility. She had recovered from whatever had laid her out the previous week, but in its place, like remnants of a chronic disease, dwelt ugly emotions she had never before experienced.

Where was everyone? How could they leave her alone in an empty house while she was ill?

She slammed out the door onto the front porch, hugged herself, and stared down the empty lane. Her Jeep sat in its usual spot, Herb's pickup beside it. No sign of Delilah's snazzy little red Camaro Richard had bought for her thirtieth birthday. A sure way to cure her pouting depression.

Spoiled rotten bitch. Married to a man born to money. Didn't even have to work, just played around with the shop.

Where in the hell was Herb, anyway?

The shaded porch was chilly, and she moved out into the sunlight of the grassy yard.

A glance toward the barn revealed movement, and she shouted Herb's name, then headed in that direction. They kept a couple of Tennessee Walkers for riding. He must be seeing to them, but why didn't he answer? As she moved into the gaping door, Herb stepped from the tack room. He hadn't seen her, was inspecting a bridle. His features were in shadow, but slanting light from a loft window outlined the shape of him, his broad shoulders and thick chest, a lock of sandy hair over his high brow. Desire thrummed within her.

"Herb, I've been looking for you. Waiting for you."

Obviously startled, his gaze skittered toward her. "You scared the pants off me. I see you're feeling better."

"More than better." She sidled toward him, a breeze blowing her hair, still damp from the shower.

He glanced around, as if searching for a place to run. He was cornered.

She snuggled against him, laid the flat of one palm on his chest and began to unbutton his shirt. His heart pounded against her hand. Leaning forward, she nipped at the warm flesh and undid another button.

"Lee?" He dropped the bridle to the dirt floor, put an arm around her, groaned when she pressed against him.

Frantically she worked the belt buckle loose, unfastened his jeans, pulled down the zipper, enclosed his erection in one fist. Twisted desire drove her, encompassed her in a blood-red mist.

"My God, Lee?"

She clamped both hands around him, unable to release his hot, hard, shaft but desperate to have him inside her. "Take my clothes off. Hurry."

"Here?" He could barely speak.

"Here and now, goddamn you."

He grew thicker, more massive within her grasp, and she sensed if she didn't hurry it would be too late. His fingers fumbled at her blouse front, glazed brown eyes pointing questions at her.

"Tear it off, damn you!"

"Lee, for God's sake. I don't—"

"Oh, yes, you do, Herb. You know you do." She squeezed him hard. "Be a man, and fuck me. Here. Now." She shoved him backward with such force that he tumbled to his butt in the loose hay scattered about beneath the loft and lay there, the erection pointing at the roof far above their heads.

Gasping, she tore her clothes off and threw herself on him, hungry mouth biting, kissing, suckling. Unable to wait a moment longer, her insides throbbing with desire, she straddled him and came down hard, screaming when he plunged deep within her.

He cried out, cupped her hips. She writhed once, twice, then climaxed as he did, both howling like animals. But she didn't stop. She wanted more and more and then more, until she was nearly out of her mind with ecstasy.

It was like nothing she had ever experienced before, and though he had gone limp, she continued to rock forward, backward. Forward again. Whimpering, crying. Tears ran from her eyes, plopped onto his chest.

"Lee, please. Stop now, please. I can't. Oh, God."

"Come on. Don't you want me?"

"Lee. Stop it. Dammit, stop." He grasped her shoulders, forced her off into the hay.

She stiffened, regarded his expression. "Is this the way you treat your whore, Herb?" Fingers curled, she clawed at his face.

Grasping her wrist he held the nails at bay. "Lenore, what are you talking about? Stop this instant."

Pinned and panting she glared at him. "He was right, you're a real bastard. You and Delilah been having a good time while you had me doped up, huh?"

"Lenore, what's wrong with you? Who was right? Delilah? That's ridiculous. I love you. Stop this, now."

"Oh, I'll stop this, all right, Herb. And you'll be sorry. You and Del both. And Richard too, for that matter. Now turn me loose."

He let her go, held both hands open while she moved off him. She gathered up her shirt and jeans, and he scrambled to his feet, yanked on his clothing, hopping on one foot, then the other and throwing harried glances her way.

"Lee, I want you to see Doctor Beecher. Let me take you now. We can straighten this whole thing out. You need help. I'll go with you."

"You'd like that, wouldn't you? Lock me up somewhere, then you'd be free to go to your whore. Well, it's not going to happen. You just get your things together and leave. I don't want you here anymore."

He took a step toward her. "Lee, be reasonable. I don't have a whore. You don't mean that. You're overwrought."

Taking a step backward, she grabbed up a pitchfork leaning against the wall, pointed the tines at him. "Don't you take another step, or so help me I'll drive this right through you. Stay away from me. Go to your whore, get out of my sight."

She tossed the pitchfork so hard it stuck deep in the dirt floor inches from his feet. Not thinking about her nakedness, she whirled and marched from the barn, across the yard and in the house. Slouched against the door, she began to shake.

What had happened to her? Dear God, what had she done?

Outside, Herb's truck growled to life.

She ran to the living room, arriving at the door in time to see the pickup barreling down the lane toward the highway. He hadn't even come in to pack his things. Tears coursed down her cheeks. Of course he hadn't. Probably thought she'd make good on her threat if he did. What had possessed her to act like that? Probably all that Valium they'd fed her. Maybe two days wasn't enough to get the medication out of her system.

Well, it served him right. He knew she didn't like to take drugs. He'd be back. As soon as he figured she'd cooled down, he'd come begging her to take him back. And she might, she just might.

Chapter 9

*O*H, YES, LENORE, *you must forgive your darling Herb,"* Alf said. Eric jerked awake, found his body doing sit ups, toes hooked under the cot. "Leave her alone, for God's sake."

"Welcome back. Leave her alone, indeed. You forget I know what you know, feel what you feel. You enjoyed our little recreation with the lovely Lenore as much as I did. What were you playing? Good guy, bad guy? I liked it, confused our poor, sweet little bitch."

Eric would never admit to enjoyment of such perverse actions, not even to himself. Let it be, just let it be. Everything would soon be over. And he would be free of this monstrosity, but then what of her?

"What is she doing?" He couldn't help but ask.

Alf laughed, paused in his exercising. *"We're getting some good looking pecs, here. Can't think why we let ourselves go for so long."*

"Stop referring to me as we. I'm not part of you. I am separate from your perversity."

"Perhaps. Whatever you say, Eric. I need a woman, after this workout. God, she

might as well have raped the poor guy. Got me hard just watching. Think I'll catch her while she's still in the mood. For a moment there, I thought she'd actually plunge that pitchfork into his chest, but she disappointed me." Alf rose, went to the sink, and splashed his face and chest with cold water, drew his shirt back on and lay down on the bunk.

Eric swore in silence. No way in hell could he force the demon not to travel out of the body they shared. God, how he craved a night of freedom from this damnable cell, even if it meant Alf would go to Lenore. Truth to tell, he looked forward to being in her bedroom, tasting her soft skin, sweet as honey, juicy as apples and tart as lemons, tastes he could only vaguely recall. He yearned to share her every breath until he felt faint. Thank God, the demon hadn't stolen his senses, but only shared them. Especially now that they had found the woman.

It had never before occurred to Eric to wonder how much of himself the demon had stolen, and what he might yet control. But he did now. Being with Lenore had awakened desire. For years he had thought his plight hopeless, but now that he had traveled from this place, connected with her spirit, perhaps he might somehow overpower Alf's control. There was even a chance that in doing so he might help her.

As always, Alf eavesdropped on his thoughts. *"That, my friend, will be the day. But if it makes you feel better to fantasize such nonsense, be my guest."*

Alf projected their mind from the cell and into the warm afternoon. Like soaring birds, they flew through an eerie world, not seen so much as sensed. Perhaps senses are truly all one in the subconscious, without need of eyes, fingertips, nose, tongue, or ears. Moving through the fluffy clouds that threw shadows across the rolling hills below, Eric mused on that possibility. And he anticipated Lenore's smooth flesh and sweet depths so unlike Alf's dark world.

Chapter 10

LENORE SAT IN Doctor Beecher's examining room, listening while he spoke, in his fatherly way, of schizophrenia, manic and clinical depression, paranoia, and the various methods of treating the symptoms.

Pushing his glasses up on his nose, he peered at her. "I'd like you to see Doctor Barbara Collins. She's a clinical psychologist. Practices in Fort Smith."

"So you do think I'm going crazy?"

"Of course not, dear. There's nothing to worry about. I'm sure it's simply a matter of stress."

He paused, and she studied the strands of white hair that stood upright around his bald spot, making him look like a confused grandfather.

"I am concerned about your refusal to move past your mother's death. You're still in denial, and that's surely distressing for you. It's been, what? Four years? And yet you keep her room as if she just stepped out to go shopping."

"Her room? You? How dare you? You had no business in my mother's room." While he was snooping, the old coot probably discussed with Herb how best to humor her.

Doc shrugged, met her challenging glare. "Perhaps not. Clean the place out, turn it into a nursery or a work space, a den, something. Anything besides a shrine. And for God's sake, go see Collins before this goes any further."

Nibbling at her lower lip, she glanced away from his steady gaze. He was way off base, wasn't he? "I'm not going crazy." She shuddered, remembering her mother's episodes that had so frightened her as a child.

He peered over his glasses. "I've been known to see a shrink a few times myself. We all need help facing our boogers sometimes."

"Boogers?" Despite herself, Lenore smiled at the unprofessional word. "Under the bed, hiding in the closet boogers?"

"That's all they are, Lee. Imaginary ghosts conjured up by that part of us that knows our weaknesses, knows without question that we are born to die but are unable to admit the possibility."

Shaking with fury, she rose and glared down at him. "Tell me, is this what you told my mother when she first consulted you? Is that why she went home and killed herself, because you convinced her we are born to die? None of your advice helped her, did it?"

Sadness filled his eyes. "My dear child. I've known your family since before you were born. Your father was my dearest friend. Believe me, I did all I could for your mother."

"If you know so much, then tell me, does madness run in the family?"

Before he could reply, she whirled and fled his office, made her way out the door into the parking lot where her knees buckled. She went down hard, knelt there in the bright sunlit morning, and gave vent to her worst fears.

"Dear God, help me." She wiped her eyes and struggled to her feet.

Glancing around, relieved to see that she was alone, she hurried to her car. Not even the God she prayed to showed his cowardly face to help her. To hell with him, to hell with them all.

Over the next few days, that conversation with Doctor Beecher haunted her. She didn't hear from Herb either, and that didn't help matters. Doctors didn't know everything, and there had to be a rational explanation for these irrational occurrences. Before she gave up and made an appointment with Doctor Collins, she would do her best to find out what was going on inside her brain.

At the Fayetteville Public Library, a helpful research librarian assisted her on the computer. She'd never even touched one, but after an hour or so was surfing the Internet clumsily. She finally located articles about the crime spree of Eric Adair in the eighties. Several had been written in *Newsweek* and *Time*, and there was a study of his crimes in a book about serial killers. With help she printed the articles and requested a copy of the book from the library. They would let her know when it arrived.

Because she wasn't ready to face the people at the grocery store in Summit Falls, she stopped at an IGA. There wasn't a thing in the house to eat except what Herb had brought in while she was sick. Cans of soup, eggs and bacon, milk and bread. He wasn't very imaginative where meals were concerned.

The next day she would get her life back on track. Deliver the carton of herbal teas still in the back of the Jeep to The Craft Basket, talk to Del like a normal person and go see Herb. If he loved her, he would help her. She didn't let herself think what she would do if he refused.

Armed with several bags of food and a somewhat grim determination, she headed for Summit Falls, a twenty-minute drive. She'd find Herb, apologize for her erratic behavior, invite him to supper, feed him his favorite roast beef dinner, and they would make up. Have ordinary sex together, not something perverted like that horrible scene in the barn.

All the while, she expected to hear from the evil voice that had possessed her into doing such a thing to Herb. But all was silent. Fearful of believing the unearthly contacts were gone lest she tempt the fates, she tiptoed through the day, ready for anything.

Before going home, she drove to the property Herb was developing southwest of town. She found him and his crew installing siding. Herb built houses styled loosely after the Ozark farm homes of an earlier era— single storied with three bedrooms, a country kitchen complete with pantry, one-and-a-half baths, a sun room with space for a washer and dryer. A ten-foot wide porch the length of the front of the house was covered with a sloping roof. With a natural wood siding of cedar, redwood, or cypress and large windows, the efficient homes sold quickly. He built one at a time on spec, using a small crew. Herb made a comfortable living, but was a cautious man.

Lenore braked the Jeep in the clearing cluttered with construction scrap and stacks of materials. She spotted two men working on scaffolding, another on the ground with Herb, sawing and passing up 1x10 lengths of cedar siding. Unobserved, she studied him. His strength and the grace with which he moved reminded her of a well-trained dancer rather than a man who built houses. Hope clogging her throat, she beeped the horn and hopped from the car. The odor of freshly cut lumber permeated the spring air. Power hammers burred rhythmically, a saw whined, echoes bounced from one hill to another. Herb paused, carrying a length of siding and squinted into the sunlight toward her. He slid the cedar up onto the scaffold, then turned and watched her approach in gruff silence.

Still angry, even a bit aggressive. Well, she deserved that. "I thought I'd find you here."

"Where else?" He waited, eyes shaded by the hard hat he wore.

"Herb, can we talk?"

He glanced at the guys on the roof staring down at them. "I'm busy."

"I know. Come to the house for supper?"

"Lee, I'm not sure that's a good idea."

The staccato hammering stuttered, the saw wound down. Three men continued to stare in unison at their boss.

"Herb, please. We can't discuss it here."

"I'm not sure we can discuss it at all." Once again he glanced upward. "You guys done already?"

The men went back to work.

"I'm fixing roast and mashed potatoes and gravy, buttermilk biscuits. Your favorites. I'll bake an apple pie."

"Stop begging."

Had she thought that, or was the demon watching… *listening?*

"Lenore."

"Herb, please. I'm sorry, I really am. Don't make me say more here. Come to the house. I promise I'll make it up to you."

She watched his shoulders lift, his head go back till he stared up into the sky, Adam's apple working furiously beneath sunburned skin. At last he looked down at her. "You see the doc?"

Unable to speak, she nodded. Tonight she'd tell him about Collins, promise to go if only he'd give her another chance.

He let out a breath. "What time?"

"I can have it ready by six."

"Make it seven. We've got to burn daylight on this place."

She nodded. A lump filled her throat, and she blinked back tears that blurred her vision. "Seven, then. See you."

"Yeah, see you." His hazel eyes glittered hard as agates.

She remained there a moment longer, waiting. What for, she wasn't sure. But he turned and deftly scampered up the scaffolding. What if he fell off there? Broke his back. His neck. She shook off the ugly thought.

When he didn't look down, but went on working as if she weren't there, she crawled into the Jeep and left.

He was angrier with her than he had ever been, and she didn't blame him. She had been sexually aggressive, and Herb never had liked that. Poor man, he must've been terrified when she'd come at him with that pitchfork. That was way past wanting a roll in the hay. He preferred to make the first move, liked her to react passionately only to his needs, never show any of her own. Ordinarily, she was satisfied to go along with that. However, lately something must be up with her libido. Some decidedly wicked desires occurred to her at the most unusual of times, like the episode in the barn.

Good God, what had come over her? What if she had carried through? Ran the tines of that pitchfork through his middle? She had a lot to apologize for. Supper better be darned good. And then afterward, well, they'd see. Herb had a healthy sexual appetite, but he wasn't an imaginative lover. He had the same taste in sex as he did food. A meat and potatoes man, he never wanted to venture toward the erotic.

Several cars were parked at The Craft Basket when she pulled into the back space reserved for unloading. Good. She wouldn't have to deal with Del's questions about her health. She propped open the wide door, dragged out the large carton and carried it inside, sliding it onto a table in the storage room. After she had carefully unpacked the tins and packets onto a small wheeled cart, she dragged it through the swinging doors into the shop.

From up front, Del spotted her. "Lee, honey, there you are."

"Yes, it's me." An unexpected suspicion crawled through her. This woman and Herb were having an affair. Of course. The bitch.

Nonsense. Where were these ideas coming from? She had to stop thinking this way. It would get her nothing but trouble. Big trouble. Del's mouth moved and she struggled to understand the words.

"It's a good thing you brought your goodies, we're running short. It seems everyone wants to go away from here with at least one of your magic potions."

She cringed, noticing several customers staring at her. Probably thought she was a witch, imagined her standing over a black, boiling cauldron, stirring, cackling, brewing.

God, she had to get hold of herself. This whole thing would be funny if she wasn't so deep down frightened. Considering her mood, she chose not to reply, but trundled the little cart to her display area, an old fashioned tin pie safe decorated with intricately woven pine needle baskets, dried wild flowers, and photos of healing herbs. She filled the baskets with colorful packets, arranged tins of tea on the wood surface, stepped back to eye the effect.

How nauseatingly precious.

Dammit, why didn't she stop fooling with such a stupid pastime? It wasn't necessary to her survival that she package herbs for silly tourists who probably never opened them but put them on a shelf to gather dust and cobwebs for a few months, then tossed them away.

"Something we bought in the Ozarks. Aren't they quaint?" She could see them preening in front of their friends.

A shudder of disgust prickled at her. Why didn't she get on with her life, do something useful or challenging? Anything. Maybe the worst thing that had come of her father's death a few months ago was all the money he'd left behind for her. She certainly didn't know him well enough to miss him. She'd have been better off poor, then she would have been forced to work for a living instead of piddling around with this trash. Now she was getting ready to marry a controlling man who would further suppress any ambition she might have.

An awful urge to run somewhere far away overpowered her, dizzying in its potency.

Frustrated, she flung her hand wide, knocked a basket to the floor. Packets of herbs scattered across the shiny hardwood, and once again every eye in the place was aimed at her.

"Oh, hell," She dropped to her knees and gathered the packages.

"You okay, honey?" Del called from behind the counter across the room.

"Sure, fine. I'm just running late, that's all. I'll just leave this list with you and pick up my invoice next time I'm in, if that's okay."

"You know it is. I'll bet we've sold all those pretty little tins before you can turn around again. Say, did you hear about poor old Mr. Stiles?"

Lenore stiffened. Stiles. He was the old man in the grocery store, the one with the black aura. "No, what happened?" She didn't want to know, prayed she hadn't been right about his aura.

"Poor old soul was run over by a tractor. Killed him instantly."

She staggered against the counter, gasped for air. It could not be possible. All these years, and the auras had never forecast death. This was surely the demon's doing.

Del ran to her side. "You're white as a sheet. I didn't know you knew him so well, honey. You'd better sit down."

She gritted her teeth. "No, I'm fine. I'll try to make another delivery in a few days. I know I'm behind."

"Are you sure? Maybe you're having a relapse, hon," Del called at the door that swung shut behind Lenore.

"Maybe you're having a relapse," she mimicked and ran to the Jeep.

Amanitas. Those funny little white buttons. Mix 'em with the good mushrooms—no one can tell the difference till it's too late. Death angels. How apt. Feed her some. That'll teach her about your magic potions.

"Shut up." Lenore yanked open the car door. Heat flooded from the interior. Twisting the key, she ran down the windows and sped from the lot, heading back toward Summit Falls. Fleeing the taunting voice. Should've known better than to believe it was gone.

Before the two-lane road dipped into the first hollow, she caught a glimpse of the skeleton of the house Herb was building on the rise in the distance. If he looked down right this minute, he would see her leaving the shop, heading home.

How many times did he look this way in the course of a day? How often did he run over here just to say hi to that sweet-mouthed little bitch?

"Just to say hi? Lenore, wake up. Invite her to dinner soon, feed them both those poisonous little death angels. Angels indeed."

Angry at herself for such suspicions, furious that the voice had returned when she'd hoped it had gone with the fever, she drove too fast over the hills and curves that led to the cabin.

"Run, run, you can't lose me." The chant like a song.

Slamming to a stop in clouds of dust, she piled out of the vehicle, unloaded the groceries, tossed and shoved them into cabinets and the refrigerator. She came back to herself staring at a slab of red meat lying on the counter, rivulets of blood running to the edge and dripping off onto the floor.

Oh, God. Oh, God. What had she done now? Where had she been? She had put the roast in the slow cooker before she left. Hadn't she?

A distant echo of laughter drifted through the open window.

"Leave me alone. Get away, and leave me alone." The scream startled jays in the trees outside the window, and they fluttered into the bright sky.

With a shudder, she turned on the cold water and splashed her face, then patted it dry with a wad of paper towels.

Okay, now fix the meat.

She opened the cabinet, took out some spice tins, sprinkled their contents over the roast, then put it in a pan and slid it into the oven. No time for slow cooking now. Setting the heat at 325, she glanced at the clock.

Get out of the house. Fresh air was what she needed. Go find mushrooms. Yes. It had rained during the night, creating the perfect climate for the delicious morels Herb loved so much. They would have them with eggs for breakfast. If he stayed all night. He would, she'd make sure of that.

"No Amanitas, thank you very much." Jesus, now she was talking to the monster.

There might be a few early herbs she could dig to plant in pots. She gathered a small basket, a few plastic bags, cotton gloves, a hand digger, and shears. Might as well harvest some fresh sassafras root. Though it was too early for sanicle to bloom, she might locate a few young plants to mark for later. The herb was one of several she used for the special mixes recommended for sore throat. If she had time, she would check a patch of St. John's wort she'd located last fall in the overgrown clearing of an old house place. Its medicinal yellow blossoms wouldn't appear for six to eight weeks yet, so she wouldn't cut it. Because that particular herb grew best in meadows, it was getting more difficult to locate. Farmers eradicated it where they could, considering it a nuisance in their pastures, and she had been delighted last fall to find a generous stand.

Properly armed and determined to ignore her unfriendly demon, she set out on the exceedingly warm afternoon. This far south March days could grow a bit hot, and so she wore only a loose chambray shirt and pants and a pair of well-worn walking shoes. Once into the stand of hickory and oak, undergrown with sumac, brambles, and wild roses, she set a quick pace along the familiar path her father and she had tread for so many years.

Not since the funeral had she thought consciously of her father. As her mother's illness had grown more severe, he seldom came home. When he did spend an evening at the house she'd hear them shouting at each other late into the night, would lie with a pillow over her head and the covers tucked securely around her scrunched up body to shut out the fury of their voices. After her mother died, she'd never been close to her father again. Perhaps he blamed her in some perverse way. She certainly held

him partly responsible for the suicide. They left each other alone, whatever the reasons. When he died suddenly of a heart attack just before
Thanksgiving, she felt nothing but relief, which was, of course, shameful.

Now here she was, striding along, thinking of a time long past when
as a child she had followed him through these woods. He had taught
her about the mushrooms and some of the wild plants, the rest she had
learned because of his enthusiasm.

She slowed, made her way carefully over a small stream fed by one
of the abundant springs on the hillside. She moved with caution on the
slick, moss covered rocks. As she stepped onto dry land, she glimpsed
the shimmer of a figure darting into the deep shadows beyond a jagged
outcropping ahead. Unearthly shrieks followed after him. Around her,
the woods darkened, as if clouds had moved across the sun. She swayed,
squeezed her eyes shut, and covered her ears to shut out the animal-like
howls. When she finally opened them, the sunlight was as bright as ever,
and there wasn't a cloud in the sky.

What on earth had that been? Too large for a black bear, more like a
tall, broad-shouldered man. A hunter perhaps or lover of the woods in
spring like herself? But why had he run off howling like a banshee? No,
more like a wounded creature. This was the Ozark National Forest, and
plenty of wild animals lived here in seclusion. That's all it had been. A
black bear screeching for her cub. The rest, her imagination. She stood
still, listening, watching, until the muscles in her neck ached, and her eyes
burned. If it was someone walking, he was mighty light-footed, for she
heard nothing. No rustle in last winter's dry leaves, no snap of dead limbs
or skitter of stones.

A flash of the nightmare, the poor creature brutally slain by red men,
blocked out her vision for an instant, and she tottered to lean against a
nearby tree. In the dream, the surroundings always appeared hauntingly
familiar, like she'd been there in real life. Of course, she probably had.

She'd wandered these woods all her life, and the subconscious stored everything to throw back in the dark of night when you could do nothing about it. Despite the warmth of the sun slanting through the bare branches above, she shivered, rubbed at goose flesh along her arms. This hadn't been such a good idea. She was still exhausted from the illness, that was all. Still seeing left-over visions just like the earlier voices. The looming forest closed around her, and she couldn't wait to escape. To hell with the morels, the sassafras root, the sanicle. All she wanted was the safety of home. She turned to run, splashing through the shallow stream clumsily, holding up one arm to ward off low branches. At the edge of the woods with the house in sight, she forced herself to stop. Only then did she realize she'd left her basket and digging tools in the woods. Such a foolish woman.

She'd go back for them later. Right now, all she wanted was inside. She hurried across the yard and through the door. For a long while she peered through the back window for a sign of someone following, or perhaps a brief glimpse of rampaging Indians and the poor luckless fellow they continued to kill over and over in her dreams.

Inside she dug through drawers until she found the Valium Herb had been feeding her while she was sick. She downed two pills and sat in the living room hugging her knees until they kicked in.

Sometime later, busy in the kitchen, she heard the crunch of tires along the dirt lane and took up the thick, rich gravy, drained the potatoes, whipped them with plenty of butter and milk, and spooned creamy mounds into a bowl. Without a word of greeting Herb went straight to the bathroom to wash up. He never kissed her until they were both clean, might not kiss her at all this time. He would have taken off his work boots on the porch like he always did. From the warm oven she rescued the tender roast—surrounded by carrots and onions the way he liked it—and the pan of biscuits. Iced tea sparkled in blue glasses shades paler than the ironware, and the kitchen smelled of bread and beef, pungent steeped tea, and the spicy apple pie cooling on the counter. Amazing what one can do under the influence of Valium.

She hugged herself into silence. Despite the experience in the woods, she felt hopeful, secure, and anticipatory. Herb was here, and everything was going to be fine, just fine. All she had to do was keep it together.

11

YOU FRIGHTENED HER," Eric said.

"Nonsense. She can neither see nor hear us. She has a vivid imagination, that's all. Still terrified. She'll get used to it after a while." Alf sounded well pleased.

Eric doubted anyone could ever get used to Alf's presence, but didn't voice his opinion. She had seen their essence, of that he was sure. "Why don't you choose someone else, someone more attuned to violence?"

"Ah. In this random universe, you suggest I choose someone who deserves what is about to happen? How terribly Christian of you."

If Eric didn't know better, he'd think Alf was actually enjoying their repartee. Until the demon set his sights on Lenore, Eric had remained silent and brooding most of the time, only venturing out briefly when Alf slept. Often his slightest action or thought awoke the monster who would then gleefully treat him to a replay of one of the ghastly killings from his past. He would awaken to the sound of demonic laughter, strapped into a straightjacket, mind blurred by drugs, unaware of what he might have done to merit such treatment from the prison doctors. But he could guess.

Lately Alf appeared to welcome their discussions. Only when Eric attempted to communicate with the woman did the demon vent his fury. Both were going through baffling changes in this search for a fresh host.

Eric ventured to continue the conversation. "I was a Christian once."

"*Born again and all that rot? Tell me, has your God forgiven you your sins?*" Alf laughed demonically, as only he could.

Eric ignored the cynicism and the shudders that crawled up his spine "If you were spawned in Hell, then you must believe in God and Heaven."

"*Oh, most surely. For to believe is the only way in which we can keep His influence at bay. Ignorance is surely deadly.*"

"I never believed in demons, and I certainly never denied God. You can see where that's gotten me."

Alf chuckled, and the action physically disturbed Eric, made his stomach churn and his head ache. How interesting that out of body, his senses remained intact. Like when he tasted Lenore's sweet breath or felt glossy strands of her hair against his cheek.

"*Indeed. What a fat lot of good your God did you. You're a fool if you think belief in demons would have helped your case, however. And tell me, where is your God now?*"

Odd that Alf hadn't chastised him for thinking of the woman he considered his alone. Maybe he hadn't sensed the fleeting thought. The idea spurred a tingle of excitement. Was it possible that when distracted by an argument or discussion, Alf couldn't sense his thoughts? More likely, he had simply chosen to ignore them.

"Where is my God? He's here with me, giving me strength to withstand your evil deeds." Eric deliberately recalled the feel of Lenore's skin when Alf caressed her in bed. Warm, vibrant, silken. Imagined his mouth at her breast and shivered with desire.

As if hands closed around his throat, Eric's air was cut off. He gasped. The surrounding woods faded to black, flecked with bright dancing lights. Caught.

As if not aware of his action against Eric, Alf went on. *"Do not deride the idea of evil. This world would be much too saccharine without terror to add its bittersweet flavor."*

The pressure released, Eric floated back to the surface of consciousness. Was it possible the punishment had been for his statement and not his passion for Lenore? He would try something more telling, but before he could continue the experiment, Alf was off, moving toward the house, mind roaring a protest.

"The bastard! He's come back. Did she invite him? How could she be so stupid? How could I? While we were arguing about your puny God, she's made a move I didn't anticipate."

Eric kept silent. How could he become so irate when he wanted Lenore to kill Herb? How could she do that if they remained apart?

Raging, muttering reproaches, Alf moved through the darkening house to the room lit by flickering candles. *"She's seducing him once more. Stupid, stupid woman."*

Eric took the brunt of the demon's anger, a pain so intense that all his senses locked down, diminished his existence to a minuscule speck in the abyss of Alf's subconscious.

Chapter 12

HERB CUT A bite from a slice of beef and dipped it in a pool of blood-red ketchup on his blue plate. "You must realize that your actions were very frightening. I've never been untrue to you, and to be accused of playing around with Delilah hurt like hell. Not to mention what happened in the barn." He flushed and stuffed the meat into his mouth, refused to acknowledge her gaze while chewing.

"I know, and I apologize. I don't know what else to say except I'm so very sorry. I was ill, but I'm fine now. All better." She smiled too widely. "It won't happen again. I don't want us to fight, to break up. I want our life together, look forward to it. I thought you did too."

"I did. I do."

"Then what?"

"I want you to see someone, get help. Unless you agree to that, I'm afraid I can't come back. You might've run me through with that pitchfork, not to mention that unseemly display. Why you practically raped me."

Not to mention you liked it, prick.

His words, her silent rebuttal, shocked Lenore into silence. She nodded, twirled her spoon through the mound of potatoes and let gravy flow around the carrots.

"I'll make an appointment first thing in the morning. Doctor Beecher gave me the name of someone in Fort Smith." She had studied enough psychology to know that she did need to talk to someone about why she could not simply go into her mother's room and get rid of her things. The voices, well that was another thing altogether. Perhaps there were reasons for them she hadn't yet fathomed. Her belief, strengthened by her recent choice of reading material, that demons did truly exist only made the experience more formidable. Which would be worse, possession by a demon or madness? Or were they both the same? Had her mother's illness begun this way? Was it, after all, only a precursor to what she had always feared and not a demon at all?

Herb laid down his fork, reached across the table to cup his hand over hers. "Good, that's great. You have to understand, this is for your sake more than mine. I can't stand the thought of you... I mean, your mother—"

"Don't bring up my mother. She has nothing to do with this."

"How can you say that? I'm sorry to distress you further, but they do say things like this run in families."

"Things like this? They say?"

"Don't make me say it. You know what I'm talking about. Your mother was quite mad."

"That's the voice of your mother talking, Herb. How dare you repeat hurtful gossip as if it were true? Your mother's a forked-tongue bitch. Would you say that runs in your family?"

Furious, she shoved away from the table so violently that she knocked over her glass of tea. The amber liquid spread across the shiny table top and ran into Herb's lap.

He jumped to his feet, mopping at the front of his pants with a napkin. "For God's sake, Lee. I've never heard you talk like this. Lately you're acting like someone else, not yourself at all."

Throwing the napkin into the middle of his plate of half-eaten food, he stomped to the front door.

She moved to stop him, grabbed at his arm. "Herb, please, don't leave."

The purpling of his face told her he was furious. He yanked from her touch, shoved open the screen. "Get yourself some help, Lee, before it's too late. Before we find you bleeding to death in your own bed."

The cruel words chopped her legs from under her, and she slumped to the floor. Arms curved over the top of her head, she hunkered there while the door slammed behind him.

"I told you killing him was the only answer." The voice came from inside her head, from all around, from everywhere, and she covered her ears and screamed.

—

DOCTOR COLLINS'S OFFICE was on the corner of the fourth floor of an old red brick building on Garrison Avenue. The ceiling-high windows looked out on the Arkansas River. Miserably hunched in an overstuffed leather chair, Lenore imagined smashing headlong through the glass and plunging into the brown water.

"Doctor Beecher called me," the youngish, plump brunette said, dragging her attention from the dark musings.

"I'm sure he did." Lenore studied the psychologist. The woman didn't look like she could possibly be a doctor with her round, dimpled cheeks and wide-eyed innocent look. Not a psychologist, at any rate.

"You don't want to be here."

"Not really."

"You think you're fine, nothing wrong?"

"I'm not fine at all."

"Then what is it?"

"I don't think you can help me. No one can."

"Why don't we give me a chance? Give you a chance?"

Lenore shrugged, stared once more at the window. She didn't even know how to dress, this so called doctor. Frumpish loose blouse, not tucked into a crinkled skirt. Lusterless hair piled on her head with strands escaping in every direction. And her aura. What a conglomeration of confusion and neglect of her own intelligence.

Oh, God, don't let me start with auras again.

"Did you come all the way down here to sit in silence for an hour and then go home?"

Lenore shuddered, raised her shoulders, glanced around the pleasant room decorated with potted plants and framed prints. Impressionistic, soft colors, hints of beauty, blur of flowers and trees and water. Men and women walking hand in hand through their fuzzy world. Perfect choice for a shrink's office. A world one couldn't quite make out. And this doctor had problems of her own, held them in with a discipline Lenore found puzzling. How could she hope to help her patients when she didn't yet understand herself?

Silence dragged out. She had to say something, admit to the reason she was here. Get it over with. In a low, trembling voice, she said, "I'm very frightened."

"Yes? What frightens you?"

A trickle of sweat ran down the center of her back. God, this was awful. Blurt it out, say it. Get past it. And she did. "That I'll go mad like my mother and kill myself."

"Why would you do that?"

"Herb says because things like that run in families."

"And you believe him?"

"I believe the voices." Even as she uttered them she regretted the words. She hadn't meant to bring that up.

Collins reacted, though obviously she made an effort not to. Her full lips pursed and one eyebrow twitched ever so slightly. She was definitely much more interested than she'd been a moment earlier. Yeah, you've got you a real crazy here, Doc. She hears voices.

"These voices," she finally ventured. "Exactly what do they say?"

"I don't want to talk about this. I want you to tell me why I can't walk into my mother's room, fold her things up, and pack them out of my house, out of my life. Paper the walls in bright yellow or blue or even stripes, for God's sake. Forget what she did in there."

"Why don't you tell me why you can't do that?"

"If I could tell you that, I wouldn't be here, would I?"

"Lenore, that's precisely why you are here. Tell me about your mother."

"I can't."

Collins perked up at that "How long has she been dead?"

"I just want to get out of here." Lenore gritted her teeth to keep from shouting.

Collins nodded. "Very well. I can see you at this same time Monday."

"I don't think so."

"Shall I call someone else? Make you an appointment with a colleague? Perhaps you'd prefer someone older or a man?"

"I don't prefer anyone. You can't force me, can you?"

The woman shook her head. "No. We can't protect you from your thoughts. Or, for that matter, protect others from them, either. Infringement of your civil rights."

Lenore sensed the sarcasm in the doctor's voice. The woman disagreed with such nonsensical laws that allowed the mentally ill to choose their own treatment or lack of it and wander the streets. At one time she had, too. People like that should be put somewhere where they could be treated, not let live on the streets just because they had their rights. Rights not to care for themselves if they didn't know how, to be homeless, dirty, bug infested, to wander around in a stupor?

Yet at this moment Lenore was very pleased with that law, for it allowed her to walk out of Doctor Collins's office, get in her car, and drive anywhere, crazy as she might be. She could probably even tell her more about the voices without dire results, but she had no intention of doing so.

Collins went on. "If I thought you were going to try to kill yourself, or harm someone else, I could put you in for observation. Otherwise...." She shrugged.

Lenore had no reply to that. Prodded by the voice, she was ready to leave the presence of this woman who needed a psychiatrist herself.

A half-hour later Lenore exited the Interstate and drove toward the safety of home. Redbuds splashed the woods with their brilliant carmine. Soon the dogwoods would bloom, leaves would swell on the trees, and the starkness of winter would disappear. Dare she hope that with spring her sanity would return?

She had to find out if Eric Adair was still behind the bars of his prison. The idea that she could do something about what was going on made her feel better.

At last, embraced within the cabin's walls, she leaned against the door for a moment, then took a deep breath and went in search of the copies she'd made at the library. All this other nonsense had distracted her, kept her from learning more about the man. He had to be the source of her problems.

She unfolded the article from *Newsweek* and began to read, found it unlike *The Comet*'s approach to the story. However, the bloody crimes Adair had committed remained undeniable. Strange how she had hoped the story was wrong. The news magazine made no mention of the killer's so-called claim that he was possessed by an immortal demon who went

around turning normal people into mass murderers of the most repugnant kind. It did quote a detective who had worked the case. What he
said sent chills through her.

> *"When I interrogated Adair, I became convinced that I was in the com-*
> *pany of true demonic possession. Evil is out there and has a presence. It's real*
> *and it's been with us since the beginning of time. Evil dwells in Eric Adair,*
> *and if the authorities were smart they'd put him to death."*
>
> *Instead they'd stuck him in an asylum.*
>
> *"That frightens me," the detective concluded. "I pray to God every night*
> *they don't decide they've cured this monster and turn him loose."*

Lenore sat for a long while, the white pages lying in her lap. Never
sure about her beliefs, she considered the possibility of evil possession,
but discarded it. Way too far out. But evil in the man who had killed
so mercilessly? Yes, she did believe in that. My God. What if they had
turned Adair loose? And somehow he had chosen her as his next victim.
The one he would murder next, after he had his fun terrorizing her.
Would that be better or worse than if she were going mad?

Darkness crept across the valley and chased the last glow of sunlight
from the mountain peaks. The songs of peepers filled the night air. If
that madman had escaped and the voices she heard were his, he could be
out there somewhere. Stalking her. Waiting. She shook herself.

Spring was a time of renewal, and here she was sinking lower and
lower into some kind of depraved nightmare. How could she believe that
Eric Adair had anything to do with what had happened to her over the
past few weeks? He was locked up for good. What she had to do was go
back to Doctor Collins and continue to see the psychologist until whatever had taken over her mind was purged.

Chapter 13

I **CAN'T LET** *her continue to see that doctor,"* Alf said.

"Why? Surely she can't hurt you?"

Alf laughed with scorn. *"I can't be hurt."*

"Well, then?"

"I'm bored with all this, bored with you. *I want her now. I want to lie within her warmth, touch her in places that will make her squirm as she never has before. Make her horny to the brink of madness, then satisfy that lust until she kills for me."*

Eric attempted to ignore the words, but Alf grew agitated. Ripped and tore into Eric's body and mind until he shuddered with excruciating pain. Howled like an animal.

"Adair, keep it down in there," a guard shouted. *"It's the middle of the goddamned night."*

Eric raised his head from where he slumped on the edge of the bed. A burly guard—they called them interns, but what a laugh—peered through the double-thick glass window in his cell door.

Eric opened his mouth to speak, expecting Alf to silence him, but the demon remained unheard, unfelt. "Sorry, I had a bad dream."

The intern gazed at him a moment longer, then moved away, the sound of his heels echoing along the corridor.

Eric ran his fingers through thick tangles of dark hair, wished it was shower day so he could clean up. Wished they would let him exercise in the yard instead of the incessant pushups and sit-ups he performed in the small cell while Alf slept. He dropped to the floor, stretched full length on his stomach and began to count, moving up and down endlessly in the dark.

Don't think, don't remember. Long lost Annie. Her sparkling dark eyes, her mahogany hair, her eager touch, the love they'd shared.

Dammit, I said, don't think. Tears mixed with sweat, and he pumped up and down, up and down. He increased the pace of the pushups until his breath came in gasps, his muscles burned, his heart thundered.

Alf surfaced, tearing his consciousness from the exhausted body and through the thick walls of their drab cell. He dragged Eric along through the endless night to the cabin where Lenore lay wide awake, all the lights aglow because she was so frightened.

Hovering over her, his dark passion setting the room ablaze with torment, Alf said, *"I want you to make love to her."*

Amazed, Eric hesitated to reply, then mumbled, "Me? Why me? I'm not sure I know how, the way we are, I mean."

"Think about it. It'll happen. I've frightened her. I need her to desire me, and I'm too brutal for her taste. Do it. Be gentle. Soften her up." Alf sent waves of agony through Eric's senses, a stabbing, wrenching pain he knew from experience would only let up if he did as Alf ordered.

A thin sheet lay over the woman's naked body, every curve outlined. Her hands clasped over the soft mounds of her breasts. She might have been dead, except for the fright that flashed in her wide open blue eyes. Midnight black hair fanned against the white pillowcase.

Passion flowed over him like warm water, and for the first time in his life he realized that desire was as much a part of the mind as it was of the body. He wanted her with a hunger that devoured his senses, overpowered his desperate need for release from this life.

Slowly he drifted against the warmth of her smooth flesh, imagined her in his arms though he had none, under his lips that weren't there, encasing the aching core of his manhood that rested in the dark cell far away.

And he called her name with all the longing he possessed.

Chapter 14

*L*ENORE. LENORE."

The voice, soft, haunting. A dream.

A gentle breeze through the open window touched her cheek, stirred the sheet draped across her. Licking lips swollen with passion, she trailed her fingers along the warm flesh of her belly. The cotton fabric drifted downward, revealing erect nipples. Aching. Waiting. Wanting.

"What? Who are you? What do you want?"

A melancholy voice whispered, *"Please don't be frightened."*

She stiffened, brushed at the side of her face as if she could somehow rid herself of this monstrous entity. "Oh, God. No, please don't." She twisted her thighs against the ecstasy that flowed between them. "Not again. I can't keep doing this." The pleasure was more than she could bear. Had she not been so frightened, perhaps she....

"No," she screamed.

"Be still, sweet Lenore. I won't hurt you." A gentle hand cupped her cheek, a thumb caressed the line of her chin.

"Who are you? Please, I can't endure what you're doing to me. I can't. I'll go crazy."

"Endure? Why, sweet Lenore. Relax and let me give you what you desire. I would never hurt you." Lips nuzzled one naked breast, then the other, so tenderly she might have imagined the warm, moist kisses.

She wanted to toss them away, but each time he took a nipple in his silken mouth, she fell under the spell. Nothing like the demon. He couldn't be real. And if only a dream, then what harm? It had been so long, so long since she'd experienced such an exquisite loving touch.

A moan of pure passion and she reached for this man who knew her body so well. But he wasn't there. Of course he wasn't real, but her lustful response was. Her body hummed and buzzed with a wild desire to have him. Voice soft, lips like velvet, fingers lingering in all the right places. Driving her out of her mind.

"You mustn't be afraid. I'm not him, the one who frightened you. I won't do anything to you unless you want me to. Tell me what it is you want, and I will give it to you."

Want? How could she not want? She twisted and turned, trying one last time to escape. "How could I want you? My God, this is awful."

"Listen to me. You're not going crazy. I can help if you'll let me."

"No, no, no." Flailing both arms and legs, she skittered across the bed and thumped down onto the floor where she crouched, sheet partially hiding her nakedness. "You're not real, not real. Leave me alone, please." The throbbing of her loins belied the plea. If he touched her again, kissed her again, she would be lost to him, lost to her own madness.

"I know how you feel, believe me, I do. I've been through this frightening and unbelievable experience. I don't want you to endure all that same horror. Let me help you." Pleading voice, sweet voice, kind voice.

Eyes wide she peered around the well-lit room. "Help me? Why should you help me?" Wrapping both arms around aching breasts, she gave in, unable to resist a moment longer. "Please, please, just put a stop to the burning, the need. I can't stand it a moment longer." She arched her hips into the air, an invitation waiting for a reply.

Flesh on flesh slipped inside her. Held there for a long moment. No violence, only a loving embrace. A sense of compassion.

How could this be? No one in the room except her and her dream lover. Wasn't that the name of an old song? A hysterical giggle escaped her, and she raised her knees, pushed hard, taking him deeper. An explosion within as he moved ever so slowly, breath against her ear when he spoke.

"How lovely and sweet and wet you are. Hot and ready. Do you feel me? Sense my desire for you?"

Someone in the room with her. Impossible to comprehend. Yet he was more than a voice, a disembodied spirit. She felt his touch, his breath on her skin, his lips at her breasts, his emotional turmoil. If not imagined, indeed if real, she should be embarrassed. Yet she was anything but. If he touched her in the same way again, she would turn to putty.

Something smooth and wet along her cheek. His tongue, moving closer to her lips, darting inside, wrapping around hers like the long, slithery tongue of a lizard *"You're cold, sweet Lenore. Get back in bed, cover up. I'll be there with you."*

She crawled onto the bed, wondering as she did if she moved through him. Under the covers, and he remained wrapped and twisted and locked inside her. Sending her senses soaring until she came with a gusto never before experienced in this bed or any other she'd ever lain in.

How is it he had no substance, yet he could touch her? Why then could she not touch him? She reached out with spread hands like a blind person testing for an unseen object.

Felt his essence.

She uttered a small, squeaky *oh*, and Eric's heart ached with sadness for them both.

"What are you doing?" Alf snarled, rupturing the moment.

That voice. The demon's voice. Lenore cried out, pawed at the quilt to cover herself, dug her heels into the mattress until her head slammed against the headboard.

Eric stilled the hatred he felt for this interloper, replied as calmly as possible, *"What you told me to do. Did you change your mind?"*

A moment's pause, Lenore rocking to and fro and crooning deep in her throat. For an instant Alf didn't answer, and Eric braced himself for the worst. This thing from hell could perform the most horrendous acts on him and his poor ravaged body. And on her too, should he choose.

This time, though, he did nothing, finally said, *"Of course I haven't changed my mind. But I told you to make love to her, not play around. Love is the singular thing that moves humans beyond the ability to protest."*

"Yes, love. Not rape or mindless sex. Love." Hopeless. The demon would never understand the difference between violence and tenderness, between love and sex.

Alf didn't reply, appeared to have withdrawn. His absence lent Eric a newfound sense of freedom. He yearned to spread his arms, raise his face to the heavens and shout with pure joy for that instant of unbridled liberty.

"Have you gone?" she asked, voice trembling. Part of her wished he had, but she understood that he had kept the demon away from her. His departure might allow him to return.

"No. I'm here. My name is Eric, and I'm with you. I promise to never hurt you." He kissed the corner of her mouth.

She jerked aside, licked where he'd touched her, put shaky fingers there. "That's it. A ghost kissed me, fucked me. I've gone totally insane. I mean, fantasy is one thing, but this, this is just loony tunes." A short pause while she digested an earlier comment, whispered, "Are you Eric—Eric Adair?"

Without answering, he slipped once more beneath the covers, nestled against her silken flesh.

She sighed, cupped one breast, and offered it to this imaginary lover. He placed his lips there, and both moaned with pleasure.

Whimpering, she offered him her body once more. Crazy. Insane. But he was there, his aura wavering to life as if it had been hidden for so very long. A shimmering umber aura, its edges flaring silver as if to overpower the darkness. She touched his essence with the palms of her hands, rubbed her cheek, her mouth, her breast. What an experience this could be if only the pounding terror that the evil one might appear would subside.

She ached to be taken again by this gentle lover, tenderly but with passion, a passion that would satisfy her own wakening desires. If this was crazy, there were worse things. No one would know. This must be, after all, merely a dream. If she did not believe that, then she must admit to an inherited insanity. But she did believe in guardian angels, had for a long while, so why not spirit lovers?

Shivers ran through Eric's mind, jarred him to pity this woman whose body so enticed him, whose very being touched the tiny thread of goodness left in his soul. He trailed slow kisses from one nipple to the other, along her flat stomach, and into the nest of dark hair below. Shuddering with delight, he moved his tongue inside her, tasted the moist sweetness, tickled the tight bud that throbbed in that nebulous cavern.

She cried out, opened her legs wide. He stroked her breasts with hands that seemed as real as the need that possessed them. She lifted her hips to him, his tongue explored deeper within her, igniting a heartbreaking intensity. Ecstasy moved her in the ancient dance of love. She clutched at wads of rumpled sheet, lost in a glistening, brilliant void. Rising, falling, crying out, she climaxed over and over with an excruciating savagery that left her limp, wrung out, panting.

Despite not having a body, he experienced a spiritual, joyous orgasm that drained him of all fear, left him cleansed of the horror that had become his total existence.

His own lust satisfied, he remained safe within her, his entire being usurped by her beautiful, lissome spirit. He never wanted to leave, for it was warm and dark and comforting there within her core.

The pale flesh of her bare hip enticed him. He yearned for arms with which to comfort her, a chest where she could rest her head. It had been so damn long since he'd cherished a woman.

Dear God, no wonder Alf wanted Lenore. He couldn't let the demon have her. He had to save her. But how?

He moved to lie beside her, desperate to rest within her arms.

"Oh, Lenore, you're so gorgeous." To Alf, *"I see why, now. I see your reason for wanting her. But please don't destroy her. I'll do anything, anything. Please."*

"You fool! She is an empty vessel waiting to be filled, nothing more. I must grant her the peace she cries out for, prepare her for her destiny." Brutally Alf yanked him from tranquility to panic, raged at her, *"I'll be back, and you will welcome me the next time and the time after that. You will do as I ask. Soon we will be together forever."*

"You bastard," Eric tried to speak to Lenore, but Alf gagged him, dragged him from her side, and into the body they shared, a body that tossed on the cold wet cell floor and moaned in sheer agony. Every muscle convulsed, drew arms and legs into a fetal mass, cradling a bone-deep tremor that radiated from heart to groin, as if it might fly apart.

15

LENORE GRADUALLY AWOKE from the erotic dream, touched herself between the legs. Wet. Had she had an orgasm in her sleep? Sometimes that happened after she and Herb made love. He would leave her unsatisfied, and she would awake later, throbbing so that she had to finish what he had only been willing to begin. Even with self-fulfillment there was never that feeling of overpowering rapture she had experienced with this shadow lover. An exquisite fulfillment of something deeper than mortal desires. She lay still so the lingering tendrils of the dream would not escape her memory.

"I am Eric,'" he had said. "'And I will never hurt you."

When she'd asked, "Eric Adair?" he hadn't replied. How could she have dreamed in that way about a man possessed of such evil? It couldn't have been real, though. She wouldn't... couldn't have it any other way. Sane people dreamed all kinds of weird things. Only the mad experienced realistic delusions, heard voices, and made love to invisible entities, for God's sake. And she would not give in to insanity like her poor, dear mother had.

What woman wouldn't welcome such a lover, one who made no demands, only desired to please. This was bizarre.

But she did believe, didn't she? The chakra made her a believer. She had touched the spirit, knew it existed beyond her body. Had seen through the third eye, experienced the power of the earth within the base of her being. How could she not believe?

The questioner in her mind, a lilting feminine voice. That of her mother, or her own inner self? She wasn't sure which. Perhaps they were one and the same.

Besides satisfying her sexually as she had never been satisfied before, the euphoric experience gave her the courage to follow her inclination and further investigate the life of Eric Adair. Having never believed in coincidences, she was convinced everything happened for a reason, no matter how puzzling. Karma, fate, God willing, call it whatever. She had believed in all these things since her mother's death. Was it only a thick impenetrable armor she wrapped around her broken heart and spirit so both would heal?

She arose and showered, taking her time soaping herself with bare hands where he had kissed her, made love to her, crept inside her. Heart, belly button, uterus, all points of the chakra, all tingling to her touch. The water grew cool, and she shut it off and climbed out. She had passed through some kind of transference that renewed her soul and spirit. Wrapped in a terry robe, she padded barefoot into the kitchen and made coffee. After drinking two steaming cups, she got on the phone to Memphis information and requested the telephone number of the Institute for the Criminally Insane. She had no idea who to ask for when she dialed the number, found herself talking to an assistant by the name of Arteria Breckenridge.

"My name is Lee Murry," she said, picking a name out of thin air and cursing herself for not being more prepared. "Uh... I'm a writer, and I wonder how I would go about arranging an interview with one of your inmates."

The woman—what sort of name was Arteria anyway?—lined out a quite complicated procedure necessary in order for her to interview Eric Adair. It included photo identification and several other steps to prove she wasn't either a terrorist, a murderer, or herself criminally insane, all of which Lenore could adhere to. After all, her madness did not embrace the criminal element. Then, of course, there was the final step. Obtaining Adair's okay to speak to her. She answered all Arteria's questions and was told they would get back to her if and when she could pay Adair a visit.

"You do know this man is violent and often not coherent?" the woman asked at the end of the conversation, a question best asked at the beginning rather than at the end of the conversation.

Lenore assured her she knew his history and was told she would hear something within a few days.

To win back Herb's trust—for she did love him, want him back, didn't she?—Lenore then made an appointment with Doctor Collins. She would bare her soul about her mother. Give the woman something to concentrate on while she made plans to go to Memphis and meet Eric Adair. Perhaps Collins would have a few useful suggestions regarding her denial of her mother's death. Lenore doubted that, though, figured the woman would want to start her on some type of medication, which, of course, she would not take. Shrink or no, she did carry the title doctor before her name, and pills and shots appeared to be the answer to everything nowadays. If that didn't work, they could always drill into her head. Maybe perform one of those newfangled lobotomies they were so damned proud of. Her belief in the supernatural was no more outrageous than that a beam of cold light could fry pieces of your brain and somehow make you normal again.

That very night, as if to strengthen her resolve, the nightmare of the man pursued by hairy red beasts returned to shove aside the shadow lover. She awoke tangled in bed clothes, muttering the Latin phrase the man had shouted, and hastened to write it down phonetically as best she could remember.

"Sic pereant omnes inimici tui, Domine."

Certainly there was some importance to it, or at least her subconscious believed so. She would find someone who could translate the words, perhaps at the University or maybe a Catholic priest. There were a few Catholics in the immediate area, and they attended a small mission church out on the old highway. Talk was it would soon close for lack of a priest, but she recalled one visited monthly to say Mass. The remainder of the time the few parishioners made do with a deacon.

She phoned city hall and asked for the name of the deacon of the Catholic Mission, got it as well as his telephone number. Daniel Klimas lived in Fayetteville, and she reached him after several tries. He spoke in a jovial tone and laughed easily. They passed the time of day before getting down to business. She learned that Father Bernard Kelly from the Little Rock Diocese was scheduled to say Mass for Easter which would fall the third Sunday of April. Not sure she wanted to wait that long, she listened with interest to Klimas's eager offer to be of assistance. He spoke with an east coast accent. That meant he must be over forty years old and probably hadn't been in the area too long. Young people today had no accent save what they heard on television, and the soft southern drawl of lifelong residents was easily affected.

"I was hoping he could translate some Latin for me, but I really didn't want to wait until—"

"Ah, well if that's all, I can probably help."

"The problem is—I mean, I wanted to discuss some scripture. I hoped he could explain the meaning of some rather strange... occurrences."

"Ah, well, if you need a Bible scholar you'd perhaps be wise to speak to Father Bernard. Or I could put you in touch with Father Peretski here in town if you can't wait."

Lenore chewed at her nail a moment. These men were all apt to think her nuts if she even touched on possession such as had been written up in the *Comet* article. Eric Adair had spoken of it as well. Could she broach the subject of the translation and the dream without bringing that up?

"Missus Maine, are you still there?"

"Umm, oh, yes, and it's Miss Maine, Lenore. I wonder, if you wouldn't mind, perhaps you could do the translation for me, and we could talk a bit, if that's all right. Then I'll decide where to go from there."

His laughter caught her unaware. It appeared he laughed even when not amused. *"Indeed it's all right. Why don't you come to services Sunday at nine-thirty and I'll speak to you afterward? We can have coffee in the rectory and discuss our strange Catholic customs. I take it you aren't of the faith?"*

"Uh, no, I'm not Catholic, if that's what you mean."

"That was, indeed, what I meant. You'll come Sunday, then?"

She hesitated, chewed at her thumb. "I'm not sure—"

"Of course, it isn't a requirement. I just thought it might set your mind somewhat at ease to see that we don't practice witchcraft, nor do we have horns."

"I'm sure I never thought you did."

His laughter boomed in her ear. *"Of course, you didn't. I apologize for even suggesting such a thing. Services are over around ten fifteen if I don't get too long-winded. It's fine if you come to the rectory then. I'll be happy to help you all I can. Of course, if you change your mind about attending services—"*

"I'll think about it. Thank you so much." Lenore hung up before he could press her about that any further. He was right, of course. Not many Catholics lived in the Ozarks, and those who did were imports. No native understood the religion, nor wanted to. He had no doubt fielded his share of questions and statements born from ignorance of the religion. She had heard them herself and for the most part ignored them. Still her perception of their mysterious rites was somewhat skewed by her upbringing.

Throwing caution to the wind, she decided to attend the service the deacon spoke of, assuming it would not be a Mass since he wasn't a priest.

Before she visited Eric Adair in Memphis, she hoped to arm herself with as much information as possible, both about the so-called possessed killer and the mysterious message in the dream. By this time she was convinced that there was a message there. She wasn't ignorant about such unusual occurrences as second sight and channeling the spirits. What her own particular visitations might be or why she was being so blessed or cursed, she had no idea, but putting sense to them beat going crazy. What she knew about possession was very little. Studies in psychology attributed possession and hearing voices, even multiple personalities, to mental diseases such as schizophrenia.

She ate a tuna salad on the back deck, so nervous about her plan that she scarcely tasted the food. Her gaze darted toward the shadowy woods lining the property, as if she expected her nightmare to materialize. Strange. Living in the wilderness had always soothed her nerves, rather than disturbing them. Yet today she sensed the presence of something or someone keeping an eye on her, and it made her wary. As if to add to her apprehension, the wind rose and rattled bony limbs not yet veiled in leaves. A branch from one of the old maple trees cracked loose and fell on the roof, rattled over the shingles, and thunked to the ground. Though the day was warm, the wind raised goose bumps along her arms. Shivering, she carried the tray and dishes inside, drew the front blinds, and perched on the edge of the couch.

This could not go on. She couldn't remain cooped up, a prisoner in this house. After all, if there was a demon attempting to possess her, four walls would not stop him doing so. She had to be out and about, feet planted on the ground, sense the wildness that lived around her. Besides, he had appeared here more than once since that scene in the grocery store when she'd gone round the bend. Something out of the ordinary was happening to her, and blaming a bout of the flu no longer explained it.

She picked up the telephone to call Herb, try to convince him to come by so they could talk, when like a shot, a door slammed in the other end of the house. She jumped to her feet, expecting to see an apparition floating toward her. What a ridiculous situation. She'd opened the windows to air out the bedroom, that's what had slammed the door shut.

Again an unexpected sound, this time the distinct opening and closing of a door.

Dropping the cordless on the cushion behind her, she crept down the hallway. To the right her room, to the left her mother's, the door kept closed since her death. Wasn't that in itself a little bit unstable of her? It was past time she opened that room up and went through Mama's things. Packed them, got rid of them. That would go a long way toward convincing Herb she was perfectly or, perhaps, not-so-perfectly sane. Nobody closed off the painful part of their life forever, not unless they were a little loony. Was that what she was, a little loony? Considering the recent episodes, she might be a lot loony.

She reached for the knob, cursing herself for trembling like a frightened child. The door swung from her reach, then banged shut. She stumbled backward against the wall, glanced at her own door. It was propped open, just as she remembered leaving it. From within a cool breeze flowed, kissed her cheeks, stirred locks of her hair. Inside the blue curtains danced, sunlight lay across the shiny hardwood floor, puddled on the braided rug.

The mischievous door swung wide, then slammed shut once again. Without taking the time to think about it, she shoved it open and took one tentative step inside. The shades were drawn, the space gloomy with abandonment. A frail web trailed through her hair and across one cheek.

"Hello, darling, I've been waiting a very long time," her mother said, melodic voice ringing in the muffled stillness.

Chapter 16

ERIC STIRRED ON his hard cot. A few minutes earlier he'd finished a hundred pushups and now lay back on the bed, panting, muscles burning. Alf appeared to be exhausted, lethargic after the previous night's adventure with Lenore, and was catching up on his sleep. Could he go to her alone without the demon? Would that be possible? Or could he only make the out-of-body trip when Alf did? Did the demon sometimes go places and leave him in the cell? Eric had no idea, for he'd only become aware of the trips when Alf had first encountered Lenore. Something about her had awakened him from the stupor in which he'd existed for so long.

Ah, well, nothing like trying. He closed his eyes, concentrated on the place where she lived, the surrounding countryside, the taste and feel of the freedom of flight, if you could call it that. It was more like thinking yourself from one place to another. There was never the true sensation of flying, like in some dreams where you spread your arms and soared high above the earth. What would happen if he fell? In dreams there was no pain or injury. He blocked the ridiculous questions and went back to the task at hand.

After several minutes of intense focus, the odor of the tiny cell altered, a slight breeze tousled his hair and filled his lungs, sunlight warmed his cheek. The house, her house, its walls, embraced him. The bedroom and its wild flower fragrance, the distinct aroma of her. His nose wrinkled, he smelled coffee, heard someone crying.

"Lenore? Don't cry."

"She's here. All these years she's been waiting for me, and I didn't know it." Lenore's voice so pathetic, so grief stricken. Heartbreaking.

"Don't cry, I'm here." He glanced around, but she wasn't there. He could hear her, smell her, sense her presence, couldn't touch her with his lips or fingertips.

Then she appeared in another room from her own, and he went to her. She must have sensed his presence, for she peered in his direction. Spoke. "Please help me. I don't know what to do. I'm not crazy. I'm not, but I don't know what to do. My mother is still in this room, but why am I frightened? I don't understand."

For just an instant, the briefest of moments, he embraced her. She clung to him. The salt of her tears warm against his cheek, a strand of ebony hair tickling his nose.

"I'll help you. I—"

A roar, a vicious grip, fingers squeezed his temples until his skull threatened to shatter.

"What do you think you're doing?" A furious Alf ripped at Eric's eyeballs, tore at his tongue, flailed his flesh until it bled. *"I'll nail you to the earth by your balls."*

In his cell Eric bolted from the bed, arms over his head, yowled with pain. Helpless to stop what was happening, he butted the wall until hot blood poured from his lacerated scalp and face.

"You bastard, I'll kill you." He screamed, backed up and rammed his head once more against the concrete wall, spiraled downward into total darkness.

The door banged open, and two burly interns rushed in, pinned him to the floor, and plunged a needle deep into his arm.

"I'm sorry, Lenore. Please forgive me." He tumbled back into the abyss. A familiar place where there was neither sorrow nor pain, memory nor regret.

Chapter 17

AGHAST WITH FEAR at the brief episode of violence, Lenore huddled in a corner until the gentle spirit that permeated the room coaxed her from her fugue. She came to herself in the closet, kneeling among the musty clothes her mother had once worn. In the dark corner she spied a shoe box filled with snapshots. With reverence she fingered the face in one of the photographs. Her young mother sat in a swing that appeared to be hung by ropes from a large tree branch out of sight above her. An expression of happiness lit her carefree features. Wind blew the long dark hair twisted with yellow ribbons and dancing around her head. She wore a dress the color of butter, and its filmy skirts had been captured in flight as her shapely legs pumped the swing in a forward motion. There was no one else in the picture, but someone's shadow lay in the dust beneath the swing. Whoever had taken the picture, Lenore supposed, with the sun behind him. Or her. Could be either one. She turned over the picture. Scrawled on the back was Emaline Dixon, Summer, 1970. Mama would have been twenty-one. Not yet married, but soon to be. Soon to go away to school back east and meet David Rourke Maine of the Connecticut Maines. Bad boy, black sheep, worthless and rich, who would choose to bring his bride back to her home in the Ozarks to escape the taut restrictions enforced by his strait-laced parents. Money in trust from his grandparents. It would never run out. He chose to build this cabin in the woods and keep his lovely wife hidden away in the wilderness where she could write her poetry and go quietly insane. What could they possibly spend money on?

Lenore laid down the photo, picked up another. Daddy holding her on his lap.

Daddy, who she once saw… heard… *dreamed* hitting Mommy over and over across the back and legs and buttocks.

A shudder of revulsion slammed through her, teeth clenched so tight her temples pounded. Had that really happened? She didn't know, had never remembered it before this moment.

She gathered the pictures, dumped them back in the box, and fitted the lid on. Mama had called her into this room, beckoned her here for a reason, but surely this wasn't it. To reveal such a horrid secret. Why had she never told her? They could have run away together. Hadn't that been what Mama had finally done? Run away? Left this earth for another plane.

"No, no, no. I love you, Mama. I'll always love you," she said aloud and waited, expecting the voice she'd heard earlier to reply. Yet there was only silence but for the song of a singular bird beyond the dirty window.

Tomorrow she would pick up some boxes from the store and pack all this stuff away. Take the clothes to the local thrift shop for resale and clean five years of dust and cobwebs from the room. Maybe paint the walls another color, hang new curtains. Yes, tomorrow she'd do that.

With a sigh she arose from her cross-legged position on the dusty floor and left the room, pulling the door shut and jiggling the knob to be sure it was firmly closed.

The telephone rang. When she answered it was Delilah.

"How you feeling, honey?"

"I'm fine, thanks."

"You're sure?"

"Yes." Lenore tried to keep a sharpness from her voice, but didn't succeed. The seed planted by the demon accusing her best friend and Herb of vile things had taken root, caused distrust of her own memories.

"I won't bother you but a minute. I was wondering if you could watch the shop tomorrow. Richard has something going on he can't get loose from, and I have to go to Fort Smith on business. If I put it off any longer, we'll be in trouble around here."

"No problem. It'll be good to get out of the house."

"Say what? Did you say you'd enjoy getting out of the house? I declare, but that bout with the flu must have addled your brain." Del laughed and didn't seem to notice when Lenore didn't join her.

"Yes, well, maybe so. Do you need me to open up?"

"No, just come on over about nine-thirty or so. I'll be back by three, four at the latest. Maybe we could do something after we close down."

"Do something?" Lenore felt a vague discomfort, as if Del had asked her to join in something illegal or immoral.

"Yeah. No big deal. Just go out and eat or something. Do us both good."

"Okay, sure. Why not?"

"Good. See you in the morning, then."

They both said bye at the same time. Del chuckled and Lenore hung up. Now what was that all about? Richard did not approve of Del doing anything without him. The business trip might be allowed, but the two of them going out to a public restaurant and leaving him behind? Hardly. She wondered what was going on.

Her mind didn't linger overlong on Richard and Del. She had too much to think about. Uppermost were her plans to visit Eric Adair.

Memphis was a five-hour drive, so she had made reservations for the night before and the night following at a motel on the outskirts of town. She would be allowed to talk to him for a couple of hours if he cooperated. There was a chance, she'd been told, that he wouldn't be coherent or would change his mind and refuse to talk to her at all, but she decided to go anyway. She could always stay over if that happened, try again the next day. Since she had spoken to someone there, all she needed to get through the gate was some sort of picture identification.

Deacon Klimas had intrigued her enough that she decided to attend services at Our Lady of the Smiles Catholic Mission. She hoped he could furnish her with information that would help clear up the mysterious dream occurring every night, though sometimes only in bits and pieces.

Still in her terry robe, Lenore was barefoot in the back yard trying to clear her mind when she heard the sound of an approaching vehicle. Running inside and through the house, she peered out the front window. Herb climbed from the car, crossed the porch, and hammered on the door once, then shoved it open so hard it almost hit her.

Eyes snapping wide, he pulled up short. "Oh, sorry. I didn't know you were there."

She nodded without speaking, only then remembering that she had been about to call him earlier and never had. He bent to kiss her cheek, and she let him. The intimacy gave her a melancholy feeling of impending loss, and she touched his arm.

He raised one eyebrow, but didn't say anything. For a moment they stood there gazing at each other.

"Well, can I at least come in and sit down a minute? I won't stay long, I promise."

"Sure. Yes, of course. And you can stay as long as you wish."

"I suppose I could." He sat on one end of the leather couch. "You shouldn't go barefoot. It's dangerous."

She nodded, but refused to get into an argument. Poor Herb. Always expecting others to be as perfect as him. Tucking the robe in so her legs didn't show, she perched on the other end.

"Del says you're feeling better."

"Del says? You could have called, asked me."

"I wasn't sure if I should."

Again she nodded. This conversation was awkward. Hard to tell the two of them had been intimate only a few short weeks ago. Planning a wedding and the rest of their life, for God's sake. Unable to think of anything to say, she waited for him to speak again. Wished he'd say he still loved her and things could go back to the way they were.

Hoped he wouldn't.

"I don't want you to get upset about this, Lee, but I have to know. Have you been seeing that doctor?"

"Once. I'm going back."

"Oh. Good. Fine. What did she say?"

"What did she say? I'm not sure I understand. You want me to tell you if she thinks I'm crazy? What, Herb? And that way you can decide if you still love me, want to marry me? Is that it?" She hadn't wanted to fight with him, but something hot and angry surged up inside her, and she couldn't control it.

His bereft expression made her want to touch his cheek, cradle his face and kiss those full lips. He spoke before she could follow the inclination, and it slipped away.

"Not exactly. No, of course not. I only meant, does she have a rational explanation for your erratic behavior? My God, do you know what people in town are saying, Lee?"

"This is the man you love?" hissed the demon. *"This shallow* toad?"

Anger exploded within her, and she leaped from the couch. Herb recoiled as if she might strike him.

"I don't care, Herb, what people are saying."

"They're saying you're crazy, as crazy as your—"

"As my mother? Thank you very much for telling me that, like I didn't have some idea already. Is that all you came for?"

"Of course not. What are you going to do?"

She cocked her head at him. "I'm afraid I don't understand."

"Is she going to admit you—uh, somewhere?"

"Put me away, you mean? What is this all about, Herb?"

"I just think—I mean, we ought to postpone—I guess what I came to say is we ought to put off the wedding until all this is straightened out."

"So this is how he treats you? He ought to be shot or poisoned. I told you so."

"Shut up, just shut up." The high pitched shout hurt her ears, and she covered them.

Herb came to his feet. "Lenore, dammit."

"Oh, God." She put both hands over her eyes, took a deep breath that enhanced the pain in her heart. "I'm sorry, Herb. I wish… I mean, I thought we could patch things up, but I've got to get this straightened out, and I can't do it with you demanding so much of me. I thought our love was strong, but obviously it's not strong enough."

"Stop being kind to this brute. Tell him what you really think, and quit being such a pussy."

"Will you leave me alone?"

"I think that's what I'll have to do, Lee."

She grabbed his arm, pulled at it. "Not you. I didn't mean you."

He removed her clinging fingers. "Some voice you're hearing? I think that only goes to prove my point." He stared at her, a sadness in his eyes. "I wish it could be some other way. If you need anything, or there's something I can do, call me. I'm at my parents' place temporarily. And see that doctor before you go completely off the deep end."

"Tell me, Herb," she said, raising her head high and swiping away the last of her tears, "Has your mother made you a list of requirements I must meet before I'm a suitable wife for you?"

"Of course not."

"Of course not," she mimicked in the voice of his mother, who could whine and screech like a harridan and did so frequently, especially where her only son was concerned.

"Don't do that, Lenore. It's unkind, and you never were unkind."

"Not that you shouldn't have been. The old bitch ought to be dead, would be if she wasn't so mean even the devil doesn't want her. She was always cruel to me, and never once did you take up for me. Not once. Did you enjoy watching, Herb?"

"You're ill, so I won't dignify that with a reply, Lenore. I hope you feel better soon."

"Oh, I feel just fine, thank you. Just fine, indeed. Now, get out of here. I don't think I want to marry you anymore. Not ever." Tears pooled, and she rubbed them away with the backs of her hands. Dammit, she hadn't wanted to let him make her cry. Especially in front of him. It told him he'd won the battle.

"I'm really sorry about all this."

She shrugged. "It's all right. I'm sorry, too. I don't think we love each other enough, that's all. Otherwise how could something like this break us up? I waited a long time for a man I could love. I guess I should have looked a little longer, that's all."

"I still love you, Lee, it's just that this is all too much for me."

"Well, I'm sorry about that. I guess you thought you were marrying someone who would take care of you, and I'm not up to it right now. I may never be."

He gazed at her for a long moment.

Lenore started to move toward the door to let him out.

"If you let him get away with this, you're really crazy."

She stopped, staggered as if pol-axed.

"He's going straight to that redheaded bitch. That's really why he's leaving you, so he can fuck her."

"No," she cried. "Stop it, stop it."

Herb eyed her. "What is it?"

"Take off the robe, show him what he's leaving.."

Lenore jerked at the belt, untied it and let the garment slip from her shoulders. She took a few steps forward, thrust her shoulders back so her breasts pointed straight at him.

Herb stared, mesmerized, eyes on her breasts, then sweeping lower.

"Come here," she whispered and walked her fingers over her belly into the mound of curly hair below.

He licked his lips and took a step backward, bumped up against the door jamb.

"I've missed you. Haven't you missed me?"

"Don't, Lee. Don't." Voice choking.

She moved closer and reached for the top button of his pants.

"Good God, Lenore, stop acting like a whore." Slapping her hands away, he reeled out the door and across the porch. She watched him go, tongue slowly moistening her lips, then began to massage her naked breast.

It felt so damned good. So what if the bastard didn't want her. She knew someone who did.

Chapter 18

THAT NIGHT AFTER Herb left, she dreamed of lying in the arms of one of the savages she'd watched kill the desperate man of her nightmares. In her most secret of hearts she'd often wished for a more imaginative love affair than that between her and Herb. Prayed he'd one day become a more skillful lover, stir her dormant sexuality. Now, God help her, that desire had culminated, but not in any way she might have expected.

The savage awakened her hidden primal passions, much as did the spirit of Eric Adair, and she enjoyed and performed unspeakable acts in the privacy of her dream. The wicked lover of the darkness was a mixture of Eric and the other one who so frightened her with his crude demands. Was that why Eric intrigued her so, because he was the other half of a demon?

She awoke exhausted in a nest of tangled, sweat-soaked sheets, and it took a few minutes to remember that she had to be at The Craft Basket by nine-thirty so Del could run her errands. Only guilt drove her to agree to sit in for Del. She'd rather provide money and the weekly contribution of herbs and teas and stay out of the other end of the business. Del knew what customers wanted and bought quality wares from local craftspeople all over the Ozarks, but bragged she had no creative talent, couldn't even put together a wreath from a kit. Together she and Richard understood how to make a success of the business and oft times performed miracles with the shop and its earning power.

Del was fond of saying, "We all do what we do best, and if we're smart we keep it that way."

Lenore was not a people person, Del had no head for figures, Richard was an accountant and CPA and had a thriving business. The partnership worked as long as they let it.

"You'd run all our customers off, if we let you take care of this place for a month," Del had told Lenore more than once. "But don't you worry none, honey. Your money opened us up, and folks just dearly love your potions. Keeps 'em coming back for more, and they always buy something else while they're here."

Dreading a full day wasted at the shop, Lenore finished breakfast, showered and dressed. Suppose she started talking back to the voices with the shop full of customers? The idea upset her, but she vowed not to let it happen and left the house determined to rid herself of this frightening mental obsession.

Eyes aimed straight ahead, she drove past Herb's construction site. Yesterday's scene had left her nerve endings raw. She had to face the reality that they might never get back together, and she wasn't sure how she felt about that. Partly sad, vaguely relieved, and mostly confused.

"Get rid of the redheaded bitch, and you'd feel better."

Lenore hunched her shoulders and ignored the barb. Good idea to practice not talking back. This voice, this so-called demon, wasn't going to leave her alone, so she'd pretend he wasn't there. She didn't have to acknowledge his existence, since in all probability he was a figment of her imagination. Once she saw Adair in the flesh and discovered that this was all nonsense, she could figure out a way to send him back where he belonged. Then she could stop having those sensual dreams about him as a lover.

She parked in the back lot of The Craft Basket, leaving the loading zone open in case someone wanted to make a delivery, and went through the storage room into the exhibition area.

At the cash register, Del counted bills and change into the drawer. There were no customers, and the place was quiet except for the tinkle of delicate wind chimes disturbed by the breeze that followed Lenore through the door. The place smelled like vanilla and citrus. The day's candles of choice flickered in mirrored wall sconces crafted from walnut, cherry and cedar. All for sale. Blow out that little ole candle, and take 'em right down off the wall, Del would tell her customers in her lighthearted drawl.

"I sold one of the cedar chests old Mr. Bradley made," she said to Lenore by way of a greeting and cracked a roll of quarters on the side of the drawer. The coins clattered into their niche, the noise disruptive.

"That's wonderful."

"Sure is, for this early in the tourist season. I splurged and ordered two more. I know they're expensive, and we have to bump the price awfully high to make anything, but I have a feeling in my bones this is going to be a good year. Sales are already running way ahead of last year. Quilts are selling faster than we can restock. Too many of our quilters have died of old age. No one wants the machine quilts some of the younger ladies make. They can get those at Walmart. Wish youngsters would get busy learning some of these folk crafts before they die out."

"Maybe we need to take a trip or two out of the area, see if we can line up some more suppliers. Nothing says we have to restrict ourselves to buying locally." Lenore adjusted her own display without facing Del.

"No, but it'd be nice to continue to do that. I hate the idea of importing anything, even from another state. I want customers to know when they come here they won't find anything made in Japan or China or Taiwan."

"Well, I wasn't suggesting that, for goodness sake. I thought maybe over in Tennessee or down in Georgia. That's not exactly foreign products. I'm going to Memphis next week. Want me to do some checking?"

Del closed the drawer and stared at her. "What in heaven's name are you going to Memphis for? You hardly ever go to Fayetteville, and now, out of the blue, you announce you're going to Memphis?"

Lenore shrugged, wished she hadn't said anything. "Just need to get away for a while."

"To Memphis?" Del's wide-eyed expression reflected her disbelief. "What in the world is there but too many people and mayhem on the streets? Oh, Lee, don't tell me you're going to Graceland. I'll just die if you do."

"No, I'm—I'm going to see someone. You don't know him."

"Him? Him? Honest to God? Honey, what's going on? So that's what's up with you and Herb. I heard he'd moved back in with his mother. Is this fella in Memphis the reason?"

Lenore cringed at how close Del came to a vestige of the truth, but not in any way she could be made to understand. For a long moment she stared through the wide front windows past the divided highway to the mountains beyond. "I'd rather not talk about it. And who told you about Herb, anyway?" Anger far out of proportion to the discussion rose in her chest.

Del shrugged and gathered her purse and briefcase from behind the counter. "I don't remember. Since when can you keep a secret in Summit Falls? Honey, all I've got to say is I don't blame you one bit for cutting Herb off. You can do lots better. He's so boring. You're doing the right thing not sitting around and pining away. And Lord knows you don't need his money. Well, we'll have to talk when you get back. You can tell me all about this new man in your life." She opened the door and turned to study Lenore closely. "You sure you're okay?"

Lenore nodded. If she were to tell Del the truth, just spout all the nonsense about demons and possession, she'd have a conniption fit, no doubt about it.

Another long glance, and Del was gone, the door closing behind her with a jingle of the overhead bell.

Lenore went to pour herself a cup of tea.

"He's so boring. The little bitch's lying to you. Wants him for herself. How can you be this naive?"

She gritted her teeth and tried to ignore the derisive words. Pay no attention, drink your tea, sweep the floor, and muck out the stock room. One thing Del hated was to handle a broom or mop. Dust bunnies resided in every corner and under the free standing display shelves. Sometimes Lenore would come over at night and clean the place when it got too bad, but she hadn't done that since her illness.

She kept her own blend of teas in a sealed tin on the shelf above the coffee maker. Setting aside the glass pot, she poured water in a small enamel kettle and put it on the burner to heat, then reached for the tin to spoon loose leaves into the tea ball. It wasn't where she'd left it. Annoyed, she dragged a step stool over and climbed to the top to search the back of the shelf.

A folded piece of paper lay under a layer of dust. Maybe a note or something. She opened it and saw in a familiar scrawl the words, *See you Thursday night, same time, same place.* It was signed with a big looped *H*, and no one had to tell her who had written it. She'd know Herb's handwriting anywhere.

"The son of a bitch. What more proof do you need?"

"It doesn't mean anything. What could it mean?"

"Are you asking me?"

"I am not talking to you. I will not talk to you because you don't exist. Now shut up and leave me alone."

"You're going to have to kill them both. You see that, don't you? How long have they been betraying you?"

"I don't care. We're not even together anymore."

"You were when that was written. He was sleeping with you and telling you he adored you, and all the time he was fucking the redheaded bitch. Besides, you still love him. What more do you need than this?"

Lenore gritted her teeth and refused to carry on the ridiculous conversation. It might be all right to talk to yourself, but you didn't go around talking to someone who was a figment of your imagination. Worse, someone you believed was a demon looking to possess your soul.

Something played over her cheek and down into the vee of her blouse. Felt more like a scaly claw than a finger. Goose bumps trailed along behind the touch.

"Is that a figment of your imagination, sweet Lenore? As for your soul, I do indeed possess that as well. And you will kill before I'm done. Everyone does. It will excite you just as it does me, and you'll no longer be able to live without satisfying your blood lust, our blood lust."

Terror stitched through her, and she dropped the note, grabbed at the counter to keep from falling off the stool. She should be accustomed to the disturbing invisible touch by now. But she wasn't. Dammit, she wasn't. Besides, she preferred Eric's sensual caress.

"What are you? Who are you? Why did you choose me?" The questions ended in a feeble cry. Elbows propped on the counter, she leaned forward, braced her head in both hands. Beside her, water boiled in the kettle, filling the air with steam.

The demon laughed, chilling her to the marrow, for his was a laugh of hateful mockery. *"Why, my dear, because it's my job, my duty. We all have our tasks in this life. In other lives, too, come to think of it. This is mine. And yours will be to rid the world of several souls that are needed elsewhere."*

"Okay. This is enough. I'm going to check into a hospital, get rid of you once and for all."

"I don't think so. Oh, by the way, we're looking forward to meeting you in person, Eric and I. That's a clever plan you have, to pay us a call. It won't do you any good. You'll still do what I tell you in the end. But, it will be fun, all the same. Eric will enjoy it. Poor boy is not doing too well at the moment. He could use a pretty woman to cheer him up. I might even allow him to speak with you, as long as the two of you don't get up to no good."

Before he finished, the significance of what he'd said hit Lenore. She reeled like a wild thing, using the wall for support, as if she could escape his clutches. He knew her plans, her thoughts, everything about her. She staggered through the swinging doors into the shop just as the front door opened with a jolly tinkle of little bells, and let in two matronly ladies dressed in purple flowered dresses. They might have been twins, so alike was the expression of horror on their carefully made-up faces when Lenore stumbled toward them, moaning and pinching at her trembling mouth.

"Get out, get out," she shrieked. "Leave me alone. I won't kill them, I won't. You can't make me."

Before the astounded women could flee, Lenore picked up a delicate hand-painted china plate and hurled it at the stockroom door. The smashed pieces flew in every direction, scattered over the dusty hardwood floor like shards of a jigsaw puzzle. Demonic laughter climbed the walls. Next her hand grasped a delicate china egg decorated with exquisite violets, flung it, then headed for another exhibit.

The women trotted out the door uttering frightened squeals, but she was barely conscious of their exit. She was busy throwing one beautiful item after another at the taunting but quite invisible demon. The china shelf swept clean, she moved to a display of hand-thrown pottery.

Hurled a heavy pitcher that struck the glass exhibit case along the back wall, shattering the pitcher and the glass. Inside were expensive carvings. Standing bears and delicate hummingbirds and a rearing horse lay dead or wounded in the mess.

She could scarcely breathe for the fear squeezing at her lungs, realized she had fallen into a nether world where she felt neither remorse nor caution. The rampage stampeded past her ability to control it, and she cast about for something else to destroy in her rage.

Chapter 19

ACCUSTOMED TO COMING to in strange places, Eric awoke and took in Lenore's rage-filled explosion. His head pounded. He struggled to remember what had happened, could only recall that he'd rammed his head into the wall of the cell. Nothing else. But Lenore was coming apart in a rage, and Alf was responsible.

"Shit, Alf. You're killing her. Stop it."

"She fights too hard. Why won't she give in? She's only a woman."

"Please let me talk to her."

"No. That won't be permitted. You tried to bash our brains in, almost destroyed us. I'm not ready for that yet. A few more days, a week perhaps, and you can do what you will with our measly shell. I'll have hers."

Lenore let out a tortured scream and raced toward the front door.

"You'll have nothing. Look at her. She's liable to run into the path of a semi if you don't let me stop her."

Alf released the hold he kept on Eric's mind. *"Do what you will. But beware. You can do nothing behind my back."*

"Of course not," Eric said. But he could and had. On at least two separate occasions.

He moved to soothe Lenore, tasting her panic like a bolt of electricity across his tongue.

"You have to stop, Lenore. Listen to me. I know what's happening to you. I can help you."

"I've gone mad. Mad." Her scream echoed in the ruined shop and she tugged at the door knob.

"No, not yet you haven't. But you might if—"

"If *what?* I can't listen to yet another voice speaking to me out of some nightmare."

Concentration made his head pound all the harder, and he wanted only to hide in the dark somewhere. But he couldn't. Something about her reaction, her desperate need, beckoned him. He had to help her. In a reassuring tone, he spoke, "It may seem like a nightmare, or worse. But it's real. You're not mad."

She hung onto the knob, hands stilling their frantic pawing. "Is that supposed to make me feel better?" She turned toward his voice, eyes wild and moist. At least she no longer tottered around like a puppet without strings. "Oh, God. Oh, God. Why should I believe you?"

"Because there's no one else." The demon drifted as if bored. Odd how he could always tell when Alf slept. And that's what he was about to do now. Nod off.

When he was sure Alf dozed, Eric whispered, *"Listen to me, Lenore. He sleeps, and when he does I can do things. Not always and not for long, but you must believe me. I'm going to find a way to help you. But we don't have much time. If he thinks you're going along with him, it will be easier."*

"You mean agree to kill Herb and Delilah? I can't do that."

"Of course you can't actually do it. But you can act as if you might. No more now. He's stirring. His kind needs little sleep. I have to leave you."

"Eric? Don't go." She reached out as if to touch him, gazed in amazement at her trembling hand and beyond it the destruction of the shop. "Oh, dear God, what did I do? How will I explain this?"

No reply, from either Eric or the demon. She'd have to figure this out for herself. The demon would probably urge her to go ahead and burn the place down, anyway. She could pretend to have been robbed, but then she'd have to call the police, and that could get complicated. Maybe just say someone vandalized the place while she was—*what?* In the bathroom?

Didn't she hear or see who it was?

No, she was frightened and hid there until they left. Saw nothing. No description of a car or a person. That would work. She hated to lie, but it was the only way she could stay out of trouble herself. If Del and Richard knew what she had done, they would have her committed for her own good or at best put in jail.

She would have to lie. There was no other way. She went to the telephone, dialed 9-1-1, and prepared a story while waiting for a deputy to arrive. She *had* to remain free, at least until she met Eric face to face.

Some twenty minutes later she faced a blond, baby-faced deputy. "The bells rang when they opened the door. I started out of the bathroom and heard something break, then something else. They were yelling and laughing, having a wonderful time. So I locked myself in and prayed they wouldn't find me."

"Did you see a car, or maybe they walked?"

"I don't know." Lenore gazed wide-eyed into the boyishly handsome face. "I was so scared I stayed in there a long time after they left. I'm sorry, but I didn't see anything."

"Their voices, do you think you would recognize them if you heard them again?"

She shrugged, pretended to think. "I don't know. I doubt it. They were shouting and laughing, horsing around like kids."

He nodded, walked carefully through the crunching glass. "Sure is a mess. I don't think it'd do much good to take fingerprints. You got insurance for something like this?"

She nodded. "Yes, of course. But most of this is irreplaceable. You don't just recreate works of art." Tears spilled down her cheeks. How awful to have destroyed such lovely one-of-a-kind pieces. "Why would anyone have done such a thing?"

"Got me, but it happens all the time. Not always kids, either. You'd be surprised how many full-grown adults do something like this for kicks. I'll file a report, and someone will get back to you. I'm going outside to look around. See if I can spot any footprints going off toward the woods yonder." His expression told her he didn't expect to find anything.

Of course, he wouldn't, but he appeared to believe her story. Now if only Delilah and Richard did too. She didn't look forward to their arrival, but there was no choice but to get through it.

"Sit down to cups of hemlock tea with them. That'd solve all your problems."

"You're back, you sadistic bastard. I'm going to solve my problems, if you don't leave me be."

"Oh, a bit of fire. You don't know how that makes me feel. Uhmm, good. I'm about to cream my pants."

The vile, vile man. Did he hear her thoughts, or did she have to speak aloud?

She'd like to cut off his balls and feed them to him.

"I wouldn't advise it, bitch. Does that answer your question?"

It did, but she wasn't pleased.

Lenore swept the last of the shattered china pieces into the dustpan, and turned to dump the contents into the trash when the front door chimed. One foot over the threshold, Del halted, face going white.

"Dear God, what happened?"

"Some kids, they just started knocking stuff off the shelves."

"Why didn't you stop them? Lee, all those beautiful china pieces." She moved along the empty shelves, hands gesturing. "How could you let this happen?"

"Let it? Stop them?" She dropped the dustpan. It clattered to the floor. *"You ready to get her now?"*

Stuff it.

"I was in the bathroom. There were too many of them. What did you want me to do, shoot them?" Resentment rose to choke her, as if her story had become real and she hated Del for blaming her.

"Well, you could've done something. You'll have to go through the broken ones, find the codes so we can inform the craftspeople just what was destroyed."

Lenore thought about that. She deserved to have that thankless job. The enormity of what she had done overwhelmed her. "Yes, yes, I'll do that. I'm so sorry. So sorry."

With an angry scowl, Del swept through the room toward the office. "Richard will have to make an insurance claim. You *did* file a report?"

"Yes, a sheriff's deputy came out. Said there wasn't much they could do since I didn't see the kids, just heard them. He said someone would get back to us and that we could pick up a copy of his report at the office." She gestured toward the trash bin that held the broken china pieces. "I'd like to take this home with me."

Del turned, gazed at her with a look of pity. "Of course you would. Wouldn't do for you to be exposed to the world for too long at a time. Go ahead, take it. Run on home with your tail between your legs. I just wish I'd been here. I'd have put knots on those brat's heads they wouldn't soon forget."

"You need to do something about this bitch. She's giving me a headache. She goes first, then Herb, soon as I get comfortable in my new digs. It won't be long now."

"I will not kill for you." A terrible feeling came over her that in the end she would. No way was she stronger than this monster that had taken up residence inside her.

Del stared open mouthed. "I did *not* ask you to kill for me, but you could've stood up to them, made them stop."

"I wasn't talking to you."

Her friend looked all around. "Well, honey, I don't see anyone else."

Lenore almost broke down and told her what was going on. The wariness on Del's face stopped her. This woman, her friend and Herb, her husband were in this together. She had no one to turn to.

"They want your money. They'll get every dime you have. You got to do something soon, or you'll lose everything."

Lenore yanked up the plastic trash liner, tied a big knot in the top, and whirled to leave. The bag swung from the bin and smacked the muscle in her calf. A shard of broken china pierced her skin. Anger fueled her actions so much so that she ignored the pain. Without hesitating she stomped out the back door, tossed the bag in the car, climbed in, and drove off. Warm blood ran down her leg. By the time she arrived home, her foot was sticky.

The demon, Alf—God, what a stupid name—nagged her the entire trip. Fear quickly turned to fury. "If you don't shut up, I'm going to slit my own throat. Then where will you be?"

Cruel laughter replied to her threat. *"Kill yourself? Like your mother? Perhaps I should find a new host."*

"That's exactly what you should do." Relief crept over her. There was a way to get rid of him. Threaten to destroy his new home. She went into the bathroom, sat on the stool, and washed her leg with warm, soapy water, then wound a bandage around it. The shoe was ruined, so she tossed both of them into the trash. While she did this, Alf continued with his rant.

"Only after you do my bidding, bitch, and kill Delilah and Herb. Only then will

I leave you be. Or you could slash that pretty skin right here and now and be done with it. There's plenty more where you came from. Dare to bargain with the devil, you foolish woman. He'll win every time."

Exhausted from her ordeal, Lenore curled up on the couch, wrapped in her favorite robe. Tonight she simply wouldn't sleep. She'd sit right there and read or put on an old movie. If she didn't sleep, she wouldn't have to dream, and while that wouldn't keep the demon away, she would remain conscious and in some control of the situation. So far she had been able to tell him no, regardless of what he demanded. But he was wearing her down. How much longer could she keep this up? Today he had proven he could cause her to go into a wild rage and destroy works of art, something she normally would never have done. Could he eventually drive her to do the killings he so craved? Up to that moment, she hadn't thought so, but now wasn't so sure. If Eric Adair or his spirit had something in mind, she wished he'd go ahead and carry out his plan.

Aware on some level that she should be careful what she wished for, she sank back onto the couch, sparing a glance at the bag of broken china, then choosing to ignore it. Her eyelids drifted shut.

"Lenore? Are you awake? He's sleeping, so I thought we could talk."

The plea came to her as if in a dream, and she made a sound down in her throat. He touched her with the tips of fingers so gentle she shivered with delight.

"Do you know how long it's been since I've touched a woman, sat and talked to a woman, felt her silken skin against mine? Have any idea what that does to a man? Being cooped up in a cell where he can't see the sunlight, smell the sweetness of fresh cut grass or flowers blooming? Or have a woman?"

"You killed your wife and child. What did you expect?" It was beyond her to feel pity for this man while being tortured by his doppelganger. They were one in the same, the two of them, and she couldn't separate one's cruelty from the other's tenderness.

"Lenore, please. It's such a dark world where I live. Allow me some light. I will not touch you unless you ask me to. I know you're frightened, and who could blame you. I can help you. I can give you some pleasure from this. Maybe we can discover a way you can be rid of him."

"You bargain for sex?"

"No, just your touch. We have had sex, you and I. Was it so bad?"

"Just the opposite. It was the best I've ever had. Do you have any idea how that makes me feel? Perhaps I should tell my best friend that the best sex I ever had was with a demon in a nightmare. Everyone already waits for me to go crazy like my poor mother. That would pretty well turn the trick. Besides, if I am insane, then you and Alf don't really exist, and all I have to do is let them commit me."

"Oh, Lenore. I assure you we exist. He will move on to someone else, but only after you have done his bidding. Then he will destroy you, just as he is destroying me."

She opened her eyes, gazed out the window. A sunset painted the spring sky in streaks of pinks, purples, and golds. How beautiful. How wonderful. Tears filled her eyes, and sadness grew all around her. Poor Eric. To never see that again. How terrible. Compassion replaced fear.

"Come here, Eric. Lie with me. Touch me, love me." She opened her arms to her invisible lover, and he settled beside her. Released a huge sigh of contentment.

It didn't take her long to embrace him, allow him inside, and they made love as if he were something more than a wispy spirit. Or as much so as they could, under the circumstances. He proved adept at making up for the shortcomings his condition created. Like not having a body.

When both were satisfied, he moved away from her. "I must go. He will awaken soon and punish us both if he finds me here. Sleep, my love," he whispered, then floated away.

She awoke some time later, starving, went to the kitchen, and made a sandwich.

Sitting at the table, pondering her situation, a feeling of helplessness came over her. Could she win this war or was she only being foolish? While the demon was aware of her planned visit to the institute, Eric might not be. She should've asked him, for it would be interesting to know what he thought of her plan.

Odd, how she'd come to accept the thing's existence as a part of her life. Almost as if he were someone she'd met and disliked, but couldn't convince to leave her alone. Maybe she'd ask Doctor Collins if all crazy people eventually accepted their paranoia as reality, their illusions as alive. Then she remembered the old saying, if you think you're crazy, you probably aren't. Did her acceptance of the demon mean she really was crazy? Or did the fact that she could consider both sides prove her sane?

The whole thing gave her a headache, and she finished off the sandwich, then laid back down, and fell asleep.

Someone rattled and banged on the door, awakening her with a start. The room was black as only night in the country can be, and she was filled with confusion and lingering fright. Rubbing at her face, she staggered to her feet and hurried to the door.

One hand on the knob, the other on the dead bolt, she called out, "Who is it?" but her visitor continued making too much noise to hear the query. Way too much noise to be a burglar or mad killer.

She unlocked the door, opened it a couple of inches, and peered through the slit.

"My God, I thought you might be dead," Herb bellowed. At least he stopped the infernal hammering. Now he was only yelling. "Let me in."

"No. What do you want? It's the middle of the night."

"It's barely ten o'clock. Dammit, let me in." He easily shoved the door and her into the room and squeezed through the opening. After he shut and bolted it, he said, "You opened up without knowing who was there. You ought to be more careful."

Groaning, she covered her temples with both hands. "I couldn't stand the noise. Go away, Herb. I was sleeping for the first time in ages."

He covered her hands with his. "Honey, I'm sorry. Ever since I heard about what happened at the shop I've been worried about you. Are you okay? Did those toughs try to hurt you?" He reached for the switch, snapped on the overhead light.

"Oh, God, Herb." She pulled from his grasp, collapsed to the couch and shielded her eyes from the glare and his scrutiny. Now she had to retell the lie once again. How could she keep this up? She took a deep breath and glared up at him. From his expression, she had no choice. Perhaps if she told it often enough, even she would begin to believe it. So she recited the fabricated story once again. It was easier this time.

While she finished, he paced circles in the center of the room, then settled on the couch beside her. She resisted his efforts to take her hands, to put an arm around her, to kiss her.

Her actions fueled his anger, and she couldn't understand why. *He* was the one who had gone off in a huff. Asked to postpone their marriage. She didn't much blame him after the way she acted, but why was he now being so conciliatory?

"What is *wrong* with you, Lenore?"

"Nothing. I just don't want us to start up again. I mean, what's the sense of it?"

"We've loved each other for a long while, that's the sense of it. I've had time to think, to put things in perspective. I want to stand by you, get you some treatment so we can go on with our life together."

"Why?"

"Why?" He threw his hands in the air. "Why? Because I love you. Haven't you been listening? Sometimes you are so damned frustrating."

"Ah, well, but still you love me?" She angled a mocking glance up at him and was ashamed to see the hurt in his eyes.

"All he wants is your money. Seduce him and slice off his balls."

A thrill of wicked anticipation washed through her. A delightful pastime, hacking off the balls of men one had no use for.

Without reacting to her look of revulsion, Herb took a deep breath and sat back down on the couch. He didn't touch her, but leaned forward, elbows on knees, hands locked together, and studied the floor between his feet for a long while before speaking.

"I saw Delilah leave the shop this morning, wondered why she was closing down in the middle of the day, but then I noticed the rear end of the Jeep out back and realized you were there. I wish I'd come down to stay with you, then this wouldn't have happened." He twiddled his thumbs, glanced at her. "They must have come in from the other side of the building and in the back door."

A tremor kicked at her insides. "Why do you say that?"

"I'd have seen them otherwise."

"What'd you do, Herb, spy on me?"

He shrugged. "Why didn't I see them, Lee?"

Stubbornly, she refused to answer. He suspected what she'd done, wanted her to admit it. Well, she wasn't about to. "I don't know, Herb. Maybe you looked away, perched up there spying on me. Maybe you went to pee."

"No, I didn't. But I was just wondering how long after Del left did they arrive?"

"Why are you asking all these questions? Do you have a point to make?"

"The point I'm trying to make is, I don't think there were any vandals. If there had been I'd have seen them. I saw Del leave, and I saw the deputy arrive. And there was no one in between."

"What about the old ladies?"

He arched a brow.

"Guess you did turn away, huh, Herb? I'd appreciate it if you left. And don't come back."

"Are you still seeing a doctor?"

"That's none of your business."

"It is. I care for you, love you."

"Well, I guess you'll just have to get over it, won't you?" Despite the pounding in her temples she lurched to her feet. "Now, will you please leave? I want to get some sleep."

20

SHE'S COMING HERE?" Eric asked, gaping around at the dank cell. "To this terrible place? You can't let her."

"It seems I can't stop her. She's tough despite her terror. Right away, figured out she isn't going insane. Besides, I think it'll be fun, playing with her in the flesh, so to speak."

The cruel bastard. Eric had to do something—*anything*. This woman ran with the wolves. She had no idea of the predator that inhabits women. A spirit that knows how to sing over the dead, she kept her creative fires dampened down. They had been sparked to flame when she destroyed much of the craft shop. If she could learn to rein in those awesome powers and gain control over them, she might well destroy Alf. He dared not think those thoughts and squelched them before the demon, who continued to dwell on his fascination with Lenore, tuned in to him again. He had to be careful or he would betray himself and Lenore.

Since discovering the woman, Alf's preoccupation had allowed Eric to grow stronger when he had all but given up any kind of existence.

He had sent her the dream, but maybe the message was too obscure. Fear that Alf would intercept kept him from revealing too much. Would she be wise enough to figure it out? The next time Alf slept, Eric would try to clarify it for her. She was in the process of having the words from the dream translated. As long as he could keep Alf concentrating on his desire to possess her, then perhaps he wouldn't connect the events in the dream and her discussion with the holy man. Somehow he must warn her, help her block thoughts as he himself was learning to do. If only there was a way to prevent Alf's reading her mind, even from a distance. But he could think of none.

Eric felt the tickle of a warning, thought for a moment it was Alf. But it wasn't. Something left in his brain wanted to survive. If Alf passed on into Lenore, then he would be free. Free of the demon, free to die and rest in peace. So why would he choose to protect her, when all he wanted was serenity? The nothingness that would come with the demon passing from him?

Alf jerked, came out of his daydreams and spiraled from the cell without warning Eric, who could only meekly trail along. That got him to thinking. Maybe Alf couldn't leave the cell without him. But that couldn't be true, for he had sometimes been unconscious or in treatment when Alf went prowling. That's how he had found Lenore in the first place. Still, perhaps his subconscious went along, and he simply had no memory of it. Why didn't Alf suffer when the body was treated with drugs and shock?

"Now that wouldn't make much sense, would it?" the demon growled and settled them into the darkness of Lenore's cabin. *"If I have the power to possess your body, I must have the power to protect my being from harm if you decide, for instance, to kill yourself. If I can't stop you, then I can pass on to another host. Or return to my home. The same applies when they torture you with drugs or shock. Mankind has come up with some devious abuse for its weaker souls."*

"You're one to judge such things," Eric said. Wait. Return to his home? Where might Alf's home be? Further conversation was cut short when Alf moved into Lenore's inert body where she still lay coiled in a ball on the couch.

With mixed joy and sorrow, Eric embraced the light within her spirit. Could he save her? Did he want to if it meant his continued suffering?

Before he could dwell on the answer to that, Lenore took him close, moaning in an ecstasy that soon transpired itself into his loins. Alf cleared his throat and stepped away to watch, as if he didn't wish to intrude. Eric understood the demon wanted to learn how best to approach her, yet he could not help himself. He made love to her with a tenderness he had learned in his wife Annie's embrace. He regretted that he had led the way into her heart and soul and prepared her for the life of hell Alf would soon impose upon her. But he could no more stop himself than he could control the hateful demon that had destroyed his life.

He whispered her name, kissed her, moved within her to touch the core that throbbed to be taken.

Happy Eric had returned, Lenore caressed this invisible man with her mind and spirit. This man who made passionate love to her, not only in her sleep but while she was fully awake and conscious.

Fingers stroked her temples, combed through her tousled hair. Warm lips breathed against her skin, a moist tongue tasted her flesh, but no body moved within the clutch of her writhing limbs. Her lover dwelled within, caressed her inner being, exposed her to songs of praise and adulation. And she slept in peace with him coiled around her heart.

Chapter 21

DEACON DANIEL KLIMAS, a large man made larger by a voluminous white robe, greeted parishioners outside the doorway of Our Lady of Smiles Catholic Mission. His aura, one of guarded serenity, embraced him like a shield. Lenore hung back while he shook hands as if each parishioner were a long lost friend. Perhaps fifteen or twenty people milled around, waiting to enter the picturesque stone building. No one was in a hurry on this glorious spring morning.

Snowy blossoms hung on dogwood trees spreading their thin limbs over the grassy grounds. The sun shone brightly along the high ridge, but in the valley far below, fog formed a filmy skirt around the foothills. She imagined the deacon's jovial laughter bouncing about down there like a loose cannon ball.

When she could no longer avoid Klimas—indeed, he watched her with an expectant smile—she drew up her shoulders, moved within his vivid aura, and accepted the large, extended hand. He possessed a rare eighth chakra of pure white above his crown. What some believed explained the halos portrayed in paintings of early Christians, including Jesus Christ. The existence of an eighth Chakra was strictly a western notion, but one she found herself subscribing to. It was a romantic idea, if nothing else.

Power flowed from his hand through hers, and a hum of heated displeasure stirred deep inside her. A warning from the demon. He feared this man, a good sign.

She met the deacon's warm gaze. "I'm Lenore Maine. We spoke a few days ago?"

His double-handed grip swallowed hers. "Ah, yes. So you decided to throw yourself upon my mercy after all. I'll try not to disappoint you." Clear cerulean eyes sparkled.

Down in her gut an inner warning vibrated so loudly she was afraid he'd hear.

As if in reply to her concern, he arched a tawny eyebrow, murmured, "Oh, my. You do have troubles, don't you?"

Pleased that he was sensitive, she nodded, held his gaze. Every sensation urged her to run before the demon called down a terrible retribution upon them both. Perhaps this man, who appeared to possess the psychic eye, though he would never have admitted it, could protect both himself and her from evil. At least she could hope so.

"Well, never mind that now. You are welcome to this particular house of our Lord. Please come on in."

He pulled the double doors closed quietly behind them, then guided her through the vestibule where a long walnut table displayed delicate crystal rosaries, missals and Bibles, postcards picturing the church and its surrounding statues, maps of the area, and brochures from nearby businesses. A box with a slot accepted any donation those taking the items might wish to give.

Beyond a second set of open doors a center aisle divided a dozen rows of pews sparingly occupied by those who had entered while she and

Klimas greeted each other. Murmurings from the small crowd quieted, and heads turned to regard her and the deacon.

After he dipped his fingers in a marble bowl of water, genuflected, and crossed himself, he seated her in the back row and strode to the altar. The long white robe swished around his ankles and projected vivid colors from his prodigious aura. Once on the dais, partly hidden behind a beautifully crafted podium, his bulk took on an austere presence. A shock of golden hair gleamed in the morning sunlight that poured through leaded glass windows along each side of the church.

Spreading his arms wide so that the robe formed wings that surrounded the smear of vivid blues emanating from his torso, Deacon Klimas gazed upward and pronounced with great exuberance, "Welcome, all you who gather in His name."

The congregation came to its feet, the sound of movement like ripples of a gentle wind through trees, and as Klimas crossed himself, they did, as well.

Lenore captured her hands under both arms to avoid her desire to do the same, and squeezed her eyes closed. If there were a God, would he strike her dead for such an act when she remained so doubtful?

Dear God, are you here? She might have asked the question aloud, she wasn't sure, but if she did, no one paid attention. They were busy with murmured responses to Klimas. And God seemed totally oblivious to the entire event.

"For those of you attending our mission for the first time, I'm Deacon Daniel Klimas. I will not conduct an ordinary mass as I'm not an ordained priest, but we will worship together in the name of the Father and the Son and the Holy Spirit, Amen." While speaking he crossed himself again.

The people did likewise and murmured the words in echo to his.

A cramp gripped Lenore's belly, and she tightened her lips to keep from crying out. That damned demon. If he was so frightened by a church, why had he come along? Surely he hadn't already left Eric's body and taken up residence in hers. Would she know when that happened? She tried to concentrate on the service and ignore the tight grip he had on her insides.

"Send forth your light, Dear God, and lead me to Your Holy Mountain," Klimas prayed.

"Your God does not show himself. Foolish child, you who have never believed. What do you think this will gain you?"

The cramp tightened, sent ragged jolts of pain into her chest, and she clutched at the back of the pew before her. Sweat beaded her forehead. The deacon's mouth moved, but she could hear nothing, as if she were in a vacuum where no sound penetrated. Grinding her teeth to keep from crying out, she collapsed onto the padded kneeling bench at about the same time as everyone knelt and lowered their heads. No one appeared to notice her writhing there. Of if they did, they must believe she had been captured by the Holy Spirit.

If only that could be. The idea of that spirit doing battle with the demon who appeared to reside inside her, at least on a part-time basis, terrified her. In their zeal to fight, might they discard her safety? Fear so filled her she could not contemplate the question further.

The demon had stricken her deaf so she could not hear God's word if he uttered one, numbed her tongue so she could not take part, weakened her so that she could not worship in body or mind. He feared the message and that she might learn to believe. Another good sign should Klimas become her ally when she fought to cast him out.

She remained huddled in the corner of the hard pew throughout the service, determined that the demon would not win and send her flying from this holy place that obviously threatened him.

Abruptly everyone arose, startling her. The deacon had finished his message and strode along the aisle past her to stand beside the doorway and wish them all a good day. The demon allowed her to rise, and she moved stiffly, one arm hugging her side where the cramp held on with ferocity. The faces around her appeared serene, their spirits cleansed by having gathered to worship God. The demon was right. Because she had never been exposed to any religion, she'd never considered its possibility, didn't believe in organized worship, though she had an enduring faith in the goodness of humankind and in a higher power.

Mama had existed only in her narrow poetic world, and her father never cared about anything outside his realm of medieval studies, so she'd been left to pretty much figure things out for herself. Growing up aware of the aura each person possessed was tough enough to handle without adding religion to the package. Perhaps she wasn't so much an atheist as a heathen, for she left room in her mind for all forms of gods. It was only her ignorance that kept her from choosing one. The cramp in her belly let up a bit when she passed beyond the deacon's space and through the doorway out into the fresh mountain air.

Odd the creature had only spoken once and that a milked-down version of his usual mutterings. Maybe his powers were weaker in the sanctity of the church, for despite rendering her deaf and mute, he hadn't kept up that constant mocking repartee she'd grown to expect. As for the cramps, those could have been real. It was that time of the month.

The fog had drifted away ahead of a refreshing breeze to reveal the earthen fields below splashed with green. The parishioners were in no hurry to leave, but stood around in small groups visiting, laughing, and chiding restless children who, released from confinement, wanted only to race and run and screech. For an instant, she was filled with a wild desire to climb in her car and drive off. What could this man of God do for her anyway? And there was no telling what punishment the demon would devise if she went any further with her plans to make an ally of Klimas.

"Lenore, how are you?" a voice said at her back.

Startled, she swung around to see Bill Crowley, the owner of the Summit Falls Grocery where she had so embarrassed herself a few weeks earlier.

She nodded, her face heated with shame. "Fine. Fine, thank you."

"Good to see you here." Crowley moved on, glancing at her warily a few times while he spoke briefly to the deacon and a couple of parishioners she recognized but couldn't put names to.

She eyed the Jeep waiting in the lot and took a tentative step toward it, was drawn instead to a statue of a woman draped in white, arms open at her sides, a golden copperhead snake coiled around her feet. So realistic was the gleaming reptile that for a moment she thought it was alive and had crawled there to catch some morning sun. Then she realized it was part of the figure that stood with feet bare, surrounded by a bed of actual yellow daffodils that looked as if they had just begun to bloom this very day. Drops of early morning dew sparkled in the throats of the flowers. The plaque, set in natural stone, read, "Our Lady of Smiles."

Bitch.

The hissed expletive jarred away the serenity Lenore felt in the presence of Our Lady.

Ignoring the demon's sharp remark, she gazed up into the placid countenance with tear-filled eyes. Did belief in God give one such complete tranquility as that expression embodied?

"It's just a statue, sweet Lenore. Anyone can paint a picture, sculpt a figure."

So much for peace and quiet. If he didn't stop calling her sweet Lenore, she would gladly—

"What? Do what? Scream at me, curse me, show these good people how completely off your rocker you are, sweet Lenore?"

"Damn you," she said under her breath and whirled to flee. Instead she ran full tilt into the broad chest of Deacon Klimas. The demon hissed into stillness like a reptile whose head had been severed.

Klimas grunted and caught her by both arms. "Here. Take it easy."

"I have to go. I can't stay. I'm sorry I bothered you. You can't help me, no one can."

"That's not true," he said in a voice compelling in tone, but he released her nevertheless. "He can, and I think you know that."

"He?"

Klimas glanced at the statue, back at the church, swept one arm to indicate the breathtaking panorama. "He."

Sighing deeply, she rubbed at her arms to quell a sudden shiver. "I'm not sure I believe."

"Whether you believe or not is of no consequence to His existence. To believe in evil and not believe in God would be both highly foolish and destructive."

She glanced quickly into his face, saw a determination she found disturbing. This man was willing to take her part, put himself in the way of danger for her. He might even believe her terrifying tale. But then what would happen to him? Could the demon destroy this good man or worse, cause her to wreak the destruction?

"Come on. The least you can do is talk to me, after I turned down a free lunch to meet with you."

"Oh, I'm sorry. I shouldn't take your time. I didn't mean—"

"Whoa, I was joking." His laughter soothed her. "People are always buying me something to eat." He patted his stomach, and she saw there wasn't near as much of him as the robe indicated. "And I could do with missing a few meals. Where would you like to talk?"

She glanced around the lovely grounds. "Could we walk?"

"Of course." He tucked her hand in the crook of one elbow and headed away from the few parishioners who continued to visit, while casting quick glances in their direction. The vague odor of incense tickled her nostrils. Probably from the flowing white sleeves.

A pickup rattled past, children in the back shouting and waving.

"Thank God for the new highway," he said. "Took all that horrid traffic away from here, left us with our peace once again. Like it was in the beginning."

"Oh, I didn't realize God built the new highway." She immediately regretted the impudent reply. She never used to be so insensitive, but then so much had changed about her behavior since the demon's arrival.

Klimas took it well, though, chuckling as if she hadn't offended him in any way. "He uses us for His own means just as we tend to use Him. But He expects us to make our own way. When we stumble and fall, He might not help us up, but He certainly eases our pain and sorrow and gives us strength to rise and plod on.

"Now, tell me about this thing that's going on in your life that you find too heavy to bear alone."

"I wanted you to translate some Latin for me, not hear my confession. That is what you do, isn't it? Forgive people their sins?"

"Lord, no. Not even the Pope could forgive you your sins, and I certainly couldn't. Only you and your God can deal with penance. I can't even hear confessions. But that isn't what we came to talk about, is it? May I call you Lenore?" He stopped beneath draping branches laced with snowy dogwood blooms and faced her, his aura like a million blue and gold butterflies dancing in the spring air.

"Yes, of course." She so wanted to get to know this man.

"Lenore, I'll be happy to translate the Latin for you. And I'll be more than glad to help ease your burden, whatever it might be. No one should have to carry their troubles all alone, and something tells me you sense yourself sorely alone, because you haven't yet reckoned on God's help."

Gritting her teeth against an expectation of the mocking voice, she dug in her purse for the piece of paper on which she had written the words intoned by the poor soul in her repetitive dreams: *Sic pereant omnes inemici tui, Dominay.*

He fingered a pair of half-glasses from his pocket, perched them on his nose and opened the paper. Pursing his lips for a moment, he studied the words, then spoke them aloud. "You've misspelled a couple. *Inemici* is *I-n-i-m-i-c-i* and *Dominay* is *D-o-m-i-n-e*. So perish all thine enemies, O Lord."

"What?"

"So perish all thine enemies, O Lord. That's what it says. Where did you get this? How did you hear it?"

She nibbled at her lip, tried to make sense of the words. Did she dare tell him? Furtively she glanced around. Everyone had gone, the last car pulling onto the highway, its tires spitting bits of white gravel from the church drive. Nothing from Alf, but she feared he listened. Feared he planned some sort of punishment for both of them.

Klimas spoke before she could. "It's from the book of Judges, the Song of Deborah. Not something just anyone would know. And certainly not a non-believer." He managed a wry grin that lit his pleasant features. He was quite handsome, with generous lips, finely drawn eyebrows, and well-set eyes that were as clear as glass marbles.

"What does it mean?"

"Mean? You want me to tell you in twenty-five words or less what this means." He waved the piece of paper above his head, anger sparking in his eyes.

"Well, yes. That's what I'd hoped."

"Perhaps you ought to take some Bible courses. I understand they have very scholarly instructions at the University in Fayetteville. The Bible as literature, or something equally politically correct." The grin disappeared, his lips tightened.

She took the paper from his hands. "I'm sorry if I made you angry. That wasn't my intention. Thank you very much for your help."

Turning, she strode away, her shiny black patent pumps kicking up last winter's dry leaves in crackly whispers.

Klimas caught her before she reached the lot where the Jeep sat beside a dusty ten-year-old sedan. From the opposite side of the church came the sound of raking. She glanced in that direction as he took her arm.

"My wife. She's handling grounds duty today."

"I didn't know you could marry. Besides I thought the Catholic Church had money. Why can't they hire someone to do that?

"I'm not a priest." He smiled fondly toward the attractive tall woman wielding the rake with vigor. "I'm afraid I don't have the capacity to deny my natural urges." Flushing, he changed the subject. "Small churches like this lovely place sadly go without a priest or enough money and have for years. There just aren't enough men of God to go around anymore. So men like myself, who have devoted themselves to their religion, but don't happen to be able to live the solitary life of a priest, are called upon to instruct those who believe and have no place to worship.

"Soon they'll all be closed down, these little out-of-the-way mission churches, and we will progress even farther away from God's intention for us. And what a pity. So beautiful, so holy.

"But we didn't come here to talk about the troubles of the Church. Talk to me, perhaps I can help you, but even if I can't, you will have shared your burden. And I promise you, anything you say to me is sacrosanct. It will go no further."

"He will hear, though."

"No, he won't, Lenore."

Eric!

"Yes. He's sleeping, claims religion bores him, but actually he's frightened of what men like this one are capable of. He tries to pretend that he doesn't believe in the strength of God, but he does. It tends to overpower him."

Klimas tilted his head. "He? You mean God?"

Klimas's question silenced Eric and startled her back to reality. Or what appeared to be real. "No. Sorry. I've been having a dream. A night-mare, really." The admission came out in stammered pauses.

He studied her without comment.

"In it a man buries this strange length of metal, iron I think, like he's hiding it, and just as he gets it covered up, chanting those words I wrote on the paper, these savages, they look like prehistoric men or early Indians, I guess. They come out of the woods and kill him. They shoot him full of arrows, these primitive stone points lashed to long lances of some kind." She took a deep breath, still didn't look at him for fear of what she would see reflected in his eyes. "I just keep having the dream, over and over. He quotes that." She indicated the piece of paper he still held in one hand.

He glanced at it, shook his head. "That's not all."

"I don't understand."

"Well, Lenore, we all have strange dreams, nightmares even. But you haven't told me what's going on in your life, what has gone on, that might be causing such dreams."

"You sound like my shrink."

He laughed gently. "Maybe because that's what I do for a living. I'm a psychologist. I counsel those lost and wandering. You are seeing someone, then?"

"Yes, but—"

"That's wonderful. Just keep that up and I'm sure all this will be resolved in God's good time."

"But you don't understand, I haven't—"

"Lenore, come with me. I want to give you something."

She nodded. For some reason he had shut her down, did not want to hear anymore, and she didn't know why. Something she'd said? Or had he finally written her off as just another crazy.

He led her into the vestibule of the church and handed her a white Bible from those stacked on the table.

"Look up the Book of Judges, read the Song of Deborah. I think you'll understand the message your dream is trying to convey. Now, I think I'd better lend my wife a hand. Come back and see me again. We'll talk some more after you've read this. About the evil that threatens you." He tapped a long, graceful finger on the cover of the Bible and went out the door and away from her before she could say more.

Strange. He knew there was more. Sensed it, yet when she mentioned seeing a shrink, he'd cut her off. Why? Was he reluctant to overstep his bounds, seeing as how he practiced in the field as well? How did he counsel people in the church and out there in real life without getting the two confused? Where did he draw the line between God and man? Or did he? Was his answer always God, when so many times much more than an unquestioning belief in the Supreme Being was needed in order to survive? It stuck in her mind, though, that he'd sensed the demon's evil. Perhaps he thought her evil as well.

So perish all thine enemies, O Lord.

She dug in her purse, found a twenty-dollar bill and shoved it through the slot in the donation box. Almost as an afterthought, she picked up one of the delicate crystal rosaries, and clutching it and the Bible in one hand, hurried across the lawn to the Jeep. She climbed in and drove away from the church, the tall white statue of Our Lady of Smiles watching her from the rearview mirror.

Chapter 22

AT HOME, LENORE laid the Bible and the rosary on the table at one end of the couch and dropped onto the thick cushions. The high-heeled sandals hurt her feet, and she slid them off, curling her toes within the black stockings. In a few moments, off came the filmy dress. The fabric puddled over the shoes on the braided rug. Panties and bra followed, until all she wore were the knee-length nylons and a copper-toned scarf holding back her dark hair.

"You are so beautiful, Lenore."

A bolt of anticipation charged through her. "Eric?" Subconsciously, she touched her throat where gooseflesh trailed over her bare skin.

Though he usually came with Alf attached like an appendage, she was no longer afraid of the man she knew as Eric. How strange, since he was a stone cold killer with blood on his hands, even though the demon had caused his unholy actions

"Yes, it's me."

"Just you, not him?" Her heart raced like a wild creature.

"Not him."

"Why? How?"

"I promised him I could make you forget about the man of God." His touch trailed through her.

She cried out. "This is insane. How can we do this?"

"We do it like this." His essence gathered her close, cradled her. *"I will not let him hurt you anymore. I promise."*

"No. This isn't possible. You *are* him, only another side. You'll destroy me just like he will. You said it yourself. You came to make me forget about Deacon Klimas. Forget about getting help to rid myself of this wicked thing. That's the only reason you're here."

"No, no, it isn't."

He ran invisible fingers over her naked breasts, and she shivered, then pulled away, as if she could actually avoid the touch of a man who resided within her body.

"I did not agree to help him. I only told him that so I could come to you."

"So you could rape me. You're no better than he. I have no say in what you do to me. Leave me alone. Both of you, leave me alone." Twisting, turning, raking her fingers over her bare body so her nails left red trails, she tried to purge him. Felt his intense sorrow that brought tears to her eyes.

"I will not rape you. Ever."

"You are inside me against my will. That is rape of the worst kind, because I can't stop you, no matter how I try."

Silence for a long moment, then a sense of freedom that made her suck in a quick, cleansing breath.

"I am so sorry, Lenore. Please forgive me. I guess I only thought of my own needs and pretended I was thinking of yours. It's been so long since I have touched a woman, felt a woman's caress, known that someone cared. God, I still miss Annie so much. I will not do that to you again. I promise."

She flattened both hands over her stomach. He had kept his word and she was free of him. If that had gained her anything, she wasn't sure. He had been an ally of sorts, though he was inexorably attached to the demon he referred to as Alf. What an ambiguous name for such an evil entity.

"It is my name for him. Certainly not his." He spoke from somewhere in the room, not within her. Like talking to an invisible man sitting in the chair opposite her.

"You're still here. I thought you'd gone."

"Only from your being."

"How do you do this?"

"I don't know. I do know that I'm growing stronger each time I travel when I'm conscious, with or without him. I'm not sure if that means he's preparing to leave me."

"When you're conscious?"

"Yes. Sometimes they give me drugs, sometimes I hurt myself to stop the anguish."

"Dear God." It was the first time she had thought of Eric as more than a vicious killer, as a human being going through torment each and every day. "That must be horrible. All these years."

"How many has it been?"

She walked naked to the back window, gazed out over the deck toward the woods. "You don't know?"

"No, I have no idea at all. Only that it must be an eternity."

A remote sadness filled her throat, as if she had just that moment experienced a terrible loss. What would it be like to exist in such a way? Then the most formidable thought of all occurred to her. That is precisely what the demon wants to do to you.

"Lenore? Do you know how long?"

"Yes, yes I do, but I wish I could touch you."

"But you said you—"

"I know, but I don't want to tell you such a thing without being able to comfort you."

He didn't reply for so long she thought he had gone, but then the scarf around her hair slipped gently away, and he was once more within her.

"I'm so sorry, Eric. It's been ten years."

His intake of breath shook her.

"You have to understand how terrified I am that it will soon be my fate. You said you think he is ready to leave you. My God, that means—"

He stirred. *"I'm afraid it does, but I made you a promise, and I intend to keep it."*

"Why? Why would you do that when you could allow what he wants and be free of him?"

"Free for what? They will keep me in that place until I die, so what good is my freedom? I can help you and truly be free in the only way left to me."

She sucked in a breath, closed her eyes against the view out the window, looked into her own heart. "Kill yourself, you mean?"

He didn't answer, and she stood there until she swayed on her feet, mesmerized by an imagined scene of inexplicable horror beyond the beautiful spring day.

Moist, hot palms covered her breasts, a cruel mouth closed over hers, sucking away her breath. She bit, clawed, and kicked. He only laughed.

"Help her now, you puny excuse for a man. Just see if you can help her now. I want what is mine, and I'm tired of waiting for it. And you will not—will not kill yourself. You will die when I'm ready and not before. Now, my sweet."

There was no place to run, nowhere to hide, as the demon invaded her body and soul, took her over and did whatever he wished while she writhed in a fury of passionate hate for what he was able to make her feel. She nearly fainted as he finished ravaging her with a roar that shook the walls, left her soaked with perspiration and exhausted until she couldn't move from where she sprawled on the hard wooden floor near the glass door.

Eric coiled around her for an instant, his words, *"I'm sorry, so sorry,"* fading until she heard nothing but the displaced songs of birds.

Chapter 23

ERIC STRUGGLED TO drag his exhausted body upright on the floor of the cell. Alf slept, and no wonder. He had attacked Lenore with a feral vengeance, draining this body they shared of every vestige of desire and energy. And once again Eric could not stop what happened. Though it was a spiritual rape, it was still a hideous thing to do to her. It gave Eric no satisfaction. Just the opposite, he felt a renewed disgust that such evil could be allowed to exist, to punish someone like her.

How long could she continue to fight to remain sane? Her mother's death had all but destroyed her ability to deal with real life beyond the tight circle she'd drawn around herself. She couldn't manage to deal with something like this.

Could the holy man help her unravel the mystery of the Song of Deborah? And even if he did, could she bring herself to do what had to be done to save herself? He didn't put the thoughts into actual words, for fear Alf would hear and somehow be able to prevent the act. She would have to hurry, for the demon grew restless to complete the possession. Did he dare warn her?

Get her to pick up the Bible, read the passages that would lead her in the right direction. That much he could do, now while the evil one rested up from his unholy conquest.

Chapter 24

ENVELOPED BY DARKNESS, Lenore stirred from where the demon had left her sprawled on the floor. She could scarcely swallow, her tongue stuck to parched lips, her body ached. Crawling to her knees, she moved to the couch, and stood shakily. After a few moments she placed one foot, then the other, scuffing along to the refrigerator and drank cold water from a jug until her head throbbed.

That bastard had ravaged her once again. She felt as raw inside as if she had been gang raped for hours.

I don't mean to hurt you, he'd repeated over and over inside her head. What a damnable lie. Of course he meant to hurt her, in the most vile, destructive way. He meant to destroy her soul, to bend her to his will.

She sipped at the water a while longer, then put the bottle back in the refrigerator and shuffled toward the bathroom. The white Bible lay on the table beside her bed. She couldn't stop staring at it. A voice urged her to pick it up, and so she did, then placed it on the pillow along with the chain of crystal beads.

After a long hot soak in bubbles scented with fern and wild flowers, she stood under a needle spray until the hot water turned cool. Wrapping her hair in a towel, she padded into the bedroom, at long last able to face the words in the Book that might explain her dream. She had no hope they would solve anything, though.

She held the rosary in her hand, the beads threaded through her fingers, and paged through to chapter four of Judges where Deborah was mentioned. It wasn't until the twenty-first verse that she ran across something that piqued her interest.

Jael, wife of the Kenite Heber, had welcomed Sisera into her tent when he fled the ten thousand strong army of Barak, who had been sent by Deborah to conquer Sisera and his people. Jael fed the man, agreed to protect him, then "took a nail of the tent, and took an hammer in her hand, and went softly unto him, and smote the nail into his temples, and fastened it into the ground; for he was fast asleep and weary. So he died."

"Good Lord." Talk about violence and mayhem. She read on through chapter five, the actual Song of Deborah and Barak. The children of Israel had prospered and prevailed after the slaying of Sisera, and they went on to destroy Jabin, king of Canaan.

Thus sang Deborah. The story of the slaying of Sisera was repeated to her by an Angel of the Lord, speaking again of how Jael nailed the man's temple to the ground with a piece of iron. And then, there it was, in the thirty-first verse of chapter five. *"So let all thine enemies perish, O Lord; but let them that love him be as the sun when he goeth forth in his might. And the land had rest forty years."*

Thumb in the Bible, she let it fall closed on her propped knees. "Okay, fine. Now, what does it mean?"

Surprisingly, despite having slept away the afternoon, she fell asleep with the light on, the Bible resting on the colorful nine-patch quilt that covered her, the rosary beads coiled next to her cheek.

The ringing telephone awoke her so quickly that if she had dreamed, its memory was jerked away.

She knocked the warbling instrument to the floor, finally picked it up and murmured a hello into the mouthpiece.

"They caught the little buggers," someone squealed.

"Who is this?" A fuzzy brain refused to register the voice.

"Del. This is Del, and can you believe it, the cops caught two little farts that have admitted to tearing up the shop. I never thought it would happen, did you? Can you come down?"

Lenore closed her eyes tight. Good God, no. How could this be?

"Lee? Can you?"

"What?"

"Can you come to Fayetteville to the sheriff's office, see if you can identify these pint-sized yahoos?"

"No, I can't. I told them I didn't see anything. How could I identify them?" How could she indeed? What was going on? Had her entire world flopped topsy-turvy so that nothing made sense at all?

Del sighed loudly, a put-on expulsion of breath calculated to change Lenore's mind. *"They want you here all the same. To take a look at them, maybe you've seen them hanging around. I sure haven't."*

"Hanging around where? I haven't worked in the shop in several months. Where would I have seen them hanging around?" This was what happened when you lied. Things went from bad to worse. It would soon spiral out of proportion.

"Lee, don't be such a dimwit. You know they have to do things the way they have to do them, even if they don't make a lick of sense. Humor them, humor me, for goodness' sake. It's your business too. I'd think you'd want these kids put away."

"They don't put kids away, certainly not for breaking a few things. They'll be home in time to eat supper with their families. Forget it."

She hung up before Del could say anything else. Next thing, they'd be knocking on her door. Well, let them. She'd be gone and for a legitimate reason. She kicked free of the tangled covers, ignoring the Bible when it smacked the floor on the far side of the bed. She had an appointment with Doctor Collins in Fort Smith in less than two hours. If she hurried she could be out of here before anyone could show up from Fayetteville. Dammit, why did lies have a way of coming back and biting you on the butt?

She was halfway to Fort Smith before she realized that all she'd had to do was appear and swear those couldn't be the boys. Their voices were too high or too childish or something, anything that would convince the cops to turn them loose. Though, if they'd been picked up for something like this, they probably deserved another slap on the wrist. Why had the little nitwits confessed to doing something they couldn't possibly have done? Since it hadn't happened. Probably just wanted some attention.

Collins let her into her inner sanctum precisely at 11 a.m. No receptionist sat at the desk in the lobby. They were alone.

"Sorry, Libby is out on a family emergency, so I'm left to fend for myself. It's good to see you. Come, have a seat wherever you feel comfortable."

Besides the straight chair that faced the woman's desk there were a pair of recliners and a blue couch that resembled those one saw in pictures of Roman orgies with a pillowed end and no arms. She took a recliner, but remained upright, sneaker clad feet flat on the floor. One white shoe had a dark smear over the toe, and she concentrated on it, refusing to look up when Collins perched on the end of the velveteen couch.

"How about the dreams? Have you been sleeping?"

"Most of yesterday and all night, as well. So I can't be having too many problems."

"On the contrary, sleeping too much is a sign of depression. Only one, mind you, but tell me, why do you think you slept your day away?"

Lenore glared at the doctor. Just tell the nosy old broad that she'd had sex with a demon and it wore her out. See what she thought of that. Nah, better not. Instead she shrugged. "I was tired?"

"At your age? Nonsense."

The brusque words accompanied by a somber stare irritated Lenore. She set her jaw and refused to say more.

Finally Collins, who had doodled over half a page of yellow legal pad, stood. "You're paying me to listen to you, to help you sort out your feelings. I can only do that if you talk to me. Why don't we try something? Lean back, hit that handle on the side and kick back. Let's just get you a bit more relaxed."

"I don't want to be hypnotized."

Collins laughed. "Lord, I'm not going to hypnotize you. I'm just helping you get in a more receptive mood. Giving you your money's worth."

Lenore eyed the woman, who today had dressed in a purple denim jumper over a gold silk blouse. Her hair, pulled high into a wrap, escaped in untidy strands. Perhaps she thought such an unprofessional appearance would help her patients relax, believe she was down to earth and didn't consider herself better than them.

For a moment Lenore studied her aura, tightly closed around her in pale colors all smeared together. Interesting. Something truly unusual was about to happen to this woman. She stopped thinking what it might be. Reading auras was the least of her concerns at the moment.

"Very good, Lenore. Now you've analyzed your shrink, so you can manage to go along with her."

She popped up the foot rest, leaned back until she was almost lying down, watched Collins roll a stool over beside her and perch there.

"Close your eyes, relax," the woman said in a soothing tone, her fingers rubbing gently across Lenore's forehead.

She did as the doctor suggested and walked straight into the oh-so-familiar nightmare.

Fighting her way out of the horrible darkness, she sat up screaming and tried to close her ears against the maniacal laughter of the demon, while Collins stared at her with a knowing smirk.

She could almost hear the echo of her thoughts. Crazy as a bat. As a loon. As her mother.

Chapter 25

SINCE ALF HAD begun his harassment of Lenore, Eric no longer slept away most of his days in some dark, quiet cavern of the demon's domain. Sometimes he wished he could, though, for to be alert meant to think and to think brought memories of Annie.

Like she used to be, before. Curled around him in their king-sized bed, joking about all that room going to waste. Teasing him about the curl of reddish hairs that grew around each of his nipples while his chest was perfectly smooth. Like those hunks who posed for calendars, she would say, while lacing her strong piano player fingers through his mop of sandy hair. She slept in the nude, her flawless skin tanned despite the warnings because she loved the sun. Loved how it warmed her bones at winter's end. They were trying to have a child, but in a lackadaisical way, enjoying the unrestricted sex.

"Mmm, I hope it takes a year or two. I like Nemo without his overcoat," she said, gripping his limp penis and massaging it once more to attention.

She had taught him how to make love because all he had ever known was violence from those who were supposed to love him. And he missed the gentleness of her. God, how he missed being with her. What a wonder to love and be loved. Something he'd never known in all his life. Alf had hurled him back into the nightmare of his childhood where hate and obsession and violence ruled. And Annie had paid dearly, much too dearly.

He shuddered, assailed by visions of her mangled body, the haunting reminder of her shrieks of terror when the man she loved, a madman, stood over her with glittering sword held high. And brought it down once, twice, three times.

"What a cool hobby, collecting such lovely swords," she'd once said.

Dear Annie, forgive me. God forgive me.

Bathed in blood, bellowing like some demented animal, he had gathered her in his arms, and waited for the police, the demon assaulting him over and over.

"Leave this place. Go, now." Claws ripped at his guts until he turned blind with agony. But he did not budge.

The police had believed his story about an intruder. The stolen sword, his own self-inflicted wounds, both her arms, both her legs hacked at. The neighbors who spoke of the couple's devotion, and the so-called butcher killer who'd slaughtered before, committing equally hideous crimes in other neighborhoods in Memphis convinced the cops of Eric's innocence.

Who could suspect this young man of such a horrible crime? He volunteered at his local church to assist the elderly, he was a member of Big Brothers and Big Sisters, he played on the softball team, coached his son's T-ball team. A model husband, father, and upstanding member of the community. Of course, he couldn't have committed such a crime.

And one day he packed a bag, got in his Oldsmobile, and drove away. Following the demon, who led him deeper and deeper into the insane butchery that was Alf's livelihood.

They would catch him, finally, some five years later, after he had bathed himself in the blood of seven more victims. All beautiful young women like his wife, like those three he'd butchered before her. From the time the demon had entered his soul, perverted his spirit, driven him raving mad, until forensic science put enough evidence together to apprehend the notorious butcher of Memphis, a total of almost eight years had passed.

Little wonder they locked him away in a hospital for the criminally insane. He could not take part in a trial, so incoherent and uncontrollable had he become when he was captured. How many years had passed since they locked him up he'd had no idea until Lenore told him. All that time he remained coiled within the darkness imposed by his own personal demon, oblivious to the passage of days, weeks, years. But then Alf connected with Lenore, and as his lust for her grew, Eric crawled up out of that hell. Became aware of a beautiful, haunted spirit badly in need of help. And he accompanied the demon in his sojourns, grew stronger, more sure of his ability to influence in a small way the outcome of some of the cruel episodes. Alf concentrated on his eventual possession of Lenore, leaving Eric free to learn more and more about her. Not everything the demon did was as brutal as the sexual assaults. Some of his antics were of a poltergeist nature like the morning he caused her to destroy so much of The Craft Basket. Sometimes he did things only meant to annoy, to back her into a corner and wear down her strength so she'd have nothing left with which to fight back. She was so strong to begin with, but his latest thing, the planting of the suspicion of sexual abuse committed on her by her father, worried Eric more than most of Alf's deceits. If it were true, the child in her had blocked that knowledge from the adult Lenore. Such a revelation could cause her immeasurable heartache, considering the suicide of her mother. If she suspected the two were linked, she would blame herself for the death of her mother more than she already did. Even if it were a cruel joke on Alf's part, God only knew how she might react.

They moved about within Lenore, Eric and his demon, tangled in her anguish while she sobbed out of control in the office high above the brown, slow moving Arkansas River.

Doctor Collins supplied her with wads of tissues but little more, scribbling notes on her pad as if she had just uncovered the secret of the universe. It was plain to see she embraced with glee this patient's revelation. What better cause for a mental breakdown than a repressed history of sexual abuse by her father? Eric could sense the doctor's subconscious euphoria. Having been exposed over and over to both the best and the worst in the field, he had little trouble seeing through Collins. If something didn't explain Lenore's depression, this quack wouldn't hesitate to plant a memory and bring it forth as repressed.

What would Collins do if she knew the whole truth? He had to keep Lenore from talking about what was going on between her, himself, and Alf. She'd end up in some loony bin with this woman wringing her hands in wild exhilaration.

"Oh, please help me."

Strength waning, Lenore's spirit reached out to him.

Somehow he had to answer her pleas. With Alf busily congratulating himself on this latest success, chortling like an imbecile, Eric felt free to dare a brief communication with her.

"You've cried enough, grieved much too long. It's time you stood up and fought back. Leave this place, this woman. She can only do you harm. Trust me, I'll be with you."

"So will he. Dear God, so will he. How will I ever escape?"

The misery in her cry broke his heart, and he contemplated committing one more murder. Get this quack out of the way, then kill himself. Rid the world of this demon who, down through the ages, had caused so much heartache and sorrow. It wasn't as if he hadn't tried to off himself and take Alf with him. But the brutal creature had always sensed his plans and stopped him. What a weakling he'd been.

Now he grew stronger because of her. Yet it was so tempting to allow Alf to vacate his body and take up residence in hers. What a relief that would be. To be left alone, to have the voice silenced, the torture ended.

But what about Lenore? He had to help her find a way to kill the demon, and the answer must lie in the scripture, the Song of Deborah. All his abused life he had gone to the Bible for solace, and that had kept him sane, made of him the man Annie could love. God help her poor soul.

Lenore rose abruptly, interrupting Eric's wanderings and startling Doctor Collins, who trotted along beside her when she left the office.

"Don't be foolish, Lenore. Stay here, talk some more, help me root out the cause of your problems. We'll get to them, believe me, we will."

But Lenore jerked from the woman's touch, fled down the narrow hall to the elevator.

Eric sensed the courage her leaving took and did his best to bolster her strength as she rode downstairs and walked the half-block to her car, barely holding herself together. Again, he wished for arms to support her, a shoulder to offer, but that wasn't going to happen. And neither could he comfort her further, for Alf awoke and goaded her every step of the way.

"That red-headed floozy doesn't have any idea what she's doing. Someone ought to do her a favor and drown her, throw her out that window into the river. You and I will accomplish that soon. Fat bitch would probably float all the way to the Gulf. Listen to me, Lenore. Your father was an adulterer, an incestuous bastard. Your mother had to know that you were having sex with him, and when she could take it no longer, killed herself over it. Only cowardice kept her from killing him, as well."

"That's not true." Lenore ground out the denial.

Eric sensed the burning fury. She was near the point where she would either lash out or submit. But he couldn't tell her that, could only listen with a numb acceptance when the demon responded.

"*Very good, you're learning. Maybe no one will notice you're crazy as a bed-bug if you don't go around ranting and raving at invisible demons, huh. Then we can get on with our plan. It's time you took care of Herb and Delilah. What an apt name for your pseudo-friend. Once she has shorn Herb of his strength, she'll move on to some other fool. Let's go back home and plot their demise. I continue to favor poison as your best bet, since you know so much about what solution nature provides. I do so like the idea. And Richard, we haven't concentrated on that piece of shit yet. I think it's time I met him, worked out a strategy for rid-ding the world of such filth.*"

Lenore climbed in the car, sat for a moment with head lowered, hands fisted around the wheel. Darkness enveloped her, and she fought her way up and out of it.

Taking a deep breath, she said aloud, "*If you don't allow me to go to the hospital and talk with Eric, I'm going to take poison myself and be done with it.*"

Eric congratulated her in silence.

"Why in the name of the Evil One would you want to do that? What do you expect to learn? We're just a beat up body, too weak to do any-thing but pass through the days. A puking, shitting, sweating, stinking body that's all used up. And Eric. Even when I allow him to surface, well, shall I say that he's only a shadow of his former self. You'd never believe what these quacks do to us in the name of medicine. You won't like your visit one bit, Lenore. I'm warning you."

"*I don't care. That's the deal. Take it or leave it.*" She stared out the window.

Alf grumbled but acquiesced and disappeared. Probably dreaming up a way to torture her into submission.

On the fifty-minute drive back to Summit Falls, Eric did his best to ease her panic with conversation. Since Alf detested car rides, espe-cially over soaring highway bridges that spanned valleys and streams hundreds of feet below, he remained spaced out, leaving Eric free to communicate with her.

"I remember once when Annie and I took a vacation in the Rockies. We'd lived here all our lives, both a little lost and a lot lonely. And to be happy at last, to view those jagged peaks crested in snow and breathe the high mountain air and wade in the icy streams for the first time. What an adventure. We were in heaven. We slept out under the stars, nearly froze some nights. It was July, and one morning we woke up with a dusting of snow on our sleeping bags and in our hair. We shivered and laughed and clung to each other until the sun came up. I'll never forget making love to her beside a creek ten thousand feet high, of rolling around in the grass, the smell of the crushed flowers, just the two of us. Her trusting me after all she knew about me. God, how I miss her. I'm sorry, I shouldn't have—"

"What happened to her?" Tears gleamed in her azure eyes.

A long, empty silence, loaded with brittle anger. "He killed her."

"Oh, God, I'm so sorry. I knew that, I mean I read about you and your wife. I'm sorry. How did he… I mean, was it…?"

"Me who actually did it? Yes, my hands, my strength, but he's responsible. I have to believe that."

"It's true. Of course it is. I can see that now. I wouldn't blame you a bit if you… I mean, you have tried to kill yourself. I don't know how you can stand it. Do you think he can make me do the same, with Herb, I mean?"

"Maybe not if we join together to stop him."

"Why couldn't you—uh, stop him?"

"It wasn't the same. Josie Lange, she'd become nothing but a blithering idiot by the time he finished with her. Twenty-two people she tortured and killed. Cut them up. Can you imagine what that would do to someone who had devoted her life to healing the sick, comforting the dying? In her state she couldn't warn me what was going on, tell me his plans.

All she could do was pray for his absence and ultimate death. As for me, I was convinced I'd gone stark raving mad."

"*Like me.*" She signaled to turn off the Interstate at the Summit Falls exit, not surprised to see her hands trembling.

"No more talking now, he'll hear. Be strong, be very strong, and listen to your dreams."

"*My dreams? I don't…. Oh, God, suppose he heard us.*"

"No, no, he didn't. Hush now."

After their first prolonged conversation, breaking contact with her filled him with a sense of loss, but he felt better than he had in a long time. Odd how he'd been able to talk to her about Annie, and he had felt closer to his dead wife for the telling. His feelings for Lenore deepened. Talking to her gentled his soul when he'd thought he no longer had one. He should have tried to explain about the dream, the song of Deborah, but desperately feared Alf had some way to overhear without him knowing. Its meaning had to be kept a secret at all costs.

A prickling in the recesses of his sensory patterns warned him of Alf's attention, and he shifted his thoughts to a distant point in the sky, floated there like a mindless cloud.

—

ON APPROACHING THE cabin, Lenore spotted Herb's pickup parked under the shade of a hickory tree. Bright sunlight blinded her, and for a minute she couldn't tell if he waited in the cab, but it was empty. Probably out on the deck, feet propped up, a beer in one hand, waiting to accost her. If he kept up this behavior, her anger might well spill over once again.

Suppose she hadn't missed with the pitchfork the other day. Dear God. Reacting in fury was one thing, but could she actually be made to commit cold-blooded murder? Plenty of people believed that anyone could kill, given the right circumstances. But how many went around possessed by a demon? God, suppose this was all in her mind? Suppose she was as crazy as her poor mother, and it was only a matter of time before she too broke. In that case, she could only pray that the only one she destroyed would be herself.

"You'll not kill yourself, Sweet Lenore. I absolutely forbid it."

"Shut up, you prickly bastard."

A claw tore at her innards, and she gritted her teeth against crying out.

Herb wasn't in the truck. He might be out in the barn. He still kept his horse here with hers, and he could be riding or grooming him.

"No, he's here, waiting inside. He's furious."

She continued to ignore Alf's comments as if he didn't exist. Refused to react in kind. Instead she steeled herself for an encounter with Herb, pushed open the door and stepped inside.

Perched on the edge of the couch, he leaped to his feet, features a study in rage. "Where have you been? The cops are looking for you, not to mention how worried I've been. Del is beside herself, nearly hysterical, and Richard is acting like some kind of maniac. What is wrong with you? I've never seen you be so irresponsible."

"I'm glad to see you, too. Why are they looking for me? I went to see my doctor. Isn't that what you wanted, Herb?"

"Don't be dense. Del said you were supposed to be on your way to Fayetteville to take a look at those two boys who broke into the shop. Then when you didn't show up, she freaked. Said if you don't cooperate with the police in this investigation, the insurance company may balk at paying off. She could be right, Lee. What's gotten into you?"

Lenore sagged onto the couch, dropped her handbag on the floor. Why had she ever started this deception in the first place? She'd had enough to handle without it. Hands over her face, she took a deep breath.

"I'm waiting," Herb said, hovering over her, his presence one more oppression to add to the weight of the others.

"Leave me alone, all of you, just leave me alone. I'll go to town and look at the freaking brats. Just go away." She bounced off the couch, shoved past him and into her bedroom. Slammed the door so hard the windows rattled.

An instant later, the front door slammed just as hard, then in a moment his truck door banged shut. She waited until the sound of the engine faded into the early afternoon, leaving behind a silence made peculiar by all the previous clamor.

It was as if she had suddenly gone deaf and could hear nothing but the sound of her own torment. Even the demon kept his thoughts to himself, giving her room to consider if she wanted to kill Herb. What a bastard he was. Killing was too good for him. Maybe she could hang him up out in the barn and stick him full of holes first. What a delicious idea.

Satisfied laughter erupted from her mouth. Hardly her own laughter. It wouldn't be long before she and the demon were joined. His voice and hers at last one. Head tilted, she caught sight of her reflection, the mad gleam in her eye, the menacing curl of her lips. Who was that woman? She covered her face with both hands.

For a long while she sat in the window seat, gazing out at the trees fringed in pale green leaves. Her favorite time of the year. The best time to walk and think, to gather growing plants that were common weeds to most, but not to her. To stand barefoot rooted to Mother Earth. To listen to her song.

"Commune with that nature bitch some other time. Go now, do what you have to do. Let's end this. I can make you forget your fears, you know that. I can touch you thus, and thus. I can do this for you, heighten your senses, prolong your passion until you scream out with pleasure and pain."

Lips on hers, tongue exploring, eager hands over her breasts. The bud within her swelling, throbbing to life. Aching with desire for this evil being. And he wouldn't stop. He would never stop. And, God help her, she didn't want him to.

Moaning with a primal passion, she rose, tore away her clothes, swayed naked in the warm sunlight streaming through the windows. He took her standing, entered her with a voracity she quickly matched, and they reached a furious, numbing climax together. She fell to the floor, crying out like an animal, sweating and panting, and his hateful, condemning words lashed at her. Every word true.

"You are stronger than your mother. She should have killed your father. Instead she killed his victims, herself and you. You must do what she couldn't so you can live again. Herb is just like your father, he must never sire your child. Now do what you must, and what we have will continue, forever. I can make you feel ecstasies you have never imagined. You know that, Sweet Lenore. You know it well."

Tearing at her hair, clawing great bloody furrows across her chest, she stormed into the bathroom, cleaned herself up, hissing through her teeth when the water contacted the deep scratches. Quickly she dressed in jeans, shirt, and walking shoes. On the deck she gathered the bucket that contained a digger, gloves, plastic bags, and clippers, then moved across the yard and into the woods, thick with the cool, damp odor of renewing life.

Nightshade. Known variously as Devil's Berries, Death Cherries, Beautiful Death, Devil's Herb. Medicinal parts, the leaves and seed. Too early for seed, the leaves and roots would do. The best for poison a bushy smooth, fetid, annual plant two or three feet in height. Taller growing in rich soil of the forest. Big fat, whitish, fibrous roots, a large, dry, prickly fruit, a capsule with four valves and filled with black reniform seeds. *Atropa belladonna* of the potato family.

Taken in small doses, it acted much like opium, was used by some as a substitute. Very dangerous, though. Never used by responsible herbalists as medicine. Large doses presented intense agony and death in maniacal delirium. An energetic, utterly lethal poison.

"Sounds good to me. Perfect."

She stomped on, disregarding his voice, taking deep breaths that entered and left her mouth as groans. If he wasn't careful, she'd feed it to him.

"It is you who must be careful, sweet Lenore. I would never tolerate such a move. You must plan well, though, these first killings, or they'll catch us. Cover your tracks so they can't prove anything. It's much easier to commit murders and get away with them nowadays, what with all our civil rights. Makes things much easier for me and my kind, this strange custom of giving rights to monsters. Let's get them all three at once. Richard, Delilah, and Herb. They'll writhe about together in agony, screaming and frothing at the mouth, doubled up with pain. All humanity forgotten in their suffering.

"Take them somewhere where there's no chance of anyone coming along. I know, a picnic. Put it in the potato salad. It will look like food poisoning. Give them plenty of time to think about what they've done to deserve such a death. And you can't imagine how it'll make us feel. How glorious is the orgasm of death."

How hateful that he used the plural pronoun rather than the singular, as if he and she were already made one. Was that how easy it would be for him? The thought sent darkness swelling through her.

Sucking in deep breaths, she tromped on through the woods, taking long strides and swinging her arms.

"Where are we going?"

"We can find the plant growing alongside most roads. The leaves are best gathered while the flower's in bloom, and they'll have to be dried in the shade. Then it will be easily mixed with water. Potato salad will never do. Alcohol would be best. A good, blood red claret served up along with bleeding steaks."

"Ah, a backyard cookout. A barbecue." More laughter trailed behind her as she trod, muttering aloud to Alf.

"How amazing that God can create such things, allow them to flour-ish so innocently, the huge white flowers unfolding as daylight wanes."

Up ahead, the animal trail forked and she moved to the left with no hesitation. The right path went to a spring where the deer and bear and foxes drank. The one she followed curved toward a country road.

A wispy warning walked on cat feet through her, leaving behind goose bumps. Nudged at her senses buried as if in the muck of a swamp. Told her to beware what was happening. Fight it. Her mother's voice called out to her, begging her to stop, turn around. Swaying trees in first bud, the sweet scent of may apple and wild azalea, the feath-ery embrace of a breeze, a whispered reassurance, flashed through the gloom of her mind. What was happening? She stopped as if she'd run full tilt into a wall.

"Why are you stopping? Have you found it?"

She stared at the bucket, turned on the path, and looked around. Dear God, what was she doing?

"Nightshade."

"No." The scream sent birds exploding from the trees.

"Yes." The roar silenced all living creatures, as if they had been strick-en as mute as the demon had once struck her.

A gentle touch, a hushed urgency she scarcely comprehended.

"Do it," Eric said. *"Do it for now."*

"I can't."

"He'll force you."

"But you don't understand—"

"Oh, I do. More than you yourself. Pretend until we can—"

"I don't need your help, you puny piece of shit. Lenore will do as I say, and there'll be no pretending. In the end I'll win. I always do. You should know that by now. And then what difference will your reluctance have made in the entire scheme of things? Evil will prevail. You can't stop me."

His rage battered her physically and emotionally, and she collapsed to the ground, dropped the bucket and spilled its contents.

"I'm through messing around with you, bitch."

Agony like the cracking of every bone tore through her until she screamed, hugged herself, rolled around on the ground. For no reason it let up, leaving her breathless, unable to move or see or feel.

A long silence, then, an icily controlled voice. *"There, see what you made me do. Sometimes, sweet Lenore, you do try me so. Now find the damned plant."*

Tears in her eyes, she rose, gathered her things, stuffed them in the bucket, and stumbled along the path, muttering under her breath until she spotted one singular nightshade, adorned with a long tubular white bud. Surprised that even one had grown enough to bloom this early in the year, her fracturing mind wondered if perhaps he had made it so. He seemed to have all kinds of powers. All except the ability to move objects. He couldn't tear her clothes off, but could force her to do so. He couldn't pick the leaves and do what had to be done, but could convince her to commit the act. The brutal act of murdering Herb, Delilah, and Richard. Who, then would come after that? The possibilities locked her throat until it appeared she might faint before she sucked air. Of course, he wouldn't allow it.

That poor nurse, the one he had possessed before taking over Eric's body, had been forced to torture and kill twenty-two souls. Dear God, deliver her from such a dreadful fate.

What was she thinking? Killing just one would be terrible enough by itself. Yet, what would really be so bad about killing Herb? She would be free of him, his nagging, his boring conversations, his need to control her.

"How very, very wise of you. Your thoughts are best kept in the proper vein, sweet Lenore. I know them all, each and every one, you know. It's only a matter of time before I become one with you. Only a matter of time. Ah, the devil take me, I've waited so long to have a woman. I see the years stretching out ahead of us and so much enjoyment."

She could not bear this. Had to do something. A glimmer of hope, remembering that he didn't always know her thoughts. He didn't. In an attempt to cover the excitement of the realization, she concentrated on a long-ago day when she had been upset about something, she couldn't recall what, and her mother had taken her in her arms and sung to her. The words and music came back, and she began to sing under her breath, blocking out this latest threat.

"Tell me why the stars do shine, tell me why the ivy twines. Tell me why the sky's so blue, and I will tell you just why I love you."

The almost forgotten song from her childhood masked her silent vow to kill herself before allowing the demon to prevail, for he didn't react. Continuing to sing, she slipped on the gloves and clipped several choice leaves from the deadly nightshade. She would practice, for there would come a time when she would have to communicate without Alf being aware.

26

AFTER ALF ALLOWED their minds to return to the prison cell and merge with the body that lay limp, battered by its latest round of shock treatments, an exhausted Eric slept into the night. Alf forced their spirits to remain out of the worn shell for longer periods each day. Both he and Lenore had little time left before Alf took over her mind and spirit. She was already reacting with less acuity to Alf's suggestions of murder. Soon it would be too late to avoid the inevitable, and she would kill. She wouldn't be able to help herself.

Once Eric had believed in God, but now he believed only in the Devil. Perhaps the Devil had cast God out of Heaven, as he had once been cast out. For Eric could not communicate with the God who had forsaken him. He had to focus on this particular event and not let his mind wander to the why of it. Question too much, and he might go insane himself. That was a laugh. As far as society was concerned he was a madman, off his rocker, crazy as a bedbug. Yet the past few weeks had shown him that a sane Eric Adair still existed, if not quite the man he once was. Locked up in this place with his horrible memories was enough to drive anyone round the bend. He had to make plans for Lenore's visit, think of ways to communicate with her should Alf decide to thwart such an action. And he had to do it while the demon slept. Time grew short.

Chapter 27

LENORE STRUNG THE nightshade leaves in the dark of her drying shed. The musty, cloying aromas of the herbs already hung there choked her. She had once enjoyed the pleasant odors, but now they nauseated her, and she couldn't wait to escape, fasten the padlock, and hurry to the house.

Neither the demon nor Eric was around, and if it weren't for the memory of their existence within her, she would have felt gloriously free. The dread of their return prevented that, though, and so she didn't enjoy the warmth of the April day, the beauty of thunderheads growing to the southwest, or the scent of rain in the wind. Would she ever do so again? If she could manage it, she would feed the deadly nightshade poison to the body that contained both their souls and set poor Eric free, then take it herself. Even if she could do such a thing, the demon would probably simply leave the dead body and find another. She couldn't be responsible for that. Surely there must be a way to kill this monster, this creature from the bowels of hell.

Odd why Alf hadn't moved into her body already, rather than carrying out this loathsome game. Perhaps he couldn't do it that way. Perhaps he had to make her do something horrible first, like kill Herb, Delilah, and Richard before he could leave Eric's body and move into hers. Was that possible?

Damn, she wished there was such a thing as a demon expert, a professional who worked in that field. Demonology. Hadn't she heard of such a thing? Maybe there were experts. She had to be very careful thinking of such a thing, for she had no way of knowing when her possessor would return. He seemed able to do so in the blink of an eye when all had been quiet only seconds before. Still, she had learned to know when he was with her. The sensation of his presence was not unlike having goose bumps in her heart. A discovery she might be able to put to good use. The idea was to be more alert and remember to sing.

Sneaking in the back door like a thief, she paused to embrace the comforting ambiance of her home. It appeared as if she had decided to fight rather than give in. Even if she didn't win, wouldn't that be better than submitting? Squaring her shoulders, humming the old song, she strode into her room, dragged a bag down off the closet shelf, and began to pack for her trip to Memphis. She would leave in the morning. There was no hurry getting down there, for her appointment wasn't for two days, but she needed to be away from here. The way Herb had talked, the cops might show up on her doorstep and drag her in on one pretense or the other. She'd lied to Herb, and maybe that would buy her some time while the demon waited for her to show up. Surely the law couldn't actually arrest her and throw her in jail for refusing to identify suspects. Could they?

As she rolled a pair of jeans to fit in the overnight bag, the phone rang. Her heart slammed into her throat, and she jerked and let out a startled cry. The reaction made her feel somewhat foolish, and she let the instrument ring again before picking it up, speaking a croaked greeting.

"Lenore Maine, please."

"That's me. I mean this is me—uh, she."

"This is Deputy Pederson, ma'am. The sheriff asked that I call you and request you come down, at your convenience, of course, and take a look at some suspects we've picked up for the vandalism out at y'all's craft shop Monday, last. When could you stop by, ma'am?"

"I'm not sure. I didn't see anyone, you know." She swallowed, trying to still the thundering of her heart. They'd put her on a lie detector, see how quickly all this web of lies unraveled.

"Shall I tell the sheriff that you aren't willing to take a look, ma'am? You see, I kinda hate to do that. No telling what he's apt to think, you see what I'm gettin' at?"

"No, I'm afraid I don't." Damn, if her voice didn't stop quivering, he'd know she made up the whole thing. "Look, I understand the boys confessed, so what's the problem?" A tiny voice in the back of her mind inquired quite gruffly if she was willing to let these two kids go to jail for something they so obviously didn't do, but she shushed it. Little urchins, probably had a garage or barn filled with stuff they'd stolen. Do them good to cool their heels in juvie for a few months.

"Well, you see, ma'am, confessions by themselves, especially now that these boys have a lawyer to keep them from pleading out, don't make too good of a case. I'm sure you'd like to see them punished for what they done. I was the one answered your call, the tall blond? We spoke, and you seem like the kind of lady who wants to see justice done."

Who was this guy? Did the sheriff employ him just to shame people who wouldn't cooperate? He was certainly doing a good enough job.

"Tell you what, deputy. Soon as I get packed, I'll just run in and take a look, satisfy all of you. When I can't identify them, then what's next?"

Silence on the line told her she'd definitely asked the wrong question. He cleared his throat and spoke softly. "They've recanted their confession. We don't have any other proof. We'll have to let them go so they can do it again to someone else."

And then everybody could blame her if and when they did. She gulped again. "I see. All right. I can be there in about an hour. Where do I go?"

After he gave her directions, she hung up and slumped to the bed beside the half-packed bag. Ahead of the approaching storm, wind whipped the trees, billowed the window curtains. What a mess she had gotten herself into. Well, she'd just stick to her story, refuse to identify the boys, and that should be the end of it. Surely.

Dark clouds blotted out the sun and thunder rumbled when she ran to the Jeep, tossed in her bag, and jumped in. She would go straight to Memphis from the sheriff's office. Great drops splattered the dusty windshield before she made it out of the lane.

Alf joined her with a shuddering of her heart, making it more difficult to see through the downpour that let go just as she turned onto the highway. She sensed his presence moments before he spoke, soon enough to shut down her rampant plans of saving herself.

"Let's fix those little fuckers."

"What, you want me to poison them, too? And maybe I could include a few of the sheriff's deputies as well."

"Sarcasm doesn't become you."

"You're alone. Where's Eric?" The moment the words were out of her mouth, she regretted them. Had let him know more about her perceptions than she meant to.

He missed barely a beat, though. *"He needed drug therapy, so I arranged it. I'm afraid he won't be in very good shape when you come to call. He'll be out of it, if you get my meaning."*

Damn him.

"You're much too late for that, my dear. I've been damned for a good many centuries now. Besides, in only a few days I won't need his paltry body any longer,

nor will I have to put up with his idiosyncrasies. All those stupid, boring exercises he does. Like that'll do him any good. Soon, very soon, it won't matter how he's preserved himself physically. When I exit, there'll only be a shell. I'm taking what's left of his consciousness with me. He understands the good side of humankind in a way I never will, and I may need that knowledge in dealing with you."

Clenching the wheel, she took a deep breath and tried to pay attention to the road. The rain had let up a bit, but the pavement of the old highway held puddles of water that tugged dangerously at the speeding tires. She should have taken the Interstate, but it was out of the way, and the old highway, despite its dangerous curves, would take her straight to the sheriff's office. Sympathy for Eric Adair tugged at her nature. He had been doomed all along, and Alf had only allowed him to hope as some kind of vicious entertainment for himself.

She thought about that for a while, then said aloud. "I hope you'll allow him to meet with me. I'd like to tell him goodbye. Surely you understand. He and I have... well, we were—uh, intimate."

"Ah, my dear child. You humans have such twisted values. You had sex. So what? He might as well have raped you, for there was nothing you could do to stop him. We overpowered you, and I allowed him some enjoyment, but if you think for one moment you were intimate, as you so coyly put it, you are terribly mistaken. Eric is too insane to be intimate with anyone. He is me, you see, as I am him."

"If that's true, you should be willing to prove it to me. Rub my face in it, if you will. Let me talk to Eric when I come to the prison, see for myself. Because, you son of a bitch, I don't believe you."

"Feisty today, aren't we?"

"Well, you know how we women are. Or do you? Eric certainly does."

"And I, as well. You'll soon see. I believe I might grant your request, just for the purpose, as you put it, of rubbing your face in it. Let you see what a madman you allowed to make love to you. Enjoyed it, didn't you? Tell your fancy head doctor about that, and see how quickly she slaps you in drug therapy."

"Well, I don't think you'd like that too well. How could I do all the ugly things you thrive on if I were put away? Isn't that your current problem with Eric? He can't get out and kill any longer, and you're bored, aren't you?"

A shattering jolt blinded her for an instant. The car headed across the road and toward the ditch, a blaring horn and squealing tires the only sound she heard while struggling desperately to control the yawing vehicle.

Chapter 28

IN AN ATTEMPT to stop the skid, Lenore overcorrected, and the Jeep shot into the opposite lane. Tires shrieking, an oncoming van took the shoulder and came to a rocking halt. She jerked the wheel back. The breathtaking sensation of the left wheels leaving the pavement made her stomach lurch and her vision blacken. Perhaps she had closed her eyes or maybe just went blind with terror.

A bellow filled her ears. *"What are you trying to do, kill us?"*

The Jeep nose-dived into the ditch, slewed sideways. Its front bumper plowed mud and grass and gravel then came to a grinding halt facing in the direction in which she'd been headed.

Both hands clenching the wheel, she laid her forehead there for a minute or two to catch her breath. Her head ached, ears thudding like her heart might burst.

Someone rapped on the window. She glanced up to see a rain drenched face, contorted with anger, mouth working. The man shouted, but she couldn't understand what he was saying. For an instant all she could think to do was stare at the poor fellow and try to read his lips. Rain plastered thin gray hair in a fringe around his forehead, poured off the end of his rather large nose, dripped steadily from his rounded chin, soaked the shoulders of his blue denim jacket.

He made a circular motion with one hand, and she realized he wanted her to roll down the window.

She nodded, punched the button, and the thing hummed open. Cold rain hit her face.

"You crazy or what? You almost killed us both. You hurt?"

"I—uh, no, I don't think so."

He glared at her for an instant, then said, "Guess I'm not either. Got a phone in this thing?"

"Phone?"

"To call a wrecker, get you out of the ditch."

She nodded again, felt scared and stupid. Suppose she had hit this man head-on? They'd both be dead.

"Hey, lady. You drunk or something? Think I'll just go call us a cop along with that wrecker."

"No. No, I'm not drunk. I'm sorry. But I didn't hit you, so why call a cop? In fact, I'm on my way to the sheriff's office right now. I'll be glad to report what happened, if you're worried about that."

His eyes widened. "You a cop?"

She didn't answer, let him think what he might.

"Well, anyway, you need a wrecker to get this thing out."

"No, look, I think I can drive it out. Stand back, and let me try. It's a four-wheel drive."

"Yeah, well, maybe so." He looked doubtful, but clambered up onto the shoulder of the road, glanced both directions, and ran across the wet pavement to his van, loafers splatting in pools of standing water. He was going to use the phone if she didn't get out of the ditch, and she didn't need to have to explain her latest foolishness. Herb would fuss, Delilah would tut and coo and hug and kiss her some more, pity vivid on her lovely face. The bitch.

She started the engine, put it in reverse and gently nudged the accelerator. The right-hand wheels slipped in the muddy ditch, but those on the shoulder bit and held. When she got it moving, she punched the foot feed, cut the steering wheel, and the faithful Jeep bounced backward onto the pavement, tires slinging mud and clumps of thick grass. With hands shaking so she could barely control them, she shifted to drive and roared off. Sheets of water poured in the open window, drenching her, but she paid no attention. In the rear view mirror, the van's tail lights flashed. To her relief it moved off into the driving rain.

Wild speculations hammered at her brain, told her if she didn't do something soon, her life would be over. And she wanted to live, free of possession, free to deal with all the guilt. She would not let this demon, or whatever it was, win without a fight he would never forget.

Deputy Pederson met Lenore when she ducked inside the heavy glass door at the police station, dripping all over the floor.

"Forget your umbrella?" His tone was less than friendly. Without waiting for a reply to the rhetorical question, he went on. "Sorry to get you out in this. It won't take but a few minutes. Just want you to look at these two kids, have them say a few words, then you're free to go."

"Yes, fine." She was through trying to explain her lie any further. She'd just look at the kids, say she couldn't tell if it was them or not. Or maybe say a flat no. Their voices were too high or something equally inane, followed by a quick thank you and goodbye.

"That's what you think. Here's the deal. You identify these little fuckers, figure out a way to convince them, or you don't even get through the front door of that place to see Eric. I'll kill him before you make it. And what I do to you won't be exactly enjoyable … well, not for you, anyway."

She stopped short, and Pederson, who held open an inner door with heavy wire over its half-glass, gave her a scowl. "Nothin' in here gonna hurt you, ma'am. Those boys are under guard."

"It's not that, I—" Could he do that? Kill Eric?

"How can you even ask?"

Damn you to hell. What's the point of hurting these boys? I think you're just playing with me.

"Pay attention, this is a test. But believe me we're not playing, and the consequences will be Eric's death. Now move before the good deputy ends up arresting you."

She stalked through the door and down the hallway. She expected a lineup like in the movies or on television, but the two boys were in a room beyond a large window, slumped in chairs on opposite sides of the table. A deputy stood against the far wall, arms crossed over his chest, a bored look on his coarse features. Two more deputies stood on the outside of the glass. One was a woman with dark hair caught in a tight knot on the back of her head.

She spoke, but not to Lenore. "Hal, tell them to stand up and face us."

The deputy inside uncrossed his arms, leaned down, and said something to the boy whose back was to her.

"The hell I will. You just go ahead and make me," the kid hollered.

Without another word, the big deputy picked the frail kid up by the shoulders and turned him around. He kicked out and shouted, but it did him no good. The other one laughed. The kind of laugh that transmitted a nervous relief to have been left out for the moment.

Lenore sighed, squeezed her eyes shut. "I don't know. That one sounds like one of them. I mean, have him yell some more. That's what they did, yelled and screeched while they were breaking things. I think—yes, it sounds like the same boys." God forgive her. "What'll happen to them?"

The woman glanced a silent question past her at Pederson. "Just sounds like. Can you be more precise?"

Lenore sighed. "It's them. I'd know that sneaky little laugh anywhere. Now, are you satisfied. May I go?"

"Have you ever seen these kids before? Someplace else, maybe watching the shop or your house?"

"Why would they—I mean, I don't understand."

"Ma'am, just think about it."

"Maybe hanging around town? I suppose I could have, the little one looks familiar."

The female deputy lifted her shoulders in disgust, then said, "Like maybe he cased the shop?"

The woman was leading Lenore to say what she wanted. Didn't these kids get lawyers or something? She couldn't lie about this, they'd find out that she didn't work regularly at the shop. "I can't say, you'd have to ask Delilah. I haven't worked there in weeks."

"Okay, Hal. That's enough." Turning to Lenore, she said, "We'll be in touch. Probably won't be a trial, not if we can get a plea."

"Please. What'll happen to them?"

"Who knows? Eventually they'll grow up to be big, bad criminals, and we can put them away for good. If we're lucky, that'll be before they kill someone."

"No, I mean now."

"Now? They'll probably go to juvie for a while. Neither one of 'em has folks that give a damn. Ah, hell. Nobody gives a damn." The female deputy shoved back an escaping strand of hair and met Lenore's gaze with sad brown eyes. "Sorry, it's been a long day. Thanks for coming by. I'm sorry we had to bother you."

"What would happen to them if they weren't the ones who tore up our shop? I mean, it could—" She broke off, gasped as a sharp pain shot through her chest.

The deputy cut a quick glance at her. "You okay? You've gone white as a sheet." To Pederson, she added, "Get her out of here before she passes out."

He took Lenore's arm, and the female deputy caught her gaze. "Don't worry, if it wasn't this it'd be something else tomorrow or the next day. Not your fault. I don't understand why they even bothered you. We had them on several other counts. Must've been somebody's idea of fun."

Lenore wanted to shout that at least part of it was her fault. If she hadn't made up that crazy story in the first place, these kids wouldn't be in here. Now they were going to be put away, and she couldn't do anything about it but walk out of there. Nothing at all. How easily Alf had controlled her actions. And if she didn't do something soon, it would only get worse.

"Not worse, better and better and better."

His gleeful tone set her teeth on edge. Though her mind searched for comfort from Eric, none was forthcoming. The demon hadn't lied, he'd done something bad to Eric. Soon this would be her fate, and she didn't think she could bear it.

"You can bear anything I see fit to hand out."

Sing. Keep singing. Cover your thoughts. She launched into a loud rendition of Clapton's "Tears In Heaven" and underneath it mulled over her options.

It was interesting to discover that while Alf might control her emotions and even cause her pain, he couldn't make her body physically do something if she refused. What it came down to was how long she could hold out under torture. Would he actually kill her? He'd threatened to kill Eric, but he'd also voiced his happiness at having a woman again. How much could she get away with before he lost it and killed her? How might he go about it? Her voice broke on a high note.

"Good God, stop that. Stop it this instant!"

She increased the volume, purposely hitting some of the notes off key to annoy him even more. It was working as long as she concentrated, cloaked the silent suppositions in music.

A vise tightened on her temples, the pain so excruciating she screamed and slammed on the brakes.

"Mess with me, bitch."

Shimmering stars danced through her vision, then cleared. The vibration hammered to a halt, left her breathless and tearful. He was an expert at striking her mute or blind. For a moment the Jeep remained stalled in the middle of the street while sweat poured over her face, stinging her eyes. A minor irritation compared to that he'd dealt her.

A car coming from the opposite direction slowed, a concerned face at the window shouted, "Hey, you okay?"

She gulped, bobbed her head up and down, for she couldn't make a coherent sound, then pulled forward to the stop sign at the highway.

On the way out of town, her mind wandered. Suppose Alf had already killed Eric and had at last taken over her body for good? All that other stuff had been his idea of a joke. When the demon made no comment one way or the other, the fear grew to tremendous proportions. She could hardly keep the car on the highway during the interminable twenty-minute drive home. She had pulled onto the lane to her house before she remembered she was supposed to be on her way to Memphis. Halting the Jeep in the middle of the road, she laid her head on the steering wheel and sobbed.

Chapter 29

ERIC OPENED ONE eye, squinted at the IV attached to his arm. Blinking once, twice, he cleared his vision so he could get a better look at his surroundings. Not his cell, but the room in which they kept him during treatments. He didn't remember acting up, but he must have, for here he was, drugs coursing through him until he felt like some sort of zombie. More dead than alive, but functioning just enough to give a damn.

He lay still, listened intently. God, it was quiet. Nothing, nobody. Anywhere. No shoes tapping through the halls, no low hum of conversation, no Alf. He wiggled, squirmed, couldn't move for the straps at his ankles, across his body, at each wrist. The demented bastard was with Lenore. Had he left him for good?

Joy flooded through him, a kind of serenity he hadn't felt since Annie's death.

Murder, you slob. You murdered her.

No, he *made me do it, and now he's gone.*

Gone to Lenore, and Eric was free. How good it felt to know the monster wouldn't be coming back. He'd recover from the drugs, and he could eat and sleep and think in peace.

He lay there, mind wandering beyond his drug induced slumber.

What about Lenore?

He rolled his head, stared at the green wall. Let the beast have her. No one had helped him. No one had cared, so why should he? Because she was lovely beyond words. Because he had touched her, felt her kindness, her innocence. Because he had promised he would help her.

The drugs took him away where he dreamed in wild, disconnected spurts. Where he saw Annie covered in blood. Where Lenore beseeched him to help her. Where he watched an ugly monster devour her beauty bite by bite.

And he awoke screaming.

God, shut up before they come and add more to your dose.

Muscles bulged as he struggled against the leather. Sweat bathed his body, soaked the loose pajamas, still he couldn't free himself. His breath came in wheezing gasps, the drugs continued to drip into his arm, clouding his mind. He rolled his head in an effort to reach the IV, tear it out with his teeth, but that wasn't possible either.

Darkness descended, and he nodded in and out of consciousness. When awake, he took deep breaths, tried to think. If it weren't for the drugs, the total freedom from Alf's evil influence would have been a most wondrous experience. Think. Think.

He wanted to pound his head, but couldn't. Had to think. Something there he needed to remember. A guarded secret hidden from his wicked possessor. What was it?

Oh, yes. Yes, that was it. He had traveled out of his body alone. Could he once again do the same? Go to her and help her? Or was he a prisoner of his own drugged helpless carcass for the rest of his life?

Well, that was what he wanted, wasn't it? Total freedom. Why should he care what happened to her? He writhed. Because he *did* care, dammit. And it was the first thing he'd cared about in a long, long time.

He cared about Lenore. If he could travel out of this body, it would be dangerous, for Alf could sense him if he chose the wrong moment for contact with her. No telling what he would do to both Lenore and himself if that happened.

Eric turned his head and stared at the wall, but the drugs kept dragging him down toward semi-consciousness. He batted his eyes, tried again. A terrible thought hit him at that moment. Suppose he was insane, and all he recalled—his possession by Alf, Lenore, the out-of-body travels, memories of killing Annie and all the others—suppose it was all a part of his dementia? Dear God, if that were true, would his knowing it be a worse situation or a better one? He actually laughed at the idea. But after a while, went back to staring at the wall, struggling to melt down the barrier, move from this place to Lenore's side. He had to do it. Had to. For true or not, he must attempt to save her, even if he died in the process.

Curious question, Eric. If he escaped this body, would the drugs dripping into it continue to affect his thought patterns? Interesting idea.

Where did that little voice come from? Not Alf.

After a while he began to doubt that he could escape, drugged as he was. It was difficult enough to do so without Alf, but he had managed it before. He pictured Lenore, the valley where she lived, the cabin tucked into the side of the hill, the sweet freedom of strolling through the woods, along the lane, stepping onto the porch, and knocking on her door. Like a normal human being going to call on the woman he was attracted to. He imagined the door swinging open, her standing there.

She wore pale yellow, the color of moonlight on a summer night. Her smile carved tiny dimples on either side of her expressive mouth, her blue eyes glittered. Not icy blue like his, but a rich deep cobalt that some-times shaded toward purple when she became thoughtful or passionate.

For an instant he stood before her, smelled her light wildflower fra-grance, felt the warmth of her soul, the touch of her beating heart. That instant ended, and he once more lay in the bed, groggy and nauseous.

But it had worked. For a brief point in time, it had worked. If he could get out from under the influence of the drugs, he could make it work again. He had to. He could not continue to live in this cell knowing he had allowed Alf to possess the beautiful Lenore.

Chapter 30

SOMEONE WAS AT the door. Lenore moved quickly, swung it open. Stood there holding her breath.

"Eric?" Lenore opened herself to him. The fresh air transmitted his essence, yet he did not speak nor communicate by touch. "Eric?"

Movement caressed her, then trailed away. He was gone, but dear God he was still alive. Alf had said he'd done something to him, what was it? Oh, yes. Some kind of therapy. Perhaps he'd been telling the truth, and Eric in his drugged state had tried to reach her and couldn't. If he had been there, he'd gone just as quickly. The sensation had been so fleeting, so vague, she might have been the victim of wishful thinking.

She had driven at breakneck speed on the way home, so recklessly that Alf had fled elsewhere to escape his bizarre fear of such things. Everyone had fears, but she was continually surprised that a demon had not been spared that all-too-human trait. Especially that he could fear something that couldn't hurt him.

Alf was nowhere to be felt, and she hurried to the phone, scrabbled

through the numbers scrawled here and there on her scratch pad. Finding
the one she'd jotted down for the Tennessee Hospital for the Criminally
Insane, she hurriedly dialed.

After the bored young voice identified herself, Lenore asked to speak
to Doctor Blaine. He had arranged for her upcoming visit to Eric and
perhaps would be the most likely to answer a few questions.

Several minutes went by before someone picked up. "Doctor Larue."

"I'm trying to reach Doctor Blaine."

"Sorry. He's gone home. Perhaps I could help you."

"I wondered, could you tell me the condition of a patient?"

"An inmate?"

"Well, whatever."

"Are you a relative?"

"Uh—yes, I'm his—I'm his sister. Eric Adair. I wondered if he's
doing okay."

"Who did you say you were?"

"His sister. My name's Constance."

"Funny, I didn't recall Adair having any relatives. Figured he'd
killed them all."

"Good God."

"Oh, sorry about that. Sick humor, I suppose. One might say we who
work here are as nuts as our charges."

"Are you sure you're a doctor and not one of the inmates?"

"Very good. Did you say Constance? Constance Adair?"

"No. I'm married. Couldn't you just check on his condition?"

"Don't have to. He had an episode last evening. He's alive, if that's all
you need to know. But he won't be battering down walls with his head for
a while yet. Chart here says he's scheduled to have a visitor in a couple
of days. That you?"

Quickly, she struggled to remember what she had told Doctor Blaine.

Of course he had her fictitious name, but did he write it down on the chart or someplace else?

"Uh, no. But I'm acquainted with her. She's coming to see him I believe for a true crime book she's working on."

"Odd. We don't usually allow visitors of that kind. Ah, well, suppose old Bruce wants to see his name show up in some gory novel. Some people'll do anything. You ever been up to see your brother?"

"I—no, I haven't."

"Can't say I blame you. Well, if that's all you needed."

"Well, only if Eric is indisposed, will he recover in time for Lee to speak to him to interview him?"

"Can't ever tell about that one. He'll be a pussycat for weeks at a time, then go berserk for no reason we can define. Hey, gotta go, someone's...."

She heard maniacal yelling and the phone slammed down.

Dear God, poor Eric. She felt as if she knew him as well as herself, having hosted him, so to speak, alongside her beating heart. And in other places as well, having felt true joy in their sexual union. He was the first man who had actually touched her soul. Literally as well as figuratively. And she didn't know the man. Except that he was a convicted killer.

She must be crazy even to think of going to see him. Probably ought to sign herself in to the psych ward in Little Rock and tell them to throw away the key. After her breakdown coming home, she'd decided to wait another day before going to Memphis. She simply wasn't in any condition to drive and went to bed early in the hopes Alf would leave her alone.

In the middle of the night she came awake as if summoned, sure someone had called her name. It wasn't the nightmare that had awakened her, though it often did. And it wasn't the demon. The room was quiet. Outside an owl hooted, was answered from some distance. Night critters and whippoorwills were silent, the early morning birds slept. The ultimate still of the night.

She peered at the lighted dial of the clock. Three a.m. The dreaded doomsday hour when every dreadful thing you could possibly imagine paid a call on your subconscious, presented you with anything to worry about so you couldn't go back to sleep. This always seemed to happen when she had something specific to do that required her to be alert. It wasn't a long drive to Memphis, but she didn't want to make it on only a few hours' sleep. Yet, the longer she lay there, the more wide awake she became. After battling with the light blanket and sheet until both had twisted around her from head to foot, she unwound herself and sat on the edge of the bed in the darkness.

"Lenore?" Small, almost indistinguishable inquiry.

"Eric?" Hard not to speak aloud.

"Thank God, I thought he might have—"

"No. I think he's gone. Isn't he with you?"

Silence for a moment, then, *"Not a sign."*

"Then where? Good God, could he be lost?" The thought gave her the giggles.

"Wouldn't that be great? We don't have long, though. I can't stay awake."

"You're hurt, I can hear it in your voice."

"I—it's okay. No time. Are you truly coming to see me?"

"Yes. Driving over tomorrow. See you the next day, if they'll still let me."

"They will. I made sure."

"But he said you bashed your head into the wall."

"He bashed my head, but let's not talk about that. I'm so anxious to see you."

"Can't you—?"

"No, not really. Only in my imagination. I know your smell, the way your skin and hair feels, the softness of your lips, the light of your spirit." The final few words faded.

"Eric?"

"Yes, what?" Stronger, but still not his normal self.

God, his *normal* self. What a stupid thing to think. "He threatened to kill you, he made me do things." She waited, but he didn't reply. "Could he do that? Kill you?"

"I think so. I'd welcome it."

"No, please don't say that. Don't."

"Lenore, listen to me. If he threatens to kill me unless you do something horrible, refuse. It would be a relief for me to go. Believe me."

"I've decided to fight him, Eric. But I need your help."

He was quiet for so long she thought he'd gone, then he whispered, *"Listen to the dream."*

"The damn dream. I've listened and listened. I can't make anything out of it."

"Look at the dream. I'm sorry, I can't. I'm...."

"No, don't go. Please don't go. Eric? Eric?"

The dark, silent room gave back no reply, but from the corner of her eye she saw a tiny flash, then another. Somehow a lightning bug had gotten in the room and was frantically signaling to its fellows. Sadly, of course, there was no one to answer the delicate flying insect, either.

Fat tears seeped from Lenore's eyes and ran down her cheeks. She put up with that for a moment, then brushed them away with the backs of her hands. She had better things to do than weep.

Chapter 31

TRAFFIC WASN'T HEAVY on I-240 skirting Memphis to the north. Lenore had left home in time to make the five-hour drive and arrive before the evening rush hour. Every muscle in her body ached, but not from the drive. She was tensed against the sudden appearance of that hideous beast who haunted her every moment. He could easily cause her to wreck the Jeep.

Following directions from the Internet, she swung south onto Highway 78 and drove to the American Way exit. Though her appointment with Eric Adair wasn't until the next day, she wanted to be sure she could find the institute before settling into a motel. There were plenty of them nearby to choose from.

Thank God Alf remained silent. What was he up to?

That worry had to be ignored. Meeting an insane serial killer who had crawled inside her and aroused her sleeping libido gave her enough to stew about.

Off to her right, she caught a glimpse of the sprawling institute where monsters were kept locked up. Too insane to be let loose among convicted killers and rapists. Dear Lord.

She signaled and turned right, drove slowly past the long building before retracing her route to the highway. The structure itself gave her the jitters. Tomorrow she would drive right up to it, get out of her car, and walk among all sorts of deviants. Well, maybe not among, but it would feel like it.

Had this been a foolish thing for her to do? Maybe she ought to turn around and go home, forget Eric Adair and her crazy plans. Even if she went to a nut house herself, she probably wouldn't be safe from Alf's attacks. She could either fight or die. Be damned if she'd give up. For that matter, she'd be damned either way.

She chose a Best Western, filled out a card for a short, bald clerk whose aura glowed vivid blues and purples above the counter, and went to her room, carrying a duffel and a backpack.

Once settled, she removed a library book on demonology from her pack and lay down to read. After a few sentences, she gasped in wonder and reread the story of the Leeds, New Jersey Devil. The story sounded more like something *The Comet* would print. The copyright date was 1998. The author had several degrees after his name. That had to make it true, didn't it?

The Jersey Devil, as he had come to be known, first appeared in 1735 to a housewife and mother of several children. Her description raised the hairs on Lenore's neck. The beast had the head of a horse, long serpentine cloven hooves, bat wings, and hind legs with cloven hooves. After warning her that if she had any more children, they would be of his loins, the creature's large wings unfurled and it flew around the room and disappeared up the chimney. Rape was not a popular term in 1735, but the young mother did claim that she was not a willing participant in the evil act.

Finger marking her place, Lenore closed her eyes a moment. Good God. A child? What if? No, stop that, no. That was *Rosemary's Baby* stuff. Pure fiction.

Uh-huh. Up until the past few weeks, she wouldn't have believed what was happening to her, either.

Back to the book. Someone had made a sketch of this demon that gave her the willies right down to her toes. At least she wasn't the only crazy person in the world. The article went on to state that the Jersey Devil was seen again on October 6, 1909 and sometime in 1995. It didn't go into great detail regarding those sightings.

Didn't sound much like her demon, anyway. Who was she kidding? He'd never revealed himself to her. She didn't know whether to be relieved or apprehensive. Tossing the book onto the bed, she cradled her head in the crook of one arm and closed her eyes. When she awoke and peered sleepily at the red numerals on the clock, she couldn't believe she had slept for three hours or that she felt more refreshed than she had in days.

Still no Alf.

Where the hell had her own personal demon got to? Perhaps he didn't like her being so close to his home.

"Well, mister, that's just too bad. You don't hesitate to invade my space any old time you please." The words, spoken aloud in the silent room, startled her.

For an instant she mistook the growling of her stomach as his reply, then realized she hadn't eaten all day. There must be a fast food joint nearby. Perhaps she'd walk, get the kinks out and take some fresh air. Motels with their policy of tightly sealed windows made her uncomfortable. Could be they thought it kept the boogers out. Boy, did they have another thing coming.

The airport must be nearby, for as she walked toward a distant Golden Arches sign, huge planes came and went overhead. Adding the traffic, the noise rose to a nearly unbearable level. The heat and stench that poured off the pavement upset her empty stomach and annoyed a lingering headache.

Why in the world had she wanted to walk? Probably better, though considering the traffic. No wonder she preferred living in the quiet countryside of the Ozarks.

She ordered a fried chicken salad and a large coke and sat at one of the small square tables near a window. Considering how tasteless their burgers were, the salad was quite palatable, the greens crisp, and the dressing tasty.

Light from the dying sun blazed in the window and fell across her lap. How had she come to be here? She, who hadn't strayed more than a few miles from home since her mother's death. Prior to that, she had enjoyed traveling, but a broken heart seldom likes to wander.

Jeez, that sounded like a country song. She smiled at a woman leading two children to a nearby table. The young mother smiled back, then turned to laugh at the antics of her golden-haired son.

The sight sent a painful ache to her heart. How could she have let her life become so lonely?

She touched her stomach. What if she had a child? Who would it look like? Dear God, she hoped it would resemble Herb and not have wings and cloven hooves. The smile died on her lips, and she pushed the remainder of her salad away.

Back at the motel, sweating and heart pounding, she swiped her key through the reader. She'd run all the way from McDonald's as if pursued by the Devil himself. Once inside, she leaned against the door, trembling. Ripping at the Velcro of her backpack lying on the bed, she took out the Bible and opened it to the marked place to reread the Book of Judges and the Song of Deborah.

Truly the world was filled with evil. Suppose this demon's killing sprees had gone on since the time of the Book of Judges. And suppose there were many others like him who wormed their way into unsuspecting people's psyches. It would explain so-called gentle, God-fearing people going on murderous rampages. But that was way too much for her to absorb. Dealing with one demon was quite enough. It wasn't in her to save the world by becoming a demon slayer.

Sitting on the edge of the bed, a trembling finger rested over the last few words of the passage. *"...and the land had rest forty years."*

She pawed through the papers she'd brought along for reference. Eric Adair had claimed possession a bit over ten years ago, when Josie Lange died. The infamous Mercy Nurse had run rampant with her killings in the late fifties and early sixties. Forty years before he committed his murders. Where had the demon been? Had Josie somehow managed to still him, like the passage in the Bible stated, by piercing his temple with a holy scrap of iron? And thus, the land had rest from his evil for forty years.

Was she being given the same chance? To somehow still this monster's rampage for another forty years? Pierce his temple with an ancient knife of some sort. In saving her own life, would she have to kill Eric Adair?

She would not come out of this without killing. Either she would obey the demon and kill Herb, or she would kill the demon and in doing so destroy Eric. Given that she could succeed in driving a chunk of iron through his temple. Some choice, any way she looked at it.

Chapter 32

A **HUGE INTERN** took Eric's arm in a steely grip, and he tried to see him through waves of color. In the center of the room, he swayed while hammers pounded at his head. The floor beneath his slippered feet rolled and lurched, and he grasped the intern's arm.

His vibrating brain floated in a mass of red-hot pain, as if not connected to his body. One arm flailing out for anything to grab, he connected with a warm, muscled shoulder. Someone on the other side of him, propping him up.

"Get him a wheelchair." The words vibrated like bongo drums.

Steadying hands on either side eased him into a seated position.

He concentrated hard. Where was he, and what was he doing there? All the faces were blurs, white patches against an ashen background.

What had they done to him? He had no name—this *place* had no name. A hospital, maybe, for surely he was very ill. In an effort to ask one of the men, his dry tongue filled his mouth like a wad of cotton, and his lips wouldn't open. The movement of the rolling chair made him dizzy.

Why didn't someone talk to him? They went about their chores like he was a stick of furniture they were moving from one place to another.

"Water," he said—or thought he did. A garbled babble issued from his mouth.

"Yeah, yeah." That was the guy who pushed him along the narrow, dark hallway, stopped, jangled some keys from his pocket, shoved the chair inside a dim cubicle, shut and locked the door.

He stared with longing toward a pitcher on a table across the room. Dim light pointed at it like a teasing finger. His hands refused to turn the wheels on the chair. They were numb and useless. His head fell forward, chin resting on his chest. Pain rocketed through his temples.

"Well, aren't we one pathetic son of a bitch?"

"Huh? Who?"

"Better get your act together, Lenore is on her way."

"Uh-huh. Who?"

"For the Devil's sake, straighten up."

The demon had returned. What had he said? *Lenore?* Lenore was coming. He strained and plopped one hand on top of the wheel of his chair, then with a long winded grunt, managed to set the other one in place. Now, push. Push.

Inch by inch, he worked his way to the water pitcher, every movement dragging a groan from deep inside his aching body. Slowly, slowly, the water-beaded container grew larger, promising relief. Sweat poured from his forehead, dripped off his chin. Eyes burning, he peered through slitted lids. Was it moving or was he? At last, he bumped into the table, but could not reach out. Arms that had done their best refused to move. Leaning forward, he touched his cracked lips to the rim of the plastic jug. Smell the water, see the water. For the life of him, he couldn't taste the water.

Oh, God. Help me drink.

With one final gut-wrenching effort, he forced the dry wad that was his tongue into the cool liquid. Lapped at it like a dog. Sucked at the surface. Anything to get the wet stuff in his mouth and down his throat. In the end, he turned over the pitcher. The precious water dripped from the table, and he threw himself onto his knees, opened his mouth, and caught the drizzle. Scraped it from the surface with the side of his hand. So cool, so good. Each swallow strengthened him for who? Who was coming?

Lenore. Lenore is coming.

A light glimmered far back in his brain. Warmth filled him.

"Lenore."

Chapter 33

MMM, THAT'S A *tasty bite."*

Lenore came awake, shoved her heels into the mattress, and scooted away from the pressure between her legs.

"Ah, you're awake. Even better. Again, mmm."

An orgasm spiked through her, her scream turning to a moan. The tongue inserted deep inside her coiled around her clitoris, squeezed, let go, squeezed again. Limp, sweating, panting, kicking, she tumbled off the edge of the bed, head first.

"Please, no. Please, I can't—why don't you—Leave. Me. Alone?" Each word gritted between clenched teeth. Her fingers ripping, tearing, clawing at her vagina. Yank him out of there. Had to somehow rip free. Pain shot from her jaw into her temples, a blinding pain so she could see nothing, hear nothing. She bit her tongue, warm blood trickled from the corner of her mouth.

Then he was gone, leaving her sobbing, sucking in air like a dying being.

Hissing through her teeth, she scrabbled on hands and knees into the bathroom, clambered over the edge of the tub and turned on the faucet. Fumbling the stopper shut, she lay there as the level rose, not caring if the water was hot or cold. Muttering like a madwoman, she peeled paper off a tiny bar of soap and using the washcloth draped over the cold, enameled rim, scrubbed herself raw inside.

When would this stop?

When would it *ever* stop?

The panting subsided one tiny breath at a time, her vision returned, though sparked through with shooting stars. Her hearing must have come back as well because a loud pounding vibrated her ear drums. Pounding and shouting.

Shaking, she turned off the water, climbed from the tub, and limped to the door, the pain inside hindering her movement.

"Yes, I'm here. I'm okay."

"Ma'am, you need to open the door." An official demand.

"It's fine, I had a nightmare, that's all."

Knuckles rapped again. "Ma'am, this is Officer Kennedy with the Memphis Police Department, and I'm not going away until you open the door and show me you're okay."

"Well, but I'm not dressed."

A space of silence. "I'll wait, ma'am."

Oh, God. What if they arrested her for disturbing the peace? She absolutely had to see Eric in the morning. Put an end to this madness. Much more, and she would kill herself.

"Like your dear sweet mother?"

A yelp squirted from between pinched lips.

"Ma'am, open the door now, or we'll open it. The manager is out here."

"Just a minute, let me put on something."

"Quickly. Now."

She pawed through her duffel, came up with a sleep shirt and slipped it over her drenched body. Hair dripping down her back, feet bare, she unlocked the door, leaving the chain on, and peered out.

"Open it completely, Ma'am."

"You can see I'm okay."

He sighed. "I'm going to kick in the door, ma'am. Stand back."

"No." She fumbled the chain loose, swinging the door wide.

Arms folded over her breasts, she took a step backward. "There, see? Everything's okay."

The tall, broad young man, who looked more like a fifteen-year-old Marine than a cop, flicked the light switch on and stepped past her. "I'll just take a look around, if you don't mind."

"Certainly. Be my guest." Again, she gritted her teeth to keep them from chattering.

Weary to her very bones, she collapsed on the edge of the bed. He returned in a moment and stood over her. "Would you mind looking up at me?"

She obeyed, and he flashed his light in each of her eyes. "Have you been drinking, ma'am?"

"Is it against the law? In my own room?"

"It is if you wake up the entire place screaming bloody murder."

One trembling finger folded the fabric across her knees. "I told you, I had a nightmare. I don't drink."

"Uh-huh." After a final glance around the room, he said, "Okay," and went to the door. "You have a good night, ma'am. And if I were you, I'd see what I could do about those nightmares."

"Yes, yes, that's exactly what I'm going to do. Thank you so much."

"You really shouldn't get so excited when we make love, sweet Lenore. One would think you were enjoying yourself way too much."

"Shut up, you piece of filth. Just shut up."

On the bed, she coiled into a fetal ball, but couldn't close her eyes.

Chapter 34

A FRAIL, BEAUTIFUL woman sat on the other side of the thick glass. Eric spotted her as soon as the intern opened the door and let him into the cubicle where they would be allowed to visit through heavy screening. But he couldn't really make out her features until he was led, shuffling, to a metal stool and helped to sit down. Still woozy from yesterday's drugs, he fought confusion to stare for the first time into the face of Lenore Maine.

"Hello, Eric."

Her voice was every bit as lovely as he'd imagined it would be.

"Yes." Why had he said such a stupid thing? "I mean, hello. You're, I mean, you look like I thought you might."

"I look like hell." She took a deep breath. Pain and confusion smeared her deep blue eyes so they looked cloudy. "You haven't ever seen me before, then?"

He shook his head, fought with his tongue. "The drug—it's hard to— to think, to talk." The words stammered out.

A nod and what he thought might be pity touched her delicate features. "Yes, I understand. But I need to know if you've ever seen me before. Come to my house." A flush colored her cheeks, and she looked down at her hands, knotted together on the scarred counter top.

A sob filled his throat, fueled by a vision of his Annie, blushing when they talked about intimate subjects. "We made love."

"What?" Her voice broke.

The guard straightened, stared at them. How had she managed to get them to let her in? He wanted to know so much, but they'd filled him with junk until he couldn't organize his thoughts. Damn Alf for bringing this down on him. Ruining his chance to talk to this beautiful woman. To decide, for once and for all, if he was going to try to save her or let her go.

He wasn't conscious that he'd spoken until she leaned forward, fixed him with that penetrating gaze, and asked, "It's true, isn't it? About Alf and the killing. And that he's going to do the same to me? All true?"

Misery filled him. "Yes."

"Listen to me," she hissed. "He almost killed me last night. Were you there, with him?"

"No. I was in drug therapy." He spat the term. "I'm so sorry. He won't kill you, though."

"No, only make me wish he had."

"Yes, that's it. You'll wish he had. If I could die this minute, I would." Against his will, his head dropped forward, and a thin stream of drool drizzled from the corner of his mouth to the table.

Disgusted, he wiped it away with the back of his hand. "I'm sorry."

She took a deep breath, and her breasts rose against the fabric of her plain white blouse. Breasts he had kissed, fondled, loved. Poor Lenore. Poor Eric.

"I'm so sorry," she whispered, then spoke up in a choppy, unnatural voice. "I'm here to interview you for a book I'm writing on serial killers.

"So, that's how—"

"And if I'm to be allowed to return we have to get to that." She signaled to the guard, and he brought a tape recorder, a tablet, and a yellow pencil to her. She smiled up at the man. "He's agreed to talk to me."

The burly man nodded, rubbed a hand over his shaved head. "Do not give him the pencil or the recorder," he said in a flat monotone and retreated once more to stand beside the exit door.

"No, I won't." Her reply trailed away, and she turned back to face Eric. "Is he listening?"

"He? The guard?"

"No, him. Alf."

Eric raised his head and felt around inside himself. "Not at the moment. He's—he's exhausted. If he did it to you last night, he has to sleep it off, if he's, you know...." He stared at her pale hands, the fingers curled around the pencil till he feared she'd break it.

Pain twisted her features, and she shifted on the metal seat. "Oh, he did it to me all right."

The poor woman. That *bastard.* "Either way, we'd better hurry."

Lenore chewed her lower lip and studied him. He scarcely resembled the photo in *The Comet.* The piercing gaze now muddled by drugs, the full features turned angular and gaunt. His once thick dark hair was splotched with white and looked as if it had been shorn with a dull butcher knife.

Not someone to fear, but not a man who had much strength left, either.

"I think I can help you, help us both." She switched on the tape recorder. "Let me know if you sense his return."

He nodded, and she told him as quickly as possible about her dream and what she'd learned in the book of Judges. He had already told her about it. He acted as if he didn't remember, so she went over the story, getting it on tape for her own purposes. She ended by quoting in Latin then in English, *"Sic pereant omnes inimici tui, Domine.* So perish all thine enemies, O Lord."

His eyes widened.

"What? Is he here? Is he back?" Heart in her throat, she gripped the pencil tighter.

"No, I know that. I've heard that before."

"Josie Lange. She knew it, somehow she knew the answer and put him to sleep until her death. Forty years. She must have told you something."

"No, I don't think so." His confused glance darted here and there, then back to her. "And you want to do the same."

"I'm going to do the same or die trying."

"Don't say that, please don't. I won't let you die. I promise."

She angled her head and gazed at him, glimpsed behind the pitiful facade the man he'd once been. The kind, gentle, loving husband and father. Tears filled her eyes.

The guard started toward them. "Time's up. You can come back tomorrow, as long as he behaves himself."

She rose and, using every ounce of energy, smiled, first at the guard, then at Eric. "Oh, he's going to behave himself, aren't you, Eric?"

The feeble curl of his lips as he struggled to return the smile almost broke her heart.

How had she ever worked up the courage to say that? This man was not responsible for the evil he had done, but he was far from sane. No telling what he was capable of in his condition.

Back at the motel, she sat on the edge of the bed, completely drained. What could she do next? She had come here to find out if what was happening could actually be more than a figment of her own downward spiral toward insanity.

Well, either she was as crazy as Eric Adair, or they were both the victims of some ancient demon who had walked the earth for centuries, torturing innocent people into carrying out dreadful deeds. Some of it didn't make sense, though.

If he wanted a host to continue to commit murder and mayhem, then why destroy them?

"I don't."

The voice, the dreadful voice.

Her heart jolted. Him. Again. She swallowed, braced herself. "You don't what?" Surprise. She could actually speak.

"They destroy themselves. Weaklings. I keep hoping I can find a human strong enough to endure my demands."

She dropped a hand to the backpack and felt the tape recorder in the open pocket. Began to sing her favorite song. "Tell me why the stars do shine." Flicked the record button. "Tell me why the ivy twines."

"What are you doing?"

"Tell me why the sky's so blue."

"I said." A roar that made her jump, the words dwindled away. *"What are you doing?"*

"Singing."

"Why?"

"You were going to tell me about the weakness of us humans."

He snorted. Well, something snorted. *"Ah, yes. But there were a few who performed quite magnificently for a time."*

"I'll bet I can guess their names."

"Enough."

Another roar, and she cringed. Tried not to think of her fears. That he would—no, no. Don't give him any ideas. "Amazing Grace, how sweet the sound, that saved a wretch like me."

"Shut up. That's vile. Tell me, how did you find our friend?"

A knot rose in her throat. He actually hadn't been there when she made the trip to Memphis.

"No, I was sleeping. Our little sexual romp left me quite satisfied. You are very good, Lenore. Your reactions give me much—uh—shall we say, satisfaction? Just thinking of it makes me horny."

A laugh, more vile than any she had ever heard, filled her head, rattled her bones, and lit terror ablaze in her soul.

"Here's a riddle. What does it take to make the Devil horny?"

And then he laughed again, on and on, until she clapped her hands over her ears and rocked in agony. But the torturous ongoing bellow continued, for it came from inside her. And that realization clenched around her belly till she gagged. Barely made it to the bathroom to retch up her guts. Collapsed on the floor, cheek lying on the cool tile, she closed her eyes against a scratching inside her brain, like bugs clawing their way through the gray matter.

"Lenore, get up off the floor. We have work to do."

The command brought her back from the edge of sanity, where she hung by her fingertips.

With an extreme effort, she obeyed. Perhaps if she did as he ordered he would stop torturing her. On her feet, hands flat against the wall to support her, she waited.

"It's time we returned and began our work."

"Return where? What work?" She couldn't think. Did he mean go back to see Eric?

"No, we're done with him. Harmless little toad that he is. Now, you'll do what I want. Herb is waiting, and so is his redheaded bitch. Together, I can see them writhing about on the floor of the house he's building for you. That will truly never do. Playtime is over. You are mine, and they are ours."

Chapter 35

SEETHING WITH HATRED for Herb and her so-called best friend Del, Lenore stuffed her things into her bags and left the room. How dare they betray her? She'd gladly kill both of them.

She checked out at the front desk, doing her best to appear normal, though she'd seen herself in the mirror. Wonder they didn't call the coroner to carry her away. The guy at the desk smirked. Maybe at her appearance, but more than likely he'd heard the story of her middle-of-the-night outburst and visit by the police. She signed the credit card receipt and fled.

Inside the Jeep, she took a deep breath, fumbled the key into the ignition, and started the engine. Shoulders hunched against further attacks from the demon, she gripped the wheel until her hands grew numb. Alf was accompanying her home, his presence like a growth of slimy moss along her spine. A gagging fear filled her with agony. Fear that he had made his final move out of Eric's used-up shell into her body. It could be too late to save herself or him.

No, don't think it. Don't think anything. *He'll hear.*

Hanging by the tips of her fingers to a fine edge of sanity, she drove back to Summit Falls, amazed she didn't roll the Jeep—or worse, crash into some innocent driver. Any plans for escape were gone. Any help she might have received from Eric were also gone. The beast rode inside her, tentacles wrapped around her soul.

Be damned if she'd think about him at all. She punched on the radio, pushed seek until she found a rock station, then turned it up so loud the windows vibrated. The terrible noise was nothing compared to the sound of Alf's voice, the bellow of his laughter. If she had to go mad, better it be from listening to the shriek of Peter Frampton. Her fellow traveler must have decided to endure the noise, though, for nothing stirred but the wind through the vents. Maybe he thought if he pulled something while she barreled down the Interstate like a maniac, he might get her killed and ruin all his plans. How very tempting was the thought. Point the Jeep at one of those tall sturdy pines lining the highway. Her luck she'd be maimed and helpless, still stuck with him.

There she went, thinking about the monster.

Think about Herb. Where was he, what was he doing? Worse, who was he doing it with? Was he really playing around with Del? She'd kill them both. And what about Richard? Maybe he'd kill Herb before she could, save her the trouble. God, how was she going to get out of this?

Drums shattered her space, guitars pulsed and wailed, Marilyn Manson squalled.

Eric had revealed to her some of the demon's weaknesses, and they came back now. Before the bastard latched on to her thoughts, she tamped them down beneath the thunderous rattle, bang, thump, and shriek of what passed for music these days.

Jesus, how could anyone stand this noise?

Well, she couldn't. Enough was enough and she turned it off. The ensuing silence closed around her like warm water.

"Thank you." A voice almost human.

"You're welcome," came up out of the shivery pit of her stomach. God, what was she doing, being polite to a demon that existed only to torment her?

He hovered ever closer. She felt him, even though he did not touch her in his obscene way. His evil flesh writhed within her, heart beating out of sync with hers so she'd know he was there. A breath that wasn't hers. How had Eric stood this for so long? Already panic drove her berserk until she was barely able to keep it together.

"What are you doing?"

Every time his voice spoke from inside her, she jumped and uttered a squawk.

When we get home, I'll mash up the nightshade with my trusty mortar and pestle, and get started on our plan to poison Herb and Delilah.

"Good, very good." He curled up and went to sleep.

Don't think, don't speak, don't even breathe. Teeth clenched, she waited, drove, waited some more.

He slept. She was as sure of it as if she could hear him snore.

Okay. *Testing, testing. Can you hear me, you piece of filth?*

Nothing.

I'd like to cut off your cock and feed it to you.

Nope, not a move.

Just as Eric had said. When he slept, he slept deep, and there were times when her thoughts could be reasonably free of his control. That would be the time to set her plan.... She let that trail off, wary of revealing her idea in case he was tricking her. Fooling him would take some doing, but if she were to survive, she had to do it. Had to.

Trouble was, she could never be absolutely sure he wasn't listening.

All the way home, stopping for gas, using the restroom, eating a snack though she had no appetite, he remained quiet. She listened for a swallow, a breath, tensed for a touch of his hand or that lustful tongue licking her insides. Nothing. He wasn't there. She had to be careful, it could be a trick. Earlier she had felt him and now nothing. Did she dare trust her instincts? Hell, that was a laugh. Her instincts might not be her own anymore.

She drove up the lane to the house. Now he would surface. But he didn't. Not when she went inside and opened all the windows, not when she bathed or fell into the bed. He would surely come in the night when she slept.

But he didn't. Lying in a tight curl, eyes wide, she stared into the darkness. Waiting. Dreading the first obscene touch. Hating even the thought of it. Oh, how he loved to move inside her, seduce her when she least expected it.

But he didn't. After a fitful night's sleep, she awoke to a beautiful sunny day. For a while, she lay and gazed out the window, listening to birdsong. So beautiful, so peaceful, so ordinary a day. What if the entire thing had not been real, but a long nightmare? And Herb was downstairs fixing breakfast. And Del was at the shop waiting for her to bring her potions.

What if? Jesus, if only.

In the bathroom, standing over the sink, she slid her gaze to the mirror and gasped. No nightmare could have turned her into the sunken-eyed hag with straggly hair who stared back at her.

"God, help me."

Breakfast—a cup of tea and a piece of dry toast—made her feel better, and she went out on the porch. Spring air smelled so sweet she breathed it in like nourishment.

He was gone. Another deep breath, cleansing her insides.

No, don't dare hope. But he is. Gone.

Remain vigilant, he likes to torture.

Best to continue preparations to kill Herb and Delilah. Not quite so hard to imagine now that she knew they were having at it like animals. But were they? What if Alf had invented the entire thing? Entirely possible. His goal to use her body to enjoy his favorite pastime, killing, would make him say anything, wouldn't it?

She had no idea what to think or what to do. If only she could speak to Eric, get his input. Jesus. Wanting to talk to the demon's alter-ego. What part of this scenario testified that she had gone bonkers?

The entire day passed with her mind ping-ponging from relief to fear to hope to dread. Wind fluttering a book's pages spooked her, a squirrel scampering across the roof jerked her from a peaceful reverie, a deer tracking through leaves in the nearby woods set her heart thrumming. Still, he didn't show up.

Okay, it was time. He'd gone back to Eric and that dark cell, and she had to work fast. If he was tricking her and caught her, so be it. Her plan couldn't wait until he rose up and forced her to commit murder.

Grabbing the basket of digging tools and supplies, she pulled out her cell phone while hurrying to the Jeep, punched in Daniel Klimas's cell phone number. Hoped he was still at the church and not off wherever it was he and his wife lived. She needed to talk to him, face to face. And fast. No time to waste. The phone rang and rang. She headed down the lane toward the highway chewing her lip and whispering please, over and over while the burr of the distant phone went on and on.

No voicemail, no reply. Finger on the disconnect, she heard his tinny voice. *"Hello? Hello? Who's there?"*

"Oh, thank God. Father Klimas?"

"Deacon. This is Deacon Daniel Klimas."

The signal buzzed and wavered as he spoke. She gazed at the signal bar that danced from one to three and back again.

"No, no. Not now." These mountains had dark holes in them through which no signal passed.

"I'm here, I can hear you."

Three bars. She braked and pulled over to the side of the road, fearful of losing him again. "This is Lenore Maine. I have to see you. Now. I mean, it's very important. Please. It's—"

"Come to Our Lady of the Smiles. I'll be—"

She disconnected, tossed the phone in the seat, and jammed the accelerator to the floor. The Jeep's tires squalled and spat dirt, fish-tailing onto the pavement. She headed for the church on top of the mountain, driving as if the Devil himself pursued her.

A hiccough, a sneeze, a catch in her breath could mean his return. Sweat trailed down her spine, dripped from her chin. It was so hot in the car. How could it be so hot? She rolled down the windows, let the wind blow wildly through her hair and batter her eardrums. There was nothing she could do if he came back. Nothing.

"And where are we going?"

She screamed like an animal in pain, pounded the wheel with one fist.

"Stop the car here and turn around. We're going to find Herb."

"No, I won't. I can't." Heart pounding, she shoved on the gas pedal until the Jeep rocked madly around a curve.

"Stop the car." The bestial roar hammered at her eardrums. An excruciating pain exploded in her kidneys. Everything went black. All she could do was cling to the wheel and gasp with the pain. Oh, Lord, she was going to die. The car left the pavement, but she couldn't see.

"Now see what you've done." He released the pressure, and a beautiful melody soothed her mind. Serenity filled her. She walked along a path deep in the woods, cheeks caressed by a gentle breeze.

"I can bring you peace, if only you let me." A voice so soft as to be unbelievable. *"Now, touch the brake."*

She obeyed, and the car rolled to a stop in front of the house Herb was building for them. His car sat outside, but he was nowhere to be seen.

How had that happened?

"Nevermind. As time goes on, you will obey me without question, and there will be rewards when you do. For us."

A warm tongue trailed down her belly. Lower and lower. Tantalizing. *"There, you like that, my sweet Lenore."*

"Eric. You came." She leaned back in the car seat, closed her eyes.

"I love you."

Moist lips on hers. She opened to them, relaxed in the tenderness of his kiss.

Inside the house someone laughed, and she jerked away, opened her eyes. *Delilah?* Inside with Herb?

Anger fueled her exhausted body, and she opened the door, leaped out and ran up the steps. Jealous? And her fooling around with a demon. Or a killer. However you wanted to look at it.

"Don't let them see you yet. Look in the window. Look."

It was Alf, after all. The treacherous shit had learned to mimic Eric! Even be tender with her to get his way. Tears poured from her eyes.

She crept along the unfinished floorboards of the porch and peeked through the framed window opening. Inside, lying on the floor in front of the fireplace on a blanket, Herb and Delilah. Naked. Panting. Her on top astride him, long red hair like a veil around them. Herb's long white legs pumping, guttural moans and mindless shouts.

Damn him, he never acted like that with her. God, but they looked silly. A laugh bubbled up from deep in her gut.

Something hot, harsh, sweating slipped over her mouth. *"Don't make a sound."*

So real had this beast become, she could taste his flesh, smell his fetid breath, glimpse of his eyes flashing, the outline of his body wavering amid the shadows.

"Now we will go to the cabin and make plans." His voice spoken aloud

outside her. How was he doing that? He could terrorize her beyond thought or deed. She couldn't move.

"You will obey me now, won't you?" He levitated before her. Teeth shone in an open mouth, drooled saliva that caught the gleam of the sun.

Sick to the depths of her soul, she nodded until her head hurt. She wanted to tell him yes, she would kill them both, but when she opened her mouth, no sound came out but a gargle.

"Very good, my sweet Lenore. Very good."

In the car, madness squeezing at her brain, a red haze clouding her vision, the demon's hands, mouth inside her. Oh, dear God, she wanted… wanted….

"What do you want, my dear?"

…only to die. Her mother's words, echoing over the passage of time. She screeched. The Jeep rocketed away from the house, down the narrow road.

"I will kill them both." A voice she did not recognize as her own came up from the depths of her mad rage.

"Yes, ah, yes." He rewarded her with a kiss, a tantalizing touch. Like a lover's. She moaned, begged for more, steered the Jeep wildly onto the paved road.

He obliged her until she could do nothing but hang on to the wheel and sob through a climax that left her too weak to maneuver the careening vehicle.

In the darkness of her subconscious, his voice sneered, *"At last, Lenore. You are mine. Completely."*

And when she opened her eyes, the Jeep sat in front of the cabin and she felt sated, emptied of the ability to deny him anything.

How long she remained sprawled in the seat, the heat of the sun warming her trembling flesh, she did not know. He awoke her with a quiet voice.

"It is time."

Nodding, saying nothing, she gathered her overturned basket from the floorboards, climbed from the car, and headed for the woods.

Chapter 36

NUDGED AWAKE BY Alf, Eric carried out his bidding with a heavy heart. Sweet Lenore. Soothed her in a way the demon couldn't. Poor Lenore. So hungry for love she would fall prey to his tender caresses. Pitiful Eric, too weak to deny Alf's commands.

Even as he kissed her, he sensed the fury that boiled over inside her. The growing determination to kill Herb and Delilah. How odd that all humans had within them this ability to kill. He had seen for himself what it took to awaken that evil, but what kept it in check? And was there no one who could resist once the possibility was offered? Did evil, after all, always overpower good?

He squirmed on the floor of his filthy cell, sat up. Shame flowed over him. His empty shell of a body had ejaculated, even as his spirit made love to her. How could that be? His member throbbed for more as if he had been with her in more than his shattered mind. What a fool. He loved her. But he wanted free of Alf so desperately, he would do his bidding and make way for him to possess such a beautiful lost soul.

"Asshole, you don't love her. You lust for her."

A gurgling sound boiled from his throat and he crab walked on his feet and hands into the darkest corner of his cell. "Go away, you beast. Leave me to die in peace."

A guard came to the door, peered through the bars of the window. "Shut up that caterwauling in there. Jesus Christ."

He covered his mouth tight, sucked down the terror. They'd shoot him up with the drugs if he wasn't careful. And if this was hell, what drugs did to him was beyond imagination. Under the influence of drugs, creatures that made Alf look tame by comparison came out to play with his brain.

Think of something else. Think of her and the joy of tasting her. How he hated that he'd betrayed her, this woman he'd come to love. What a sniveling coward he was. He sensed her spirit weakening, giving in to the beast's evil domination. It wouldn't be long now, and as Alf spent more and more time with her, Eric grew weaker. Perhaps, in the end, Alf's possession had been all that kept him alive.

In another life, he might have been fascinated enough by the subject to delve deeper into it. Had anyone ever succeeded in denying the commands of this demon or any evil being for that matter? Once Alf vacated Eric's body for good, he would be left alone in the cell, a victim of whatever fate awaited him. What he hated most was that he would no longer be allowed to visit with the beautiful Lenore. But she would soon not be beautiful.

Lenore had tried, but all seemed lost, for she was on her way to the woods to escape for a moment and think. She'd told him it was to gather the poison that would begin her killing spree. That was a lie. The nightshade she would use hung drying in the shed, for it needed to be dried and turned to powder so it would dissolve in the wine.

Alf nodded off, bored with her trek through the woods, and Eric crept to the surface.

"What happened to your plans? Have you found the weapon that will defeat Alf?"

"Leave me alone. I'm doing what you asked."

"No, it's me, Eric."

"I don't believe you." She swept a hand over her cheek. "He came to me as you, made love to me."

"No, that was me. He asked me to. And it was so wonderful. I wish we could, I mean, if only we could——"

"Eric, is that really you?" She stopped and rubbed a palm over her breast. "It aches so, yet I want it so much. How can he, I mean, you, do this to me? Why?"

"I wish I knew. But I will never understand what such a force can do. He made me kill my wife, and I loved her more than life. I thought it was because I'm weak, but now I know that wasn't it at all. It was because evil is so much stronger than good."

She dropped to her knees in the soft loam. "No, I won't believe that, I can't." Eyes wide, she gazed into the surrounding shadows, searching. "Are you sure he's not here?"

"He sleeps."

"Oh, God." She dropped her things, buried her face in both hands. "I thought you were gone for good."

"Shh, don't speak. Just think. I sense your rage. It is what he counts on, you know."

She nodded. "I know nothing else. Herb has betrayed me, and so has my friend."

"But if you did not have Alf within you, what would you do about this? Surely not kill them."

She staggered to her feet, picked up the basket. "You're right, of course. I would cry a lot and grieve the loss of yet more loved ones. I would feel miserable and alone and suicidal. Like my mother. But Alf has given me strength I didn't know I had. The power to fight back instead of lie down and let them walk all over me. Don't you understand? He has given me the ability to survive?"

"My heart aches for you. This isn't the way your life should be."

"Oh, yes? And how is my life supposed to be?" A shriek that frightened birds from the trees overhead.

"Please, he'll awaken."

"Go away, Eric. It's way too late for my life to change. Besides, I want to kill them. I do."

"And how long do you think you'll survive committing the ugly killings he demands? No, I don't believe you really want to kill. Please go to your priest, find a way to break this spell."

"How do you know about him?"

"I heard you talking to him. He can still help you."

"No, it's too late. Way too late."

"Please, Lenore."

"Ah, there. See. I knew I'd find it." She gathered the leaves of the deadly nightshade and put them in her basket.

It was no use. He must give up. She was mesmerized, overcome by evil. *"Goodbye, my beautiful Lenore."*

Back in the cell once more, Eric lay sprawled on the floor, arms akimbo, while tears flowed.

Chapter 37

HUMMING, **LENORE WORKED** with the mortar and pestle until the dried leaves and seeds were a fine powder that she poured onto a sheet of paper. Folded it carefully around the deadly poison. Inside the kitchen, she washed her hands and wiped them on a towel, fetched her purse, and hurried out to the Jeep. Fayetteville was the closest place to buy wine, and she drove in with all the windows open, singing along with the radio.

At last she was loved by someone who would remain with her always.

At the liquor store on the south end of town, she gazed with wonder at her reflection in the sliding glass door of the cooler. Her cheeks flushed, eyes sparkling, hair wildly tossed by the wind, lips full as if with passion. He had made of her a beautiful woman.

The transformation had been painful, but worthwhile, and she smiled. This was what real love had done for her. She would never be alone again.

She reached inside, took out two bottles of a dark red wine that would not show any discoloration, paid for them while the college student clerk flirted with her, then winked boldly, and left the store. His eyes followed every twist of her hips, giving her diabolical pleasure.

"Mmm, nice." Alf pinched the rigid nipple through her blouse.

"Yes, indeed."

Back at the cabin, she picked up the phone and dialed Herb's cell phone. He'd had more than enough time to exhaust his weak sexual desire with Delilah. Still, he didn't answer, so she left a message.

"Herb, darling. I wanted to apologize for the way I've acted. Darn, I hate to do this on voicemail. Why don't you come for supper tonight? I promise no more foolishness. I've been an absolute idiot. Please come, darling. I'm fixing your favorite meal. Rare roast beef and wine. Say around seven?"

She smiled, disconnected. "Bastard." She dialed Delilah's number. A voice bright and gay answered, pricking at Lenore until she could scarcely control her own.

"Dee? You sound happy." *You bitch.*

"Lee? My God, are you okay? Herb said you—that is, we've been so worried about you."

"Okay? Yes, I'm fine. I feel better than I have in years. I wanted to invite you over for supper. It's been so long since we've talked, just the two of us. Please say you'll come. About eight?"

What if the two talked, discussed the invitation? All would be lost. She had to hope they didn't. By the time Delilah arrived Herb would be dead on the floor, and she would be next.

"Well, I don't know. Tonight? Sort of short notice, don't you think?" Her tone had gone a bit stiff, perhaps a little wary? Did she think Lenore guessed at her treachery? Probably feeling guilt, the little cunt.

"Oh, please. I feel so bad over the way I've acted, and I can't stand us not making up. Please say you'll come."

A sigh, then, *"All right. But don't worry. All is forgiven. You know that."*

Forgiven, indeed. "Eight o'clock, then?"

"Yes, I'll be there."

Lenore hung up with a smile. "Bitch."

In the kitchen, she fetched a corkscrew, opened the wine, and used a funnel to pour the crushed nightshade into one bottle, then another. Digging about in her supplies, she found two corks, fitted them into the necks of the bottles, wiped them clean of her fingerprints, and set them both in the refrigerator.

Singing, she fetched a roast from the freezer, placed it in a roaster in the oven and turned it on. A tossed salad and baked potato would finish out the meal neither of her guests would be allowed to eat.

"How do you feel now, my dear?"

Ah, her lover. He sounded pleased. "Wonderful."

"Good. Wouldn't you enjoy a hot bath? I know I certainly would."

His tongue tantalized her until she squirmed with desire.

"Yes, but hurry." In. Out. Wrapping around. "Hurry. Supper." Blind with passion, she stumbled down the hallway, tearing at her shirt and unbuttoning her jeans.

"Oh, we won't be that long."

His laughter trailed after her as she ran into the bathroom, stoppered the tub and turned on the faucet. Shedding her clothes, she scented the steaming water with lavender and climbed in.

He writhed about within her, and she gasped in eager expectation.

"It's been so long since I've possessed a compliant woman."

The exquisite agony set her on fire, then a pain bright and shiny locked onto her, hard and harder till the climax erupted. White hot lava gushed over every pore, set her organs burning.

The demon shrieked and moaned, hammered and writhed, bit and clawed until her insides grew raw. Blood dribbled from her nipples into the water. The flogging within her grew in intensity. Convulsions bent her double, and her mind shattered, slivers exploding into murky space.

With a final remnant of sense, she prayed to die. Babbled with a tongue floating in blood, begged for her dead mother to help her. As if in reply, a steaming darkness closed over her and dragged her away.

38

YOU'VE KILLED HER." Eric gazed through Alf's bleary vision at the beautiful Lenore, head draped limply over the edge of the claw-footed tub, wet hair hanging to the floor. Her eyes were closed, her flesh a pale blue but for the ashen shadows beneath the curl of her fluttering lashes. Blood drizzled from her nose and one corner of her mouth. Crimson rivulets trickled from her nipples into the water.

"Do something." The demon's roar burst like thunder into the steamy room. *"She cannot die."*

Uncomprehending, Eric gazed down at her. "If you don't learn to control yourself, you will not have a vessel for your evil deeds."

How was it that he and Alf hovered over Lenore's body? They should be inside her or nowhere at all. Alf's speech sounded through his ears, rather than his brain. A shimmering outline, the glimmer of eyes, a slobbering mouth, floated before him. What was happening? He felt ripped to shreds.

"Do not tempt me. I'm finished with your weak carcass, I can leave you lying back there in your cage and go into her for good."

"Not if she's dead, you can't." He dragged in a ragged breath. "Why don't you? I'm tired of this."

"You are a weak sniveling coward. I would not give up so easily the woman I love."

"It is too late for me and her. Leave me be."

"Perhaps you are right." A howl of delight. *"First I need you to teach me what it is I do wrong, then I will leave you be, as you wish."*

"Teach you? Lord knows—" A white hot force slammed into Eric, and he saw stars.

"Do not use that name. Not ever."

Gasping for breath, Eric waited for what was to come next. Amazing that Alf had allowed him to function at all at this point. Perhaps the change was underway, and it was too late for the beast to stop Lenore's suffering.

"Do something for her. Now. Please." Alf broke off. *"She's dying."*

My God, the demon was terrified.

She stirred, her eyelids flickered, blood bubbled from between her slack lips. She was alive, but was she sane enough, strong enough, to carry through with the plan to free both of them? He had to be careful.

"She lives. Go to her. Now." Alf physically put hands on him and shoved. The transformation had begun.

"Yes, yes, all right. But leave us be. We can't both function within her at the same time. You know that."

The depraved presence fled in a draft of hot air, and Eric drew in a breath. To exist for long, Alf would have to return to the body they shared. Would that give them time? He sent a tentative probe to Lenore's spirit. She was so weak, her emotions so damaged he feared that even if she survived, she would be too crazy to function.

"Lenore." Would she be able to hear his voice as he could?

Hands flailing, legs pumping along the bottom of the tub, she mewled like a tiny kitten. Pity mixed with a growing desire to destroy Alf, whatever it might cost his own soul.

"Oh, sweet one. I'm so sorry. It's me, Eric. He's gone."

"No, no, no, no." Under the waxen lids her eyes darted. Her head rolled from side to side against the rim of the tub.

She'd heard him. He yearned to pick her up and carry her to the bed, but his nearly depleted body lay on the cold stone floor of the madhouse where it was caged. A waving image of himself of arms, legs, and body floated before his eyes. But they weren't real, rather were perceived by his imagination. Alf had fled, needing the body that lay in that dungeon. There he rested, waited for Eric to do his dirty work with Lenore. Could she see what he saw? He doubted it. In spite of the vision he had no arms to hold her, no hands to soothe her battered flesh. All he had was his mind. Somehow, that had to be enough.

He continued to soothe her, sensing a restless cessation of terror. Perhaps she was too weak to climb from the tub. The water had gone cold, and gooseflesh spotted her skin. Her lips were blue and trembling.

"Lenore, you're cold. Turn on the faucet, the hot water."

"Go away." The plea in a voice harsh from screaming.

"Listen to me closely. You want to live, I know you do. If you don't help yourself, you are killing yourself. And you don't want that, do you? Not like your mother."

She cried out, lifted both hands to scrub at her eyes.

"You can do it. Lean forward, turn on the hot water. Left hand, that's right."

One pale arm reached forward, the fingers clawing.

"That's it, a little farther. Move forward. Yes, that's it."

Grunting, she shoved herself with one arm, reached out with the other. One inch at a time, bent forward from the waist until the tips of her fingers brushed at the handle.

"Yes, you have it. Now turn it on."

"Eric?"

"Yes, Lenore, I'm here."

She slapped at the faucet, splashing water into her face. *"Where is he? Is he close by? I can't stand him. How could he do that? I was doing what he asked. He hurt me so much. Don't, don't, don't let him hurt me again."*

Eric could barely understand the garbled words, but hurried to reassure her, stroking at her spirit with a light emotional touch. "Lenore, turn on the water. Now. You have to get warm."

The deep caress calmed her, and she made a final lunge, grabbed the faucet, and turned it. The running water grew hot after a moment, and he sensed her body warming and reviving. He curled around within her, held her close, all the while aware of the urgency that must soon drive her to seek out the priest.

Somehow he had to get her dressed and into her car and up the mountain road to the church. Him with only a vestige of arms or hands, a nearly depleted spirit. The priest could help them find what they needed to defeat the demon.

But they didn't have much time.

Chapter 39

DANIEL STARED AT the phone a long while before discon-
necting from Lenore Maine's frantic call. The woman sounded more than simply desperate. If ever he'd met someone
possessed by evil, it was her. And so when she didn't arrive in a timely
fashion, he decided to go look for her.

She had told him at their first meeting that she lived off Old Sawmill
Road and that her cabin was about three miles from the Interstate. The
area was sparsely settled. He should be able to find her. Or perhaps run
across her on the way. She might have had car trouble.

A sense of urgency drove him to run to his car, keying in his home
phone number as he did so. When Emily answered, he hurriedly told her
where he was going and that he might be a while.

"You know, honey," he added as an afterthought, "if you don't hear
from me in a couple of hours, why don't you call the sheriff? Just to be
on the safe side. Tell him there might be trouble at the old Maine cabin.
He'll know where that is."

He started the car, pulled the door shut, and shifted into drive, all with his right hand while the left held the instrument to his ear.

"Daniel, what kind of trouble? What's happened?"

"Probably nothing. A woman with a problem. You understand."

"Yes, of course. Don't I always? But the sheriff?"

He pulled onto the deserted highway and headed north. "Now, don't worry. Just do as I ask." The afternoon sunlight flashed in his eyes as he headed down the mountain.

"Okay, but call me as soon as you can."

"I will. Love you."

"Love you, too."

He tossed the phone into the seat and shoved on the accelerator, a sense of black dread creeping into his heart.

The Church did indeed believe in evil. It believed in possession and exorcism, but how he himself felt about that, he'd never been sure. He feared he was about to learn.

Chapter 40

CRIMSON WATER LAPPED at Lenore's chin and flowed over the rim of the tub, splashing onto the floor. She squinted, but her eyes wouldn't focus.

Where was she? A bathroom, but whose? And what had happened?

Fire licked through her, scorching her insides. Any movement shot excruciating pain into every organ. Like she'd been run over by a truck. Memory floated back in waves. The demon. He had... *they* had... oh, God. Muscles, flesh, bones throbbed. Incessant bolts of lightning erupted from her skin, pommeled her lungs until every breath was agony.

A small voice urged her to stand up and fight. Fight? She couldn't move, let alone fight. She wanted to tell him that, but her tongue was a club, swollen and sore. Even her teeth ached.

"Lenore, you can get up. You have to."

She squinted into the steam, listened to the steady flow of water onto the floor. "Who is that?"

"It's me, Eric."

Frantic, she flailed at the water, screamed in a voice like the caw of a mad raven.

"Calm down, it's all right. He's not here. It's just us, and we don't have much time. Get out of the tub. We have to find the priest. If we don't, you'll live like this until he kills you."

"I want to die. I only want to die."

"Like your mother?"

"Yes, why not?" Fury sent hot, shiny knives into her gut.

He was quiet a moment, and she listened to the water. How soothing, running water. *"Because I love you. Because you have to save us. Because it's not just us. It's all those he will kill if you don't stop him."*

"Why me?" Oh, God, that hurt so bad. "I don't have the power."

"You do, yes—you do have the power. You know how to save us, save them. Now, get out of that tub and put on some clothes."

Like a woman birthing a child, she bore down, struggled to rise from the bloody water. Grunting, moaning, she pulled herself to a crouch, hugging her aching belly against both thighs.

"That's better. Now, out."

She lifted one leg, kicked the side of the tub, and cried out. Tried again, this time cleared the edge and flopped a foot into several inches of water on the floor. Bending, holding the rim with both hands, she worked the other leg out. For a moment, everything went black, the room whirled around her, and she hung on, making funny noises she herself didn't recognize as human.

"Good, that's great."

"Oh, shut up."

"That's even better."

The long haul down the hallway, slippery with water, and into the bedroom exhausted her and she collapsed onto the bed.

Oh, so good, so very good. To lie there and never move again. But she couldn't. What was it Eric said? The demon would be back. He'd do the same to her over and over until she died.

"Why?"

"*Why what?*"

"Why does he want to kill me?"

"*He doesn't. He wants you for his own for a very long time. The only problem is, he doesn't know how not to hurt you. In the throes of his dark passion, he only knows what he must have.*"

"And that's me. My body."

"*And your soul.*"

"I'll kill myself."

"*He'll simply find someone else, and the killing will start all over again.*"

She sobbed, the tears like acid on her cheeks. "I don't know what you want me to do."

"*I want you to stop him.*"

"I can't." A wail. She curled up, knees under her chin. "I can't."

"*Yes, you can. You know how. Remember the nightmare and the Song of Deborah? You found out how to stop him.*"

She lay in silence, closed eyes staring into the darkness of her own mind.

Finally, "He's afraid. Is there a rosary here? A crucifix?" She pawed at the night stand, fingers closing around the crystal beads.

"*Yes, yes. He fears God.*"

"He fears all things good. Even the symbols. The priest—well, he's not really a priest—but he's a man of God. When I spoke with him, Alf was very afraid."

"*Okay, that's good. But that alone won't stop him.*"

Weary and sore, she sat on the edge of the bed. Sensed Eric touching her, trying to ease her pain. "You are a good man."

"*Good men don't murder their wives. Come on, we have to hurry.*"

And then she remembered it all, the legend and what she must do.

"Eric."

"Yes?"

"You will not survive if I do this."

"I know." He took her hand, and she sensed the gesture. *"Neither will he, but you will."*

A loud banging on the door rattled the windows, and Lenore started in terror. Wanted to babble like a child.

"He wouldn't knock, it's not him. Not yet, but he's coming soon."

A voice cried out her name, fist banging again. She limped into the living room, leaning on the wall for support. Before she could reach it, the door burst open, and there stood Daniel Klimas, the lowering sun surrounding his large figure.

"My God," he shouted, and she looked down, saw that she was naked and bloody.

Chapter 41

THE MAN OF God who had appeared at her door helped her dress, as if she were a small child. Asking no questions, he guided her feet into the legs of jeans, holding her upright to pull them on and fasten them. He went through dresser drawers and found a tee shirt, slipped it over her head, pulled it over her bruised breasts. The sympathy in his eyes soothed her.

"There, that will have to do." He looked at her bare feet on the wet floor. "Where is this water coming from?"

"The tub. In there."

He followed her gesture, and soon the sound of running water ceased. Surely he noticed the bloody water, but he said nothing when he returned.

"I'll need shoes."

"Of course." He supported her into the living room, and she sank to the couch, where he knelt to slip tennis shoes on her feet. The same shoes she'd kicked off with such abandon earlier when the demon had come to seduce her. A shudder grabbed her in its eerie embrace.

Klimas glanced up. "Are you okay?"

"Okay? I don't think I'll ever be okay."

"Tell me." He remained on his knees beside her, eyes an earnest gray.

And so she told him everything, from the very beginning. Always, as she spoke, Eric hovered impatiently. There was so little time, but this man had to know it all to help her. She could not do this alone.

When she ended her story with the nightmare and her resolution, she waited. No one would ever believe such an outlandish tale.

"And so we must find this place, then? Where he buried the iron rod. And then you have to drive it into whose temple? Describe it to me, this place from your nightmare."

How odd that he could repeat the outrageous deed with such belief. Perhaps to a man of God, faith was faith.

She nodded. "Yes. It is an old Indian trail. They chased him up the mountain out of thick trees into a clearing. There is an overhang, and near it a huge slab with Indian writing, drawings? Perhaps a place where wagons once traveled? There was the skeleton of such a wagon, and that's where he buried the iron cross."

"Cross?"

"Well, not exactly. One short piece of iron crosses the other, like an old sword only the blade is short."

Daniel nodded thoughtfully. "More like a dagger?"

"Yes, only it's not shiny." Urgency filled her, yet there was something else, something she'd forgotten in the nightmare. She struggled to recall, then remembered. "A tree. Bent funny. I've read about them somewhere. The Indians bent saplings so they'd grow pointing at water?"

"Signal tree. A signal tree. I know where there's one. We—my wife and I—walked the Highland Trail through the Ozarks. Let me make a call."

She gave him the cordless and watched hopefully while he dialed. Spoke. "Russ. You know that old Indian trail on your place? About halfway down the mountain there's a signal tree. Are there any overhangs or caves, a slab of rock with drawings? Perhaps the partial skeleton of an old wagon?"

He listened, nodded at her. "Well, this may sound strange, but I'd like to bring someone down to take a look, if that's okay." Again, he listened, watching her. "Yes, I understand it is part of the Ozark Highland Trail." He paused. "A friend. Nothing sinister." He attempted a chuckle that didn't quite come off.

Painfully, Lenore rose from the couch, fear stirring in her. This was taking much too long. If Alf returned before they could finish this task, all would be lost.

Klimas turned away, and she couldn't hear him for an instant, but then he said, "Good, thanks. If you don't mind, that'll be fine. I appreciate this."

Nodding, he said goodbye, handed the phone back. "Are you sure you're up to this?"

"I have to be. Don't I?"

"You need to hurry. He's getting restless."

Klimas glanced around, gaze stopping where Eric's shimmering essence hovered. "Who is that? What is that?"

Eric. She'd almost forgotten him. How could she explain his presence? She'd left him out of her tale, thinking that to be too much. How weird she could talk about being possessed by a demon and yet not explain Eric.

"No time now. You must trust me. Have faith that he is going to help us." Clasping a hand over her mouth, she cried out.

"What? What is it?"

"I have to get the rosary, in case he comes. I must have left it on the bed."

Daniel headed for the bedroom. "I'll get it."

By the time he returned, she'd made her slow, painful way to the front door and leaned on the frame, panting.

Without speaking, he curled an arm about her waist and helped her through the yard to his car where he opened the door and placed her in the seat, then ran to the other side and climbed in. If he noticed the essence hovering in the backseat, he didn't mention it.

The small Honda roared to life, the tires threw gravel, and they barreled down the lane. He steered onto the highway, tires screaming.

To the southwest, black clouds rolled up to cover the sun, and thunder drummed in the distance. Trees on either side of the pavement swayed and bowed to the wind. Daniel's profile against the darkening sky appeared strong, determined. All the same, she feared for him and what she'd gotten him into. If she had to die, she didn't want to take anyone with her, especially not this kind man of God.

"When we get there, I'll go by myself. I can't let you take any chances."

"We'll see. Where is he now, can you tell?"

"No. Only that he's not within me."

"How do you know?"

"I can't feel him breathing." Her reply dropped to a whisper.

"Oh, my dear God. This must've been hell for you. How long has this been going on?"

"Days. Weeks. I've lost count."

He slowed the car and pulled into a wide spot near a log house built on the rim of the ridge. He parked next to an SUV with U.S. Forestry Service printed on its door. Behind the house, the tree-covered mountainside fell into a valley far below. Beyond stretched the Ozark peaks, streaked with spring's first greening, brilliant with the magenta of redbuds and snowy with dogwood blossoms. Lightning flashed, and rain spotted the windshield.

She caught her breath. "Hard to believe his kind of evil can exist in such a beautiful world."

"It always has. We can only fight it in each generation."

She sat for a moment, gazing again into those gray eyes. "Thank you for coming this far with me. Thank you for helping me. Now I have to go on alone."

Cranking open the door, she stumbled and held on a moment to get her bearings. "We'll need something to dig with. I forgot. It's buried. I watched him bury it before they killed him."

"Wait here a minute. Russ will have a spade." He ran toward the cabin and soon returned with a short handled camper's shovel. "I'll just point you along the way."

She clutched the rosary in one hand, grabbed him with the other. "Promise me you won't follow. You have to promise. I have to do this by myself. Wait here, and if I don't come out, well, I'd say run like the hounds of Hell were at your heels." She paused a moment, caught his wary glance. "Because they likely will be."

He closed his fist around hers, holding the rosary. His strength poured through her. The reassuring expression on his face soothed her. The task at hand seemed not so enormous.

He lowered his eyes as if he couldn't meet her gaze. "Go with God."

A knot clogged her throat, and she swallowed over it, then ducked into the brush where he pointed, following a faint trail. The rain intensified. Deep in the woods great drops splatted from the canopy. Daylight bowed to the storm, umber shadows crept along the ground. The trail zigzagged back and forth down the steep incline. Rocks punched sharp points out of the soil, tree roots laced one side of the trail to the other. If she wasn't careful, she'd trip and end up at the bottom of the mountain. Fear and the need to hurry shot adrenaline through her dampening the pain. A cold sweat battled drops of rain splatting on her skin.

In places she found signs that a road had once passed along a bench. How would she know which one to follow? This footpath had never been a wagon trail. No horse or mule could have pulled it. So the road had to follow one of the flat benches. But which one? And would the demon leave her be long enough for her to find out?

Her clothing grew soaked, rain dripped from her chin, ran between her breasts. Streams raced down the path.

Off to her right, pointing up toward the sky, a huge flat rock was almost hidden by blooming paw paw and a gnarly old dogwood. An ancient legend about the dogwood tickled at the back of her mind. Something to do with Christ and the crucifixion, but she couldn't remember what. Ahead was the signal tree, and not many yards from it the skeletal remains of a wagon wheel. This was it, the exact place. But where were the writings? Leaning against the huge bent trunk of the signal tree, she pulled away the branches of paw paw, and there they were on the wet face of the stone. The black scrawls depicting animals and stick figures from centuries before, exactly like in her dream. Clambering into the underbrush on hands and knees, she pushed aside a branch hanging thick with creamy blossoms and saw the crude figure. A beast of some sort, standing on its hind legs. Cloven feet, arms reaching outward, the face of a monster stroked in single lines. Her heart clamored in her breast. She had seen this drawing before, and it sent newborn fear through every pore.

Exhausted, heart hammering so hard against her ribs she feared it would fracture the bones, she crabbed her way to the wagon wheel and began to dig in earth changing to mud.

Even as the shovel cut the soil, she remembered the photo in the book containing the Jersey Monster. The same dreadful being Eric called Alf. The one who brought evil into the lives of ordinary people, making killers and worse of them.

Her brain, her heart, her very being jolted. Her feet lifted off the ground, and she clawed air before they slapped back down. She scraped at the dark mud. A damp, ancient smell washed from the darkness. The sky lit brightly, revealing piles of bones. Digging madly, ignoring aching muscles, she unearthed arrowheads of red chert less than a foot down. Cool to the touch, the sharp edges so perfectly crafted so many centuries ago.

Forty years and forty years and yet another forty years, stretching back to the beginning of time. This monster and others like him had possessed the best and the worst of humanity. And always someone had found a way to quiet the beasts. Yet never could they destroy them. Was she to be the one to quiet this one, or would he overpower her, wreak havoc by using her body?

Not if she could help it, by God. Not even if she died trying.

"Hurry, hurry." Eric urged her on. *"He's coming. I feel him."*

In a panic, she dug and dug some more, the hole growing larger and larger in the loose, black soil. running water pouring into the hole. The shovel unearthed small bones of birds and squirrels and other animals that fed the tribe that once lived here. She envisioned the wild men of her nightmare attacking and killing the man who buried the shaft of iron that would destroy the demon. Chopped and dug with renewed vigor till the muscles in her arms burned with the effort.

Sweat mingled with rainwater to plaster her shirt and jeans to her body. Cool rainy wind gave her the shivers. The flashlight, lying nearby so she could see by its glow, flickered. Her heart skipped, went silent, and she held her breath, stopped shoveling. Listened. Nothing. No one. Only the renewed beating in her chest. She was alone.

"Well, almost. You know, we have to go there, don't you?" Eric, still with her.

She lifted the digger, plunged it deep and hit something solid. "Where, go where?"

Using both hands, she pawed away the earth, and there it was. The shaft of iron shaped like a crude cross.

"Where my body is. We have to go there."

Pausing, she stared up into the stormy sky. Rain drenched her face. Her heart sank. "We can't go there. It's too far."

Denying his words, she cleared away the soil, and lifted out the iron cross with hands that shook.

Then someone came crashing through the woods. A deer? A bear? A mountain lion? Could be any or all. Clutching the shaft across her breasts, she turned and in the flash of lightning saw the figure of a man.

"Who are you? What do you want?" Her voice shook so she could hardly make the words understandable.

"It's just me, Daniel."

"You promised you wouldn't—"

He took a step toward her. "No, I didn't."

Grimly, she considered him. No, he hadn't promised. He'd talked his way around her request. So here he was, and she could well be responsible for his death as well as her own. She took a deep breath.

"Well, at least you aren't a bear."

He chuckled. "Did you find what you wanted? Is that it?"

"I don't know, I hope so. But he says we have to go there. To Memphis, to the—to where…." She gave up trying to explain, broke down sobbing. "It's too late, too late."

"Who says? Go where?" He joined her, picked up the flashlight, and together they looked over the ancient piece of iron, bent and twisted into a Celtic-style cross by some long dead blacksmith.

The metal felt warm in her hands, as if just cooled from the fire. "Daniel, touch it."

He reached a finger out, rubbed it over one of the twists. "Warm. It feels alive." His voice rose no louder than hers, as if he too were afraid of who might hear them.

"It is, I think."

"*Sweet Lenore.*"

She jerked, dropping the cross, and staggered backward against the signal tree.

Daniel shined the light on her. "What is it?"

"He's here. Oh, God, no. Please help me." *Eric?*

"Where is he?" Daniel slashed the beam of light around the clearing. "I don't see anyone."

But she did. Caught the flash of his yellow serpent eyes, the gleam of his drooling teeth, an outline against the darkness when lightning played over the sky. She clenched a fist over her heart. Hammered at her flesh. "Here. In here. He's here, and he won't let me—"

"Fight him, Lenore," Daniel urged and bent to pick up the iron. He held it out to her. "Take it. Take it, and hold on tight."

She could not see Daniel's face for the light in her eyes, but the cross lay in his hand. All she had to do was reach out and get it. But her hands wouldn't move. Her arms hung limply at her side. Numb, tingling.

"Yes, take it, foolish Lenore, and I will smite you down."

"I can't." She shuddered inside. Too late, much too late. "Eric, where are you?"

No reply.

"Yes, you can." Daniel pushed it toward her. "Yes, you can."

His voice, so certain, so reassuring. She lifted an arm, hand hanging limply. Struggled to touch the cross, to latch her fingers around it.

"Fight him, Lenore. God will help you. I will help you."

"No," bellowed the demon. *"No one will help you."* Thunder bowed to his roar, trees shook, and the ground quaked.

Something tugged at the cross. In the flash of lightning, a shadow moved between her and Daniel.

"No!" She screamed and latched onto the cross with both hands.

He had moved outside of her and outside Eric's body both to fight this battle, and that might mean he had little strength left to do so. If he had his own strength, then why did he have to possess a real live body to do his killing?

"*Bring him here,*" a familiar voice from far away said. "*Come to me, and he will follow.*"

Eric!

"*Yes, Eric. Come to me.*"

Nodding, she closed her eyes. Clutched the cross and pictured the rank cell where she had once visited with Eric Adair. The place where they kept him imprisoned because of this terrible monster. A demon who thought nothing of ruining lives, killing, destroying good people.

"You are a piece of ugly, dirty filth. Not fit to walk the earth." She hugged the iron cross to her chest, felt it grow hot, but didn't let go. "God cast you out because you aren't worthy of his love. And I cast you out too. Eric casts you out. You have no place to go." With each word she raised her voice until the last word was a scream.

And he replied in kind, the demon roar echoing off the surrounding mountains. Thunder crashed in reply, shaking the ground under her feet.

Daniel fell to his knees, his prayers drowned out by the storm. The flashlight rolled around on the ground, casting weird shadows into the trees, and she moved, jerky at first, then fleeing through the dark night. Falling hard, sprawled on a cold stone floor, the cross beneath her. Burning, burning her chest. There was little light in the cell, but she could make out an astonished Eric Adair, sitting on his bunk staring at her as if he couldn't believe what he saw. Indeed, she didn't blame him.

"Where is he?" Eric finally said.

"*In you, and you are going to kill her. She will forever disobey me. I must find another. Kill her, you feeble creature. Do it now.*"

The demon's voice sounded as clearly as if he stood beside her.

Eric gazed at her for a long moment, eyes bloodshot and hopeless. Then he nodded his head, fell to the floor on his back, and stretched his arms out on either side. "Do it now. I'm ready."

"*No, no, no.*" The roar threatened to shatter her eardrums.

She dragged in a deep breath, lunged across the tiny cell, and drove the sharp point of the cross into Eric's temple. The crunch of bone and spurt of blood filled her with disgust and a deep and abiding sorrow, still she held all her weight against the iron bar, pinned the writhing body to the floor. At last he lay still, the expression on his face one of final peace.

She knelt beside him for a long while, till she was sure there was no life in his body. Not his own or that of the demon he'd called Alf. With a deep sorrow for his passing, she yanked the iron cross free and as she raised it above her head, found herself looking into the concerned, cloudy gray eyes of Daniel Klimas. With disbelief she gazed around the clearing, past the signal tree and the message rock and the skeletal wagon wheel.

"Are you all right?"

Confused, she darted another look around the clearing. "I'm not sure. What happened?"

"Nothing. You stood there with that cross, like you were in a trance, then you plunged it into the earth, and after a while, you rose and came back to yourself."

"He's dead, Daniel. I'm not sure how or why, but I only know he's dead, and I killed him."

"That can't be. You never left this place."

"Yes. Yes, I did."

He gazed all around. Then like the man of faith he was, shrugged and said, "Well, okay. Are you going to be all right?"

"Yes, yes, I am."

He nodded, a strange look on his kind features. "Well, then, I guess we can go."

"Not yet. I have to put this back where I got it."

She knelt, and he shone the light so she could place the cross in the hole. Wet blood gleamed on its point as she scraped black earth over it.

"And for forty years the land had rest," she quoted.

Chapter 42

DELILAH DIDN'T WAIT for Lee to answer her knock, but went in the cabin. Water on the floor. Strange. The place was much too quiet. "Lee, honey. You here?"

No reply.

Shrugging, she went into the kitchen. Well, she *was* early. Lee had said eight o'clock. The oven was on, and a delicious smell filled the place. Nothing else done. Table not set. Funny. She opened the refrigerator. Two bottles of wine lay on the shelf. Pulling one out, she fetched a glass from the cupboard, removed the cork, and poured it full of the sweet red wine.

Outside, the storm moved on, leaving behind the joyful song of peepers.

Herb pulled into the lane, in a hurry because he was late. A light shined in the cabin, and he parked next to Delilah's car. Something told him her presence did not bode well, but he was past caring. He might have agreed to come here, but he had no intention of making up with Lenore. She was way too crazy for him. So if he and Delilah had to fess up and go their way, so be it.

He climbed from the car and waded through the wet grass to the front porch. No one answered when he knocked, so he stepped inside into an inch of water. Now what had she been up to?

His heart kicked. Water? Bathtub? Oh, God. Suppose she had decided to do away with herself and wanted him to find her body. That'd be just like her, the bitch.

Her mother had killed herself by slashing her wrists in a filled bathtub.

He sneaked down the hallway and stepped into the bathroom. Gaped at the tub of bloody water. Fell to his knees and reached in.

No body. No Lenore.

He turned, glanced over his shoulder. Someone there? No?

Rising, he left the room, checked out her bedroom, then went through the living room into the kitchen. A bottle of opened wine sat on the table. She was playing games with him. Trying to scare him. Well, to hell with that.

Casually, he opened the cabinet, took out a glass and filled it with wine. Taking a long drink, he stepped out the back door onto the deck. Something lay there, in the shadows, and he took another swig before snapping on the light to take a look.

Delilah lay sprawled on the pine boards, mouth a rictus of horror, eyes wide, white foam around her once gorgeous lips.

He knelt to touch her, and the first cramps hit his belly.

Chapter 43

DANIEL KLIMAS SAT across the table from Lenore, stared at her through the screen that would not allow them to touch. "I was sorry to hear about Herb and your friend Delilah. Do they know what happened?"

She shook her head. "A detective came and talked to me. They seem to think they took poison because—because of their affair. It was some sort of suicide pact. At least that's what was decided." She smiled. "They never found any trace of what they might have taken. Thought that a bit strange."

She didn't mention that nightshade left nothing in the system. It was best he not know for sure that she had done away with them. It was indeed a sin, no matter her motive.

He nodded. "How tragic. I'm so sorry about everything that has happened to you. Hold on to your faith."

Again, she couldn't hold back the tiniest of smiles. She had been taking instructions in the Catholic faith ever since the demon's exorcism. But this was the first time she had seen Daniel since that dreadful night a month earlier. He had been on a sabbatical. No doubt what had happened tested his faith, and he needed to recharge. The church probably didn't call it that.

He studied her with those peaceful gray eyes. "How are you doing?"

"Well, at least they say I'm not crazy." She smiled wryly.

"Are they going to let you go home?"

"The doctors say next month."

"Are you really all right?"

She nodded, feeling more at peace than she had since the day she'd seen Eric Adair's picture in *The Comet*. "We did it, didn't we?"

He grinned. "You did it. I just stood by being amazed and terrified."

"Maybe so. But without you I could not have made it through. I'd have chickened out." She sobered. "I wish we could have saved Eric, though."

"Yes, it was too bad, but it's done. At least for the next forty years and with this one demon. Evil still stalks the earth in all kinds of forms. We must remain vigilant."

Again she nodded. "Best I don't talk about it, or they'll think I've gone off my rocker again." She chuckled. "You, too, I suppose. You haven't told anyone, have you?"

"Good Lord, no. I wouldn't want to be shut up in here, too."

Together they laughed.

After a moment, "Sometimes it feels like it was all a dream."

"I understand." He gazed around him at the bright, airy room. "This place isn't so bad, is it?"

"Not really, but I'm ready to go home."

"I had your place completely redone for you, just like you asked."

She picked at a fingernail, thought of her mother, and smiled. "It's time, you know, that I let go of that life. You've been a good friend."

"Yes, well, we all need friends."

Unless they betray you. That little voice inside her no longer disturbed her. The doctors said it was just her subconscious and certainly not a demon of any kind. Perfectly normal for people to talk to themselves occasionally.

"Let me know, and I'll come pick you up."

"Thank you."

"Well, I'd better go. Take care of yourself."

She smiled at him. "You, too, Daniel. And I thank you. For so much."

After he went out the door, she padded to the heavily screened window and watched him cross the parking lot and climb into his little Honda.

Maybe she should've told him she was pregnant, but the opportunity hadn't come up. Besides, he'd want to know who the father was. He would know in due time.

She rubbed her belly and stared out across the mountains, a niggling fear growing alongside the demon's child.

VELDA BROTHERTON writes from her home perched on the side of a mountain against the Ozark National Forest. Branded as *Sexy, Dark and Gritty*, her work embraces the lives of gutsy women and heroes who are strong enough to deserve them. After a stint writing for a New York publisher, she has settled comfortably in with small publishers to produce novels in several genres.

While known for her successful series work—the Twist of Poe romantic mysteries, as well as her signature Western Historical Romances—her publishing resume includes numerous standalone novels, including *Once There Were Sad Songs, Wolf Song, Stoneheart's Woman, Remembrance,* and this, her magnum opus, *Beyond the Moon.*

Facebook: Author Velda Brotherton
Twitter: @veldabrotherton
www.veldabrotherton.com

www.ingramcontent.com/pod-product-compliance
Lightning Source LLC
Chambersburg PA
CBHW031942240626
47153CB00003B/828